LINE MATES & STUDY DATES

CU HOCKEY BOOK 4

EDEN FINLEY

SAXON JAMES

LINE MATES & STUDY DATES

Copyright © 2021 by Eden Finley & Saxon James
Cover Illustration Copyright ©
Story Styling Cover Designs

Professional beta read by Les Court Services.
https://www.lescourtauthorservices.com
Edited by One Love Editing
https://oneloveediting.com

All rights reserved.
This book or any portion thereof may not be reproduced or used in any manner whatsoever without the express written permission of the publisher.
For information regarding permission, write to:
Eden Finley - permissions - edenfinley@gmail.com
or
Saxon James - permissions - smjamesauthor@gmail.com

DISCLAIMERS

While we stuck as close as we could to the NCAA guidelines and rules in regards to hockey, we took creative freedom with some small details, because fiction is supposed to be fun.

Names, colleges, characters, businesses, places, events, and incidents are either the products of the authors' imaginations or used in a fictitious manner. Any resemblance to actual persons, living or dead, or actual events is purely coincidental.

1

ASHER

I'm going to go do something stupid.

Those were the words I said right before I followed through and overshot it. Because I didn't do something stupid last night. I did something fundamentally messed up.

Well done, Asher, you eternal man-child.

The heavy weight spooning me shifts, and I close my eyes and mutter silently, "There's no place like home. There's no place like home." Except there's a gigantically big, huge, stupid problem with that. This *is* my home. It's Ezra-fucking-Palaszczuk who needs to get out of my bed and this house before any of my little brothers and sisters see him in here with me. Or worse yet, if my older brother sees him.

I elbow Ezra and whisper, "You need to go."

The deep moan in my ear was sexy last night when I was drunk, but now it makes me cringe. Not because he's a dude but because of who he is. "Come on, I thought we could have some more fun before you kicked me out."

"My brother will kill you."

"Westly? Please, he never stays mad at me long. He loves me."

I know. That's why I fucked Ezra in the first place.

Alcohol is an evil mistress. It takes those devious "what ifs" and turns them into reality. Sleeping with my brother's best friend should have been reserved for when West really pissed me off. Instead, on a drunken whim, I thought fooling around with Boston's hottest defenseman was a brilliant idea.

No one has ever accused hockey players of being smart. Even I know this is crossing a line.

Which yeah, I would have been prepared to do when I really wanted a reaction, but for once, this wasn't one of those times.

Why, why, why did Ezra come visit my brother while I was all … I shudder, *vulnerable*? Eww, that's gross. *Go away, you useless emotion.*

Ezra runs his big hand down my chest, and I elbow him again.

"Get out," I mumble.

"Fine." He stands and pulls on his sweats, but he only gets them up to his thighs when footsteps thump down the stairs and my bedroom door slides open. I use the term "bedroom" loosely because it's actually the basement of our parents' old clapboard house. It's dark and freezing, and the makeshift sliding door West installed for "my privacy" doesn't have a lock, but unless I wanted to share with one of my siblings, it was this or camping in the damn yard.

"Asher, you have to—" West's voice cuts off when he sees Ezra pulling up his goddamn pants. My brother's hardened gaze turns to me, ire filling his green eyes that match mine.

"Knock much?" I snap.

I don't even know where my hostility comes from half the time. It could be a number of things. The top of the list would be losing our father and stepmother in a car accident a year ago and

West guilting me into giving up my spot in the NHL to help him raise our siblings. He said he needed help and didn't want to hire a nanny, that he didn't want to uproot the kids' lives more than they already had been after losing our parents. West gave me the choice, of course, but it didn't feel like much of one. I wasn't going to leave them in the sole hands of Westly Dalton. Yeah, there's a part of me that wants to escape, but another part has the obligation to stay. If West can give up his career in the NHL for them, I can postpone mine.

Maybe Buffalo will still want me when I graduate from college, and maybe they won't, but by then my draft contract with four-year exclusive rights to Buffalo will be over, and I can try my hand as a free agent.

Until then, my life is no longer just mine but also West's, Zoe's, Rhys's, Hazel's, Bennett's, and Emmett's.

Okay, maybe I do know the source of my hostility, after all, but that doesn't change anything.

Acknowledging I'm being an irrational shithead doesn't make me stop being one. It's impossible to rein in the asshole inside me. I've given up trying.

West folds his arms across his wide chest and avoids looking at me as he says to Ezra, "Now you've gotten what you wanted, you can go back to Boston." Then he turns in my direction. "You need to take Hazel, Bennett, and Emmett to hockey practice." He spins on his heel and leaves the room.

That's *it*? That's all I get for screwing his ex-teammate? I don't know whether to be pissed off or scared.

When West is angry, he yells. Our screaming matches over the years have been the definition of sibling rivalry. But ever since Dad died, he doesn't give a shit about fighting. Either that or he's holding it all inside and will one day explode.

I turn to Ezra. "What did he mean you got what you wanted?"

"Your brother used to be fun, but ever since he moved home, he's all 'I can't go out. I can't leave the kids. I'm a big boring bore.'"

I rub my temples. "I'm sure there were more options for you back in Boston."

"Yeah, but I was hoping if I made the drive out here, your brother might finally take me up on the offer to go out."

I scoff. "Not likely. Don't know if you've noticed, but his life has drastically changed in the last year."

"Which is exactly why he deserves a night out."

I desperately want to ask Ezra what exactly a night out with the two of them would entail because my brother is … elusive when it comes to his party life.

The rumors swirling around him in hockey circles are full of wild stories even I wouldn't be able to keep up with, and I've never had the guts to ask if they were true or not. There are some things I just don't want to know about my brother.

I roll onto my stomach and throw my pillow over my head. I'm hungover, and Ezra is still rambling.

"Suddenly West is all Mr. Serious and Responsible. It's *weird*. And unnerving. There's been a cosmic shift in the universe, and that shit's unnatural."

Can't he take the hint?

"Why are you still here?"

"You were a lot nicer last night."

"Alcohol makes me nice. Get. Out."

"I'm going."

I peek under my pillow as Ezra throws my clothes at me.

"But you need to get up and take the kids to hockey."

I'm like a damn taxi service. Although, if I'm honest, I don't mind driving them around and taking them to hockey. They lost both their parents and now have two fuckboys who don't know what they're doing trying to make sure they get through their teen years safely. They're dealing with enough shit without adding my ruined life plans to their conscience. It's not their fault our parents died. It was a damn moose in the middle of the road that left them parentless and West out of his element and needing help.

West may be acting responsible, but he isn't fooling me.

Once a fuckboy, always a fuckboy.

It's why I don't fight it anymore.

I finally get up and dress. It's the beginning of what is going to be a long-ass summer. West is coaching at CU for their summer camp. Zoe and Rhys are old enough to be left on their own, but I'm responsible for Hazel, Bennett, and Emmett, who are luckily going to their own private day camp. All the while, I get to go to summer classes because my freshman year didn't go well. I don't expect my sophomore one to go any better, but if I want to play hockey, I need a C-grade average. At this point, I can only see me reaching that with extra-credit programs. Fun times.

I just want to play hockey. If the universe wasn't a cruel bitch, I would be in Buffalo living my NHL dream instead of playing college hockey.

I pause at my bedroom door. How the hell am I supposed to play this?

If it's true that everyone has an angel side and a devil side, my angel side is telling me to apologize, but the darkness inside me won't allow it. The words *I'm sorry* don't fall from my mouth often. Or at all.

I make my way upstairs and hear West and Ezra in the kitchen.

"Are you kidding me?" West hisses. "My little brother?"

I stay hidden around the corner where they can't see me.

"It was only sex," Ezra says. "Who cares?"

West sighs. "It can't be like that for me, and it shouldn't be for him either. Don't you get it? One wrong step and our siblings end up in foster care."

My stomach churns, and I don't think it has anything to do with my hangover.

"Okay. I'm sorry. Won't happen again," Ezra says.

"You're damn right it won't. Go back to Boston, Ez."

"If that's what you want." Ezra's loud footsteps move toward the door, and then he appears in front of me. He gives a cocky smile. "See you round, Little Dalton."

I hate, hate, hate being called that. Little Dalton, Mini Dalton … everyone in hockey does it, and it's annoying. I'm always being compared and always have to live up to the expectations Westly Dalton set.

Ezra leaves, the door clicking shut behind him.

When I round the corner, West is packing the kids' lunches to take to camp. This is where I'm supposed to speak, but I've got nothing. I'm surprisingly flat. I usually thrive off tension, but I know I messed up this time.

His stormy eyes meet mine, and his mouth opens, but then Bennett drags his ass past me to get to the fridge.

In an epic brother stare down West and I have perfected over the years, words are said without actually speaking.

Bennett picks up the OJ and leaves again with the whole carton. I swear that kid is half orange juice. And thank fuck nine-year-olds can't pick up on tension in a room. Or, maybe they can and he's smart enough to get out of here as fast as possible.

"Why are you the way that you are?" West starts.

That's a good question. I go to answer that maybe it's because I've already lost too much in my twenty-one years and that everyone and everything else can go fuck itself, but he holds up his hand.

"Never mind. I know why you do the shit you do." His whole body slumps in defeat.

"It didn't mean anything." Like that makes it any better. Teammate code. Don't date siblings. Not that Ezra and I have ever or will ever date in the conventional meaning of the word. Like he said, it was only sex.

"There you go missing the bigger picture again." West plants his hands on the countertop of the kitchen island. "What's it going to take for you to put your head down this summer, study your ass off, and help me around here without all your attention-seeking behavior?"

"Fuck you." Even if he has a point. Just … fuck him.

"You almost flunked out freshman year. Get your shit together and stop testing me. Your life for the next eight weeks is kids, study, and more studying. Got it?"

"Yay. How fun for me." Though it's not like I have anything better to do. The only friend I made this last year is moving to Montreal.

Without Cohen, my social life is pretty much nonexistent.

"I need to go," West says. "Finish packing these, and then get on the road. They can't be late for morning warm-up."

I know that, I want to bite at him but don't have the energy.

West pushes past me, and it takes all my strength not to throw the kids' lunches at the wall.

Even though our mom died when I was too young to remember, I do remember being told my whole life I need to find healthier coping mechanisms than my "outbursts." It used to be hockey. Now it's sex. And adrenaline. That feeling of pissing someone off so much to the point where I don't know if they're going to hit me or not. I long for that.

"Are you and West fighting again?" The small voice of my eleven-year-old sister, Hazel, makes me flinch.

"Not at all," I lie. I turn to her.

Where West and I look like brothers, dark hair, green eyes, Hazel and our other half siblings take after our stepmom. Lighter hair, blue eyes.

I soften my gaze. Of everyone in this world, my younger siblings are the only people I can honestly say I love. "I slept in, and West is pissed you're going to be late for practice."

"Is that all?" She doesn't believe me, but I'm not dragging her or any of the others into our shit.

"Promise."

"Are we ready to go?" she asks.

"Yep. Just need to finish these lunches."

"I'll help."

We get on the road five minutes later, and as soon as I drop them off, I resist the urge to ditch school. It's hard, but I do manage to drag my ass to campus. If I want to keep playing for Colchester, I need to take these classes.

I regret it as soon as my first class starts because all the information goes over my head.

It's definitely going to be a long summer.

2

KOLE

Summer went way too quickly.

I spent most of it interning for the Stem Cell Foundation in New York, and then like every year, I flew to Miami for the last two weeks with Mom and Dad. It's the only two weeks of the year we get away from Dad talking nonstop about the love of his life. No, not my mom. *Hockey*. As head coach of the Colchester University hockey team, it takes up most of his time. Dad and I never get along better than when we're in Miami.

It sucks because we used to be great, right up until I turned fourteen and realized that playing a sport I hated wasn't enough to gain Dad's approval. When I told my parents I was gay, they hugged me and said they love and support me. When I told them I was quitting hockey? Dad barely spoke to me for a month.

So heading for the hockey arena instead of study group right now feels like a giant waste of time.

"I still can't believe you made that dumb bet," Katey says. Her hair is bubble-gum pink this year, and she's recently had her nose pierced, but her face is delicate and doe-eyed, so she pulls the look off like some kind of cartoon, jerk-off fantasy. If you're into that sort of thing. I'm not, which is why we're best friends.

"In my defense, without Foster Grant, I really didn't think Dad's team would make it to regionals last year."

"Defending Frozen Four champs? Not make it to regionals? Do you need a head check?"

Okay, so maybe literally everyone in my life is more focused on hockey than I am. Mom occasionally drags me to the home games out of support for Dad, and I put up with it because the three of us go out for dinner afterward. It may not seem like it, but Coach Hogan is a *family man*, and it's amazing to see that not only are he and Mom still together, but they actually *like* each other.

That's what I want one day. Not so much the traditional marriage and kids, but someone who'll be there for me the way my parents are there for each other.

Until then, there are a lot of queer men on campus I haven't had fun with yet.

"Why are you smiling?" Katey asks.

"No reason."

"You'd have to be the only person I know who'd be smiling over losing a bet. Do you really wanna play errand boy for a whole year?"

"*Equipment manager*, thank you very much." I fail at forcing a haughty tone. "And of course I don't. I had to give up my spot on the LGBTQ community committee for this, but I lost, so now I need to make the most of it. There's always a silver lining."

"Ugh. Your optimism is unnatural."

"What's the point of moping? It won't change anything. Besides, it's not like I'll need to talk to anyone, so I'll put in my earbuds and listen to coursework."

"What a riot."

"Supportive face, please."

She bats her eyelashes, and the sweet smile she uses on our professors appears. "A few things, babe." She counts on her fingers. "The blue line is *not* a euphemism for drugs, you can't pet puck bunnies, and for the love of all that is good on this earth, when it comes to hockey players, remember Momma's rules: look with your eyes, not with your hands."

"Don't worry, they play hockey. That's an instant boner-killer right there." Between my teammates when I was younger and Dad, it's become clear to me that the only thing hockey players are interested in is hockey. Guys with zero personality instantly lose ten hotness points.

"See you tomorrow, ball boy," Katey sings.

"Even *I* know hockey doesn't have balls."

"Yeah, but it sounds better than puck boy. Laters."

I heft my bag higher as I push my way through the doors. Thankfully there are no jocks around yet, seeing as there's still a good hour until practice, but Dad wanted me to get here early to meet some of the assistant coaches.

I walk down a hall filled with trophy cabinets and slow in front of the huge photo of the Frozen Four winning team from a season ago. Even though hockey and I will never get along, it makes me happy to remember Dad's excitement that night.

Last season was a different story. They were a mess to begin with, somehow pulled it together to make it to regionals, and then food poisoning and injuries plagued them. It's actually kind of unfair that they lost because it wasn't that they played horrible—they were four players down. It's a shame it didn't happen a few games earlier, though, because then I wouldn't be here now.

I wish I had the same passion for hockey that Dad does, but being on the ice felt like a chore, and seeing how different Dad would treat me when I played made me resent it.

At home, he's always been warm and calm. On the ice, he treated me like any of his other players. It's not like I wanted special treatment, but Dad in coach mode is intense and intimidating and someone I didn't like very much. It made me resent playing, but Dad could never understand that.

Note to parents everywhere: don't judge your kid based on what *you* like.

I make it to Dad's office and push inside without knocking. There are two others there already, and Dad introduces Assistant Coach Dalton and Beck, who I recognize as one of Dad's players from last season.

"This is my boy, Kole," Dad says. "He didn't think we'd make it to regionals last year, and because of that bad call, he's our equipment manager this season. Anything you need, just let him know."

"I'm happy to serve."

Dad sees right through my sarcasm and levels me with a look. "You *will* take it seriously. This might not be your scene, but I expect things will run smoothly."

"You've hired a hockey-phobe, not an idiot. I've got this."

"See that you do."

"No offense ..." Beck says, sounding exactly like he's about to be offensive. "But do you even know a thing about hockey?"

"I know enough."

"He played for seven years," Dad says, and there's that twinge of disappointment, clear as day. You'd think six years later, he'd be over it. "We've been through what I expect. He'll be fine."

"It's not all about the equipment though, is it?" Dalton asks, eyeing me. "He's going to be dealing with the team as well. Do you really think you'll be able to handle testosterone-filled divas?"

That turn of phrase reminds me of the guys I normally sleep

with, and I can't help a quick laugh from slipping out. "Yes, the *divas* will be fine. The equipment will be fine. I know what all the thing-a-ma-bobs are called, and when I'm counting, I can do this thing called adding and subtracting—it's wild." Three jocks stare back at me, not appreciating my teasing. "Fine. I've been top of literally all my classes since the seventh grade, and as much as I've tried *not* to, I know hockey and I know what's needed. I can handle the jocks, because I really don't give a damn about what a bunch of athletes think of me, and if any of them get too much, I'll play the *daddy* card."

Dad sighs like he was really hoping I'd be on my best behavior. But despite me being flippant and not wanting to be here, I do plan on taking it seriously. It's one season, and then I'll be released into the wild again.

"Come on, the team will start arriving soon." Dad stands, and Beck moves to follow him.

I'm about to head out the door too when Dalton calls me back.

"Coach Hogan speaks highly of you."

"I should hope so. He's my dad. It would be kinda shitty of him to talk down about me."

For some reason that makes Dalton hesitate. "Well, umm, I just want to make sure you really do know the ins and outs of this job."

"Lug equipment around, order new equipment, and have twenty-five hockey players treat me like their bellboy. How hard could it be?"

"There's other things. Like ..." Coach Dalton averts his gaze. "Keeping the players in line. Making sure they're not sneaking out of the hotel at away games. Telling us if you know of any drug use or rule breaking."

My eyes narrow. "I didn't realize being a snitch was in the job description." That's exactly what I need, angry jocks trying to find the guy who ratted them out for having fun.

"My brother Asher plays on the team. He's an excellent player but a bit of a loose cannon. The problem is your dad won't keep him on the roster if he gets into shit."

"That's not my problem. That sounds like yours."

"Like he listens to me about anything," Coach Dalton says. "Look, all I'm asking is you keep an eye on him and tell me if he's doing anything he shouldn't be."

"I mean this in the kindest way possible, but why would I want to do that?"

"You said you don't care what a bunch of hockey players think of you. Did you mean that?"

"Well, yeah …"

"Then you're not going to care about locking him in his room if you have to."

"*I* might not, but last I checked, the law is pretty clear when it comes to holding someone captive."

He finally manages a small smile, but even that looks like it takes effort. When I look at Dalton, all I see is bone-deep exhaustion. From his tired eyes to the slump in his shoulders … It makes me feel sorry for the man.

Sorry enough to do as he asks? I'm not sure if he's lying about equipment managers taking on that sort of warden role or not, but am I willing to do it anyway?

"I'm kind of out of options here, and I don't know what to do anymore when it comes to him." Dalton's voice is soft. No, it's downright *defeated*.

One more look into Dalton's expressive green eyes, and I have my answer.

"Fine," I huff. "I'll attempt to rein in the wayward son. But I'm not making any promises."

"No, totally." He runs a hand back through his hair. "Just knowing there's one extra set of eyes on him helps."

How bad can this guy be?

I get my answer half an hour later when a younger version of Coach Dalton stomps into the locker room a few minutes late. They both have the same dark hair and green eyes, but Coach Dalton has a few days' growth on his jaw and chin. His brother is clean-shaven. He throws his bag into his cubby with a loud *thump*, then drops onto the bench like he doesn't care that every person in the room is staring at him.

He'd probably be good-looking if he wasn't scowling, but with a single, menacing look, one thing is clear:

Asher Dalton is trouble.

Already I can tell that I'm not going to be looking out for the guy—I'm going to be babysitting him.

And let's face it, probably failing.

3

ASHER

"Sloppy!" my brother yells when my attempt to make a pass fails to hit my teammate's blade.

Hey, it's more words than he's spoken to me all summer, so there's that.

Apparently it took a couple of hours for the shock of seeing me and Ezra together to register, and then he hit a whole new level of angry. Silent treatment: achievement unlocked.

And shit, maybe it worked, because all summer, I did what he'd told me to do. I studied my ass off. I dropped the kids off at hockey. I went to school. I kept my head down. And I still only scraped by with a C in all my classes.

What do I have to show for it? A weakened body and slack playing. Hell, I'm slower than a lot of the freshmen out here. This is what happens when you spend all your time indoors and not working out. I don't know how nerds do it.

After my brother's torture, then comes Coach Hogan with skating drills.

"Blue Red Crossover, go."

We don't get a break before he's calling out the next one.

"Dot Drill."

Over and over again, drill to drill, Coach Hogan doesn't let up.

My lungs burn, and my muscles are starting to cramp. I am so unfit compared to a mere eight weeks ago. Note to self: learn to read while running on a treadmill or something.

Coach Hogan blows his whistle. "Box skate!"

We all groan.

He's never like this. He's a hardass but never this sadistic during training. Some of the guys in the locker room said he goes all out for the first practice of the year, but I wouldn't know—I was a late recruit last season.

A few newbies ask under their breaths how I was drafted to the NHL when I skate slower than a turtle in mud, but they're not as quiet as they think they are.

I'd like to tell them all to fuck off, but I can't even breathe, let alone speak.

And then the worst thing that could possibly happen does. My gut churns, and my lunch tries to make its way back up. It's a sprint to the sidelines so I can throw myself into the team box and hurl into a trash can.

"That might be a new record," Coach says. I turn my head to find him looking at his watch. "All right. Practice over. Someone make sure Dalton is hydrated."

Rossi, this year's captain, helps me off the ice.

Kill me now. I'll never live this down.

The familiar need to fight someone flares up. At least if they're distracted by my being an asshole, they won't focus on how weak I am. I'd rather people hate me than think I'm a joke.

And yep, even though I hold my head up high as I walk into the locker room, I'm met with snickers all round.

Great. Just great. Maybe I should've spent last year getting closer to Rossi or Simms, but instead I made friends with a guy who was graduating. Then again, that would've been difficult considering I took first line center—a position both Rossi and Simms were gunning for.

I start stripping down at my cubby and ignore everyone around me. I'm down to my jockstrap when a bottle of Gatorade is thrust in front of my face.

"Thanks," I murmur.

"No problem. I know from experience how hard Coach can push." He says that, but when I turn my head, it's not any of my teammates standing there.

It's a guy maybe an inch or two shorter than my six-one frame with dirty-blond hair, warm hazel eyes, and a cute smile. He looks too thin to be a hockey player.

He leans in. "He always goes too far on day one. Likes to pretend to be tough for all the new kids, but I'll let you in on a little secret." He lowers his voice. "He's a big teddy bear underneath all that."

Coach Hogan a teddy bear? Is this guy high?

"If you say so."

"I'm Kole." That killer smile widens. "Kole Hogan."

My face falls. "Coach is …"

"My dad. And this year I'm your equipment manager, so if you need anything, let me know, and I'll give it to you."

My cock twitches. What he said wasn't supposed to sound sexual, but apparently my body is going to take it that way. I mentally tell it to calm the hell down because having sex with a cactus would be less dangerous than fooling around with Coach's son, even if that destructive part inside me is already reveling in the fallout that tryst would bring.

As I watch Kole's gaze move over my almost naked form, I have to wonder if there was sexual innuendo implied after all.

I clear my throat. "Thanks for the drink."

Move away, Asher. Move away before you do or say something Asher-like.

"No problem."

I step away from him and head for the showers, realizing I still have the bottle of Gatorade in my hand and not my towel.

Fucking hell. Kole's still standing by my cubby when I march back in there and trade them out. He chuckles as I walk away again.

Only, now I realize I still have a jockstrap on. I strip that off and throw it across the room so I don't have to go back another time.

WEST BEATS me home because we took separate cars, and as soon as I step inside the house, it's obvious pandemonium has broken out.

Welcome to my life.

The twins are yelling at each other over whatever Xbox game they're playing, Zoe's yelling at West about being too young to look after four kids while he and I play stupid hockey, and Hazel's at the dining table, noise-canceling headphones on with her laptop open in front of her.

Okay then.

I turn to Bennett and Emmett. "Find a way to problem solve between yourselves, or guess what? Neither of you get to play the Xbox."

That shuts them up fast.

Now, Zoe's turn. "Why are you too young to look after the others?"

"Because they don't listen," she screeches. "Rhys went out. I don't know where. I've been trying to call you. He just ... *left*."

"He left," I say. "He's thirteen." Why in the fuck did he think it was okay to go out this late at night?

"Yes! What was I supposed to do? Leave the others here and go after him? This is too much pressure. This is *unfair*."

Oh, honey, you want to talk to me about unfair?

I give her my "Are you fucking kidding me?" glare, but then her blue eyes fill with tears, and I remind myself she's fifteen. I'm twenty-one and can barely handle all the chaos three preteens and a thirteen-year-old bring.

Last year, our system worked. Zoe was with the kids in the afternoons until West and I got home from practice, and West would stay home while the team was at away games. But I guess all the kids have had a hormonal surge, or maybe last year they were all too depressed to act out. Maybe Zoe's tired, which I understand. Either way, it's obvious it's not working anymore, and we shouldn't be putting that much pressure on Zoe.

I soften my voice. "Okay, here's what's going to happen. Zoe, go ... have a bath or whatever you womenfolk do to relax. West, you make some calls to Rhys's friends' parents, and I'll go for a walk and see if I can find him close by. He can't get far on foot."

West nods at me and moves into the kitchen to find the school binder with parents' names and contact numbers in it. "Wait, who are Rhys's friends?"

It speaks! Though, I don't know if it was directly to me or everyone in general.

"There's Tom, Harrison—actually, try Harrison's first," I say. "He lives close by, and they've been besties since they hung out all summer."

West blinks at me as if to ask how I know this, but it's not hard. I pay actual attention, unlike him, who seems to be checked out most of the time. He's here, but he's not really *here*.

"Okay." He looks down at the binder.

"Last name Ford," I say.

He lifts his head. "There's a kid named Harrison Ford in Rhys's class?"

I laugh. "No, but you should see your face. Real last name is Greer."

West flips me off, and I actually welcome it. Yes, a sense of normalcy for once! He finds the number and dials, but while he does that, I turn to Hazel and give her my best "I know you know things" stare.

I can communicate with all my siblings with one single look. "Where is he?" I ask her.

She points at her headphones and shakes her head.

"Where. Is. He?"

Hazel sighs and moves one side of the headphone away from her ear. "He was going to meet a girl. At the park."

"A girl? From school?"

She shrugs. "Online, I think."

"He's meeting a girl from online?" I screech. "Which park?"

"The one with the dog park in it. I think. I dunno, he said something about her walking a dog. I thought he was being gross, so I stopped listening."

That thing where I said I love my siblings? They make it really hard sometimes.

"West, I'm going out to look for him." Even though I'm dead tired after that grueling practice and it's pitch-black outside, I run to the park. It's only a block and a half away.

I swear to God, if my little brother has been trapped into some sex trafficking ring, I'm going to go full Liam Neeson on their asses.

I reach the park, breathless and sweating, but I can't see anyone anywhere. The streetlights illuminate the area to a certain degree, but not completely.

The only person I can see is a dude with a dog in the fenced-off play area beside me. Other than the occasional bark or growl, the whole place is silent.

I pant, sucking in sharp breaths, but I'm not sure if I'm winded because of the running or that I have no control over where Rhys is.

Fucking Christ on a cracker, Rhys can't be gone. We can't have screwed this up already.

I spin in a circle and grip my hair. Real fear shoots through me.

This can't be happening. This *can't* be happening.

Pressure grows in my chest, and I rub my sternum to try to dull the ache.

"Hey." The voice behind me is familiar, but not the one I'm hoping for.

I turn to find Kole, and I blink at the coincidence. "Are you following me?"

"Yes, I'm stalking you." He lowers his voice and mutters, "Fucking hockey players and their egos."

"Sorry. I'm not thinking clearly."

"Are you okay?" he asks.

I glance at him and then his … what I'm assuming he calls a dog. It looks like a hellhound of some sort.

"Asher?"

I shake it off. "Uh, my brother. He …" I can't push the words past my lips.

"Coach Dalton?"

"No. My younger brother. He's thirteen. He went out while we were at practice, and—"

A loud laugh sounds behind us, coming from the kids' playground. I'd know it immediately.

"Rhys?" I yell.

Then I hear, "Shit, it's my brother," in a loud hiss.

I charge over to the climbing tower and find two pairs of legs sticking out. Relief and anger surge through me in equal measures. I'm fully prepared to yell at Rhys for being stupid for meeting some rando, when the girl's face comes into focus.

"Wait, I know you. You go to Rhys's school." I look at Rhys. "Hazel said you were with someone you met online."

Rhys scoffs. "You really think I'm that dumb? I ain't telling Hazel shit. She'll tell everyone at school."

"Go home before I call your parents," I say to the girl, and then I eye my brother. "You need to get your ass home before West kills you. And then kills me for the fun of it."

They both scramble away, and even though I know he's safe, adrenaline is still kicking through me.

Taking a deep breath, I try to compose myself before I head back home. My hands tremble, and my chest burns. Ouch, no, it aches every time I suck in air.

Oh, shit, is this what a panic attack feels like?

I can't let anything happen to my younger siblings. The thought of losing another person …

I swallow hard and wince. Everything. Fucking. Hurts.

A calming hand lands on my shoulder. "Breathe. He's okay. It's okay."

I want to pull away and put my usual walls up—be the asshole I'm known to be. But I'm tired. So damn tired.

I blame it on utter exhaustion that I let Kole see me like this.

Kole sniggers, and at first I think it's at me. My hand fists at my side, and I grit my teeth, raring for a fight, but when I lift my head, Kole's focus is on something else. "Shit, I think you lit your brother's ass on fire. I swear he's leaving cartoon steam as he runs home."

I huff and follow his gaze to where my brother is indeed running faster than I could probably skate. I take out my phone, my hands still shaking as I try to come down from the adrenaline, and message West that Rhys is on his way back.

"Your parents should sign him up for track," Kole says.

"Mm, maybe." I pocket my phone, and just like in the locker room earlier, my gaze rakes over Kole's soft features.

His dirty-blond hair looks more brown in this light, but his hazel eyes are brighter.

A growling mutt nuzzles his way between us, and I jump back a bit.

"Hades, stop being such a whore," Kole says.

I almost choke. "Uh, what?"

"He growls whenever people are paying attention to anything but him. He's an attention whore."

"He looks like he'd bite my hand off if I tried to pet him."

"That's why he wants the attention." Kole kneels and pats his dog, who pants happily at the affection. The sight is so ... pure and ... the opposite of what I am.

"Strangers don't give it to him because he looks so fierce. Who's a fierce boy?" Kole's baby voice is kind of adorable.

No, not adorable.

What the hell is wrong with you, Asher? Get your head together.

I need to get out of here. "I should, uh, get back home. Make sure West doesn't kill Rhys, that the twins aren't killing each other, and that Zoe's calmed down from her panic attack." My eyes widen. "Oh, wow, I just realized that's a whole lot to dump on someone. Let's rewind that. I'm ... going home."

Kole tilts his head. "Why do you have to do all that and not your parents?"

This is the perfect opening for me to play the *woe is me* card. My parents are dead. My siblings and I are orphans. If the word "orphan" doesn't make someone uncomfortable, my blasé attitude when I say it usually does the trick, but tonight, my mouth doesn't cooperate. I couldn't stand to see the usual pity on Kole's face after what just happened with Rhys.

"They're … uh … not around."

"That sucks. Want to walk together? We're going the same way." He points in the direction Rhys ran.

Again, the urge to shoot him down is there, but I suddenly have no voice at all. All I can do is gesture for him to lead the way. I can do this.

I made friends last year … well, *friend*. But I can do it again. Maybe. Cohen seemed to like me in spite of my attitude. I tested him and his boyfriend repeatedly with my stupidity. They both took it in stride, though I'm fairly certain Cohen's boyfriend wanted to punch me a few times. I would've welcomed it if he did.

That said, making friends with Kole, specifically, seems like a recipe for disaster. I'm a fuckup. Sometimes on purpose. And fucking up with Kole is risky when Coach holds the entire season in his hands.

"Asher?" Kole asks, and I realize I spaced out.

"Right. Walk."

Just a walk.

With Coach's son.

4

KOLE

ASHER DALTON IS ... UNEXPECTED.

His hands are shoved deep in his pockets, and his shoulders are drawn up like he wants to retreat inside them like a shell. Everything about him is coiled tight. Defensive. It's a difference from earlier in the locker room. Before, his green eyes were intense and dark. Out here, under the streetlights, they're dull and weighted with defeat.

His lips are turned down, and we slip into silence as we leave the dog park.

When I'd seen Asher tonight, my first thought was that he was meeting a dealer or something. The way Coach Dalton asked for help, my immediate thought went to him being into the kinds of things that could get him kicked off the team, and with the way he was antsy and pacing ... Well, yeah, him looking for his little brother was the last thing on my mind.

Knowing the real reason behind his anxious twitching, I can't help being intrigued.

This afternoon, I labeled him as a *troubled asshole*. Now, he's ... loving brother?

It doesn't add up.

I try not to smile as he glances my way again. "Do I have something in my teeth?"

"I'm wondering how long it's going to take you to explain—" he waves a hand toward Hades "—*that*."

"My dog?" I play dumb but know exactly what he's asking.

"Yeah, what happened to the poor guy's face?"

I've had him for years, so I'm mostly unaffected by it, but every time Hades meets someone new, the questions start. "He was a shelter dog. All they could tell us is he has bull terrier in him, but it's obvious he's a mix of a million different breeds too. He's a true mutt. When animal rescue saved him, he was in a pretty bad way." Clearly. "They mentioned it was acid burns." It's not often I get angry, or want to hurt people, but thinking about what poor Hades went through always sets off a twist deep in my chest. He lost an ear, and one whole side of his face has been burned, so his eye is fused shut and teeth are exposed in places. They were worried his experiences would mean he'd be too aggressive and untrusting to be rehomed, but he's just your average puppy wanting love and affection—who happens to have a mangled face.

"You named your dog, who's had his face burned off, after a cartoon character with fire on his head?"

The disbelief in Asher's tone brings me back to the moment. "Hades was god of the underworld. If my dog hasn't mastered death, I don't know who has."

"Still think Hellhound suits him better."

"You sensing a kindred spirit?"

"Mutual troublemakers. He looks like he hates being told what to do too." He points at where Hades is tugging hard on his leash. He's never been great at walking. "What made you pick him out of all the other dogs?"

"Not sure, really. It was a feeling. There were a few others I wanted, but you know that moment, where you set your eyes on something and just *know?* We were meant for each other."

Asher stares at Hades. "Can't say I know the feeling."

I can sense his mood taking a dive again. "So, do you get all your general knowledge from cartoons?"

"Pretty much. They're about my intellect level." Asher grins. It almost reaches his eyes. "But, uh, having a heap of younger siblings will do that."

"Are they all younger? There were ... four, did you say?"

"Five. Plus me and West."

"Wow."

He shakes his head roughly. "What about you?"

"Only child. Wish I had siblings."

He opens his mouth to throw something back but stops himself. "They're mostly okay."

Silence slips between us again. Normally, I'm great at small talk. I can hold a conversation with anyone. Professors, my friends, the researchers at my internship. When you grow up ugly, you learn to accommodate. *He has a great personality* applied strictly to me until senior year of high school.

Asher, apparently, is terrible at small talk. Or at least, he is with me. It shouldn't bother me, shouldn't even be on my radar, because befriending jocks isn't something I tend to do. And if I'm honest, if it weren't for Coach Dalton asking me to keep an eye on Asher, I probably would've kept walking tonight, but I'm glad I stopped. Pleasantly surprised, even.

I try not to stereotype, but the jocks I've met—and I've met *a lot* through hockey and Dad—only want to talk about sports.

"Do you feel better now?" I ask, trying to revive this conversation.

His expression tenses. "I'd convinced myself Rhys was meeting up with some sick fuck from the internet. I was a little panicked, okay?"

"I was actually talking about hurling at practice today, but yeah, I can understand why your brother was your first thought. Has he ever done something like that before?"

"Not that I know of. But until last year, I was away playing for the juniors, so who the hell knows."

I almost ask if his parents are going to be angry, but they seemed like a touchy subject for him, so I turn the conversation somewhere I'm sure will hold his interest while boring me to tears. "Think you'll make the Frozen Four this year?"

Instead of the immediate uplift I'm expecting, Asher's tense shoulders slump. "Probably not."

"Already writing it off? Don't let Dad hear that."

Finally, *finally* that gets a real smile. "I can't believe Coach Hogan is your dad. What's that like?"

"Like any dad, I suppose. He has high standards for me, he loves me, but ever since I quit hockey, there's always been a little … distance and disappointment."

Asher snickers. "*You* played hockey?"

"Hey …" I shove him playfully. "I did. And I was good too."

"Get out."

"I was."

"No fucking way. I don't believe it."

"I quit when I was fourteen. You can imagine how that went down."

"I'm surprised he didn't kick your ass."

"Me too, actually."

"So … why did you? Quit, I mean." Asher sounds like he's curious when he really doesn't want to be.

"I didn't like it, for one. And around that time, I was figuring myself out. Working through what I wanted in life. Sports wasn't one of those things. Boys were though."

Asher turns to me, and I look up to meet his eyes.

"I'm gay, by the way. I always make sure I get that out there early on, because I don't have time for assholes."

Asher looks stunned for a moment. I'm lucky in that I've never felt like my sexuality has made me a target, and with all the queer guys who've passed through the CU team, I'm pretty sure it won't now either.

"Sounds to me like you'd have plenty of time for assholes. Literally."

I laugh hard. I was not expecting that response. "I take it you're cool, then."

"You won't get any trouble from me." But there's something in the way he says it that makes me not so sure. It's almost teasing. And not in a bad way. Asher's broad smile has completely taken over his face, and he almost looks like a different person.

I could see Katey being attracted to him instantly.

Luckily, I'm smarter than that. It takes more than a pretty face to draw me in.

We reach a corner, and Asher slows. "That's me down there."

I'm about to say goodbye, when he drops to his knees and scoops Hades up into his arms. My dumb dog barks excitedly in his face as Asher squeezes him tight and scratches his head furiously.

"Ah, shit," Asher says. "He peed on me."

I catch my laugh. "He does that when he's excited."

"Thanks for the heads-up." Asher eases Hades off his lap. "Anytime Hellhound wants a pissing post, you let me know."

"Will do." I drag my gaze from the dog up to Asher and find

him watching me. This close, I can make out the bright shade of green in his eyes, and when he's not scowling, he seems like someone I could be friends with. I hesitate over offering him my number, because while he's okay now, I sense that overall, he's not. I've come to learn that offering guys your number after letting them know you're gay can be taken the wrong way. Asher seems cool, but I really have no idea of his sexuality, and most people still think straight is the default—so when he didn't offer up details on his preferences, it makes me lean toward that assumption. "I'll see you tomorrow."

I watch him leave before walking the three blocks home.

Dad's in his office when I first walk in, so I let Hades off his leash to run outside and throw myself in the armchair across from Dad's desk.

"You'll never guess who I just ran into."

"Oh, yeah? Who?"

"One of your players. Asher Dalton. You'll be proud. I'm being nice already."

Dad stops whatever he's reading and rubs his wide jaw. "Asher, huh?"

Uh-oh. I know that tone. "Yeah. He was looking for his kid brother at the park."

There's silence for a moment, and I know Dad's trying to work out what to say. "The Daltons are … they've been through a lot. I like that you're being nice to Asher, but keep it at that. Nice. Professional."

"Nice? You made him throw up at practice."

"That's hockey, that's not personal."

Hockey. Of course. Everything is *just hockey* like I wouldn't understand. "He seems okay to me."

"Well, deep down I'm sure he's a good kid. But he's troubled.

He's got a lot on his plate. And so do you. Being premed, you don't have time to take on another pet project."

"Pet project?"

Dad waves his hand. "You know. There's always someone, or something, that needs saving. I love that about you. But you'll do that as a doctor, and Asher ... leave this one. Trust me."

Great. Because that will help with me telling Coach Dalton I'd keep an eye on him.

I knew being the team narc wasn't in the job description, but that now has me curious.

First Coach Dalton, then Dad. Why is everyone acting like Asher is a lost cause?

The *pet project* comment pisses me off. Though I know Dad doesn't mean it to be offensive, it's rooted in the type of deep-seated toxic masculinity that says a man shouldn't *care* about things.

Well, I do.

I like making people happy. I like helping them. It's *why* I want to be a doctor.

The fact Dad's told me not to give Asher a second thought has the rebellious side of me awakening. It doesn't happen often. Only when it's something I feel strongly about, and not turning my back on people who could use help is one of them.

Quitting hockey and being true to myself, also one of them.

People are wrong about Asher. I have no idea how I know that, but even watching him during practice gave me that feeling, and then tonight cemented it.

Asher isn't who he pretends to be. He just needs to prove it to people.

Except the next afternoon when I get to practice early and start to haul the equipment out onto the ice, Asher seems determined to prove *me* wrong.

I pause on my way into the locker room when I overhear voices. I have no idea who's talking, but it's about me.

"Why do you reckon Coach hired his son this year? Think it's to keep an eye on us?"

I tense as the locker room quiets down. When the voices start talking, I can't work out who is who.

"You think that's what it is?"

"Why else?"

"Fuck. Think Coach knows about the puck bunnies we smuggled into the hotel last year?"

Jocks are not smart. Dad could walk in here at any moment, and they're barely keeping their voices down. He doesn't need me to snitch when they're doing it themselves.

"Why don't you guys shut up already?" That voice, I know. It's not that Asher has a distinct sound, but it's definitely him. "Don't worry about the coach's kid. He's just a bag bitch who got his job because of daddy. Worry about yourselves. You'll all look pathetic out there if you can't keep up with me, and if any of you are hoping to score NHL contracts, you better up your game."

"Says the guy who puked during first practice."

Insults start getting fired back and forth as I slowly retrace my steps away from there.

I try to ignore what he said about me, but that familiar disappointment whenever people show their bigoted side kicks in. *Bag bitch.* It's not quite an f-bomb or some other slur, but it makes me feel as small. Even if it's technically true. I *am* the team's bag bitch this year—but there are so many other ways to say it. He used that phrasing, knowing I'm … me. The term *bitch* adds a level of ick.

I thought he was cool with the gay thing, but maybe he's not.

And it doesn't matter. We're not friends. He's perfectly entitled to his opinion. Like I'm perfectly entitled not to have time for people like that.

Maybe Dad was right and Asher is more trouble than he's worth.

I don't know what Coach Dalton expects, but if Asher's determined to live up to his reputation, nothing I do will help.

ASHER

When deciding on a major, I weighed up two different options. Athletic Training or Dietetics, Nutrition, and Food Sciences, but the ultimate plan is still the NHL. On the off chance the NHL doesn't want me when I graduate though, I need something to fall back on. I figure I could go into coaching or become a dietician for athletes.

I didn't want to follow in West's footsteps, so I ended up choosing nutrition. And I'm regretting it.

I didn't know how many health and biochemistry courses I'd have to do.

And as I get back my weekly assignment from medical terminology class with a big fat D at the top, I realize I might have bitten off more than I can chew.

These weekly grades don't count a whole lot toward my final mark, but it's a hit nonetheless. Maybe I should change majors.

At first I'm disappointed in the grade, and then I'm pissed because I shouldn't even be at this damn school. By the time I head for practice, that adrenaline that makes me do stupid shit is already coursing through me. My usual scowl is in place.

Then I see Kole coming the other way down the hall of the hockey rink, and a smile finds my face for what feels like the first time all day. "Hey."

His eyes meet mine for a split second, and he gives me a nod, but he keeps walking.

And the scowl is back. Along with the dark cloud hanging over me, urging me to be the guy I don't want to be but can't seem to help when it comes so easily.

I thought that night at the park Kole and I were on our way to somewhat being friends. Learning he was gay should have scared me off because I know me, and I'd likely take advantage of that at some point—whether to piss off West or just because Kole is hot and it would be fun, fuck the consequences—but I still decided to be friends anyway. Since then, he's basically ignored me. It's very possible I did *something*, but I have no idea what.

Doesn't matter anyway. If I don't get close to anyone, I can't hurt them. Or vice versa.

I enter the locker room, and like always, the rest of the team stares but mostly ignores me. I can't say I blame them.

We get suited up and hit the ice, and after a few warm-up drills, we're put into a scrimmage. Coach is playing with the lines, and he's moved Simms from second line center to first line winger.

We're both not happy about it. He's not used to playing left, and the freshman, Kaplan, on my other side has amazing raw talent but is still green. Since that first practice, I'm back on top of my game, but it's obvious everyone else is still on vacation.

Our line is getting pummeled by Rossi's, and we're supposed to be the best. This is really what Coach Hogan thinks will get us the W?

We're switched out for another line, and all three of us sit next to each other in the team box, slumped with scowls on our faces.

Beck skates over to us. Last year this guy was playing with us. Now he's an assistant coach. "You're gonna have to do better than that."

"Thanks, Captain Obvious," I mutter.

"Gelling with new line mates is hard, only made harder if you're all more stubborn than Jacobs and I ever were. We put our personal shit aside on the ice and still managed to work as a team, even when we hated each other. Put your egos aside and get it done."

I liked him better when he wasn't an authority figure.

The next time we hit the ice, instead of doing what Beck says, Simms decides to play his own game. Kaplan tries to keep up with me, and I try to work out what the fuck Simms is doing, while our captain, Rossi, fires bullets at our goalie.

I manage to get the puck off a rebound from Schofield's pads, and I pass to Kaplan. We make some ground, and Kaplan passes back to me, but before it hits my blade, Simms cuts across me, comes into my goddamn zone, and takes the puck ... from *me*. His *teammate.*

And even though Coach blows his whistle to get us to stop. Even though he, my brother, and Beck will handle it, my inner asshole comes flying out.

I shove him. "What the fuck was that?"

"It was reflex," Simms yells. "I'm not used to being a winger yet."

"Where'd you learn to play? At the school of narcissism?"

"That's rich coming from you. I'm surprised you even know the word 'narcissism.' Wouldn't have picked it with your ... grades."

Ooh, hitting me where it really hurts. My intellect. Joke's on him, because I don't give a shit about grades.

"At least I'm not a pigeon."

Simms's eyes fill with the kind of ire I thrive on. The kind that leads to getting exactly what I want.

It urges me to keep going. "Hope you can find your girlfriend's G-spot better than you can the net."

The team's collective "Oooh" and Coach's "That's enough" is drowned out as Simms tackles me to the ice.

My head hits the cold surface, but I don't feel it. Stupid helmet saving my life and whatever. Simms manages to land a punch to the left side of my face, and I'm thankful my helmet at least doesn't have a cage because I can feel the entire force of his fist.

It hurts.

It burns.

Most importantly, it reminds me I can actually feel pain.

He gets another punch in, but it lands on my pads, and then he's hauled off me.

Beck helps me up, and I smirk at Simms.

"You hit like my eleven-year-old sister."

It sounds like an insult, but it's really not. Don't piss off Hazel. She's fucking fierce.

Either way, the taunt works. Simms launches for me again, and I'm disappointed when he's held back.

Coach Hogan's face is beet red as he yells at both of us to get off his ice.

Gladly.

"Kole," Coach Hogan calls. Kole gets up from where he's sitting in the stands. I didn't even know he was watching. "Make sure they don't kill each other in the locker room."

Kole mock salutes his dad.

"Everyone else, get back to work. We have first line spots to fill."

Okay, now that hurts. A tip for anyone wanting to piss me off:

you can say shit about my parents dying, you can say shit about me being a dumb jock with shitty grades, you can even dissect my sexuality and call me any slur under the sun because screw your opinions of who I sleep with. What you can't do is take hockey away from me.

We trudge down the chute and into the locker room, both Simms and I still full of adrenaline and the urge to fight.

Simms throws his helmet across the room and glares at me, while I cock my brow, just daring him to come at me again.

But then Kole steps between us, and I deflate. I deflate so fast I have to wonder if he's an antidote to adrenaline.

His hazel eyes bore into me, his lips pulled into a thin line, and I suddenly feel about two feet tall.

Simms undresses quickly and heads for the showers, leaving us alone.

"Have fun out there?"

Yes. "Being punched isn't supposed to be fun."

"That didn't answer my question."

"You heard Simms. I'm barely keeping my grades up to stay on the team. I'm not very smart. Why would picking a fight be fun?" *Yes, Asher, why would it be?*

"Do you feel any better?" Kole taunts.

I don't like his tone. "Better than what?"

"I get it. You play the dumb card or the asshole card to get out of expressing any kind of emotion."

Bam. Direct hit.

Apparently, calling me on my shit is also on the list of things that can hurt me. I just didn't know until this very minute because no one ever fucking does it. They call me out for my bad behavior. Not the cause of it.

I swallow hard. "I don't know what you're talking about."

"So, instead of being thrown off the team for not keeping your grades up, you'd rather be kicked off the team for fighting. Got it."

"They won't kick me off the team. This school needs me."

"Funny. They won the Frozen Four without you two seasons ago. What did you guys place last year again? Oh, wait ... you were knocked out at regionals."

"I had food poisoning and couldn't play."

"All I'm saying is, if you want my dad to keep you on this team, you might want to think about becoming a team player. No one is irreplaceable. I've seen him cut more talented guys with less shitty attitudes."

Here comes the guilt again. The high I get from hurting never lasts long. It's always replaced quickly with *Why the hell did I think that was a good idea?*

Kole sighs. "I'll go get ice for your face. Your eye is starting to swell."

Ooh, fun.

6

KOLE

When I get back with an ice pack, Asher's exactly where I left him, except now he's stripped right down to his jock.

Because of course.

I guess I should thank my lucky gay gods that he's still wearing that because Asher's body is … well, you don't train every day and wind up looking like me.

It's a damn tragedy that athletes have to look so good.

I throw the ice pack his way and sit down on the bench opposite him. "So what was the fight about?"

"What do you mean? You saw it."

"I saw him cut you off, sure, but it's not like it's the first time it's happened today. Or all week. And he's not the only one who's done it out there."

"Why do you care?"

"I don't." I lean forward. "Dad sent me, remember?"

"Always do what daddy says?"

"When I'm working and he's the boss, sure."

Asher doesn't have a comeback for that. It's sort of fun, watching him struggle to hang on to his scowl when he's clearly not feeling it anymore. "Some of the guys think you're here this year to spy for him."

"Do they?"

"Yeah, so it probably won't work."

"Noted." I don't point out that *his brother* is the one who asked me to spy because I get the feeling that will set Asher off. "Did you have a plan out there at least?"

"For?"

"Oh, are we pretending you're dumb again? Fine. A plan for after you got your lights punched out and Dad screams himself hoarse. What happens then?"

"I shower and go home."

"Well, I'm glad you have it all thought through."

This time his scowl is genuine. "If you want to call me an idiot, do it. You'd be right. Then I can go shower and put this shit-hole of a day behind me."

"If only it worked like that." I eye him and the way his muscles are coiled, wanting another fight. His hand is tight around the ice pack in his lap. "You realize that can't help your eye unless you actually, you know, put it on there."

He tosses it onto the bench beside him. "Fuck my eye."

Pleasant. I stand and cross toward him to pick it up and do it myself.

"What are you doing?"

"My job is to make sure the players have what they need." I step forward. My finger gently rests under his chin as I tilt his head up before pressing the ice pack over his injury.

Asher cringes for a moment, from the cold or the pain, but it sort of serves him right.

"You want to be careful." I nod in the direction of his helmet sitting next to him. "Those things aren't foolproof. You can still get hurt."

"Maybe that's what I want."

My eyebrows jump up. With the ice pack still pressed to his face, he's uncomfortably close. His body heat is coming off him in waves and matches the way he's studying me. He wants a reaction from me, and I'm confused about whether he's telling the truth or whether he's trying to shock me. I get the feeling with Asher it could go either way.

But then I replay the fight in my head. His anger, the taunting, and then as soon as Simms was on him, he went limp.

"That's why you didn't fight back." Finally, I look down at him.

His glare is more intense than I'm ready for, and I almost want to look away again. "I'm surprised you noticed."

"I do have eyes."

"Yeah, but most people see what they want to see." He tries to play it off like he doesn't care, but there's something in his tone that makes me think it's all bullshit.

"Why have you been ignoring me all week?" he suddenly asks.

"I haven't. We talked on Monday."

"Yeah, four days ago."

"Technically three if you don't count today, which I don't, because look—we're talking."

"Now who's playing dumb?"

That makes me laugh, but I quickly cut it off when I remember *why* I've been keeping my distance. "I didn't think *you'd* notice. I'm just the *bag bitch*, after all."

Understanding slowly takes over. "You know I was saying that to get them to shut up about you, right?"

"Yeah, but it's the word you chose. Gay men get called *bitch* to make them sound weak and feminine. And yeah, I'm not some tough jock like the rest of you, but—"

"It's only a word. I didn't mean anything by it."

"Words have meaning though."

"I call people bitch all the time. It has nothing to do with their sexuality."

"In that case, I'm surprised you don't get punched more often."

He looks like he wants to argue back but stops himself. For one wild moment, I think he's going to apologize. "Fine. I won't call you a bitch again." That's *close*, I suppose.

Asher stands suddenly, and I'm so shocked I forget to step back. His body presses against mine as a slow smile takes over his face. "So you know, I don't give a shit about the gay thing." He drops his voice. "The last person I had sex with was a guy."

Nerves shoot through my gut, but I force myself not to react. He's playing with me. It's what Asher does. "Is your whole starting lineup queer?"

"Only last year. Besides, I don't consider myself queer. Not really. More … whatever floats my boat if you get what I'm saying. Whoever gets the sails going. Whoever pops my … tent."

I hold up my hand. "I get it."

"For instance, the last guy was one of West's old teammates. He was hot and had a wicked mouth, but he was a means to an end. He served a purpose. That's all."

My skin flushes because while I don't know if he's trying to tease me or turn me on or make me uncomfortable, his rumbly voice near my ear has my body auto responding.

I force myself to step back and put distance between us. "You slept with Ezra Palaszczuk? Intimidating much?"

"You know Ezra?"

"You don't think every time an NHL player has come out, Dad hasn't been all 'Look, you *can* be gay and play professional hockey' like that was why I quit?" I roll my eyes.

"Oh. Umm, well, yeah, he and West are best friends, so …"

"Ah, so you slept with him to make your brother angry. Were you hoping he'd hit you too?"

"Westly doesn't hit. Believe me, I've tried."

I can't work out whether Asher wants me to like him or to push me away. Sleeping with people to hurt others isn't a stand-up quality in a guy, but with Asher, I get the impression it goes so much deeper than that.

He turns to grab his towel from his cubby, and my stare immediately drops to his bare ass.

"Are you checking me out?"

I jump at being caught, but he's smiling again. "Just objectifying you."

"And that's better because …"

"It's not personal. You have a nice butt." It might be my imagination, but I swear he flexes.

"This is hockey. Literally everyone here has a nice butt."

"And I'll objectify them too."

I won't, because I have better self-preservation skills than that. I'm not Asher. But now I know the thought of being with a guy—or having a guy check him out—doesn't bother Asher, I'm not worried about admiring all that lean muscle.

Katey said to look but don't touch, after all.

That I can do.

"Careful," he says. "I can't imagine your dad being cool with you checking out his players."

I pretend to draw a halo over my head. "I am a sweet, innocent angel."

"You were eye fucking my ass."

I shrug. "Again, it's a nice ass."

"You're lucky I know better than to think you're flirting with me."

I don't answer, because yes, I *am* flirting, just a bit, but I don't actually want it to go anywhere. First, because hockey players are a solid no, and second, he's right. Dad would *hate* it if I hooked up with one of his players. Especially when he's already warned me away from this player in particular.

Asher starts for the showers and then turns back to me. "Hey, do you wanna be friends?"

"What is this, grade school?"

"Forget it."

"Asher." I can't help laughing at how ridiculous he is. "Yes. We can be friends."

The sound of the running shower suddenly cuts off, and Simms walks back into the locker room. He's glaring at Asher, so I wait until Asher's disappeared into the showers before I check Simms is okay and leave.

I don't know what I'm getting into by being friends with Asher, but if he's consistent, I'm sure he'll do something soon enough to piss me off or push me away.

Fun times.

Dad and Coach Dalton are on their way down from the rink, and I make a split-second decision to say something.

"Dad, wait."

"I don't have time, Kole. I have a pair of dumbasses I need to deal with."

"That's what I wanted to say." I quickly step in front of him and block his path. "You should go easy on them."

"What for? You of all people know there's no fighting on my ice."

"Well …" *Think, Kole!* "Simms was provoked—we all heard it. And Asher, *technically*, didn't fight. You can't punish him for taunting, because the other teams do that all the time. Your players need to be ready for it."

Dad clenches his jaw so tight I can tell he still wants to explode. I don't doubt for a second that no matter what he decides, he's going to head into that locker room and tear into both of them. But hopefully they can get out of this unpunished.

"You know I'm right," I point out.

Dad shakes his head. "They're both on thin ice."

"Literally."

And now Dad's scowling. How new for him. "If they pull this shit again …" He's about to say they'll be off his team, but he hesitates. Maybe Asher's right that Dad wouldn't kick him off. He's undoubtedly the best player, and they need him.

Dad storms off in the direction I've come from, and I let out a long breath. I *think* that means they're okay? Dad's intense when it comes to hockey, but he's logical too.

Coach Dalton doesn't make a move to follow him. "I can't believe you did that."

"What?"

"Stuck up for Asher." He turns to lean against the wall. "Sometimes I think I'm the only one who'll fight for him. And I mean the *only* one because he won't do it for himself."

"I'm getting that impression."

"Is he okay?"

"Yeah, his eye is a bit swollen, but he'll be fine."

Coach Dalton sighs. "I don't know why he has to be such a hothead all the time."

I'm not so sure Asher *is* a hothead. Yeah, he gets angry, but it's more of a calculated burst than an uncontrolled explosion.

"He's always been like that, but it's gotten worse since our parents died."

His words hit me right in the face. "Your parents are dead?"

"He didn't tell you?"

"He said they weren't around. I assumed he meant they worked a lot."

Coach Dalton blinks at the opposite wall. "Normally Asher tells everyone. He shoves it in people's faces like he's forcing them to pity us."

Pity? No. Asher isn't the type to want pity. Though I'm definitely feeling something similar toward him right now. "Or ... like he's trying to make them hurt the way he is."

Coach Dalton's head snaps toward me. "You think that's it?"

"I have no idea. I barely know Asher." Though I'm starting to suspect no one does. Considering he's dealing with school and hockey on top of losing his parents and looking after his siblings ... Wait, does that mean that Coach Dalton and Asher are raising those kids?

That's a lot to take on, and not having a support system would only make it harder.

I think I'm starting to understand him more than I ever wanted to.

He's ... lonely.

Well, that, at least, I can help with.

Asher Dalton just gained a new best friend. Whether he wants it or not.

7

ASHER

"Give it back!" one of the twins screams.

"It's my turn!"

"Shut up, I'm trying to do homework!" Hazel yells.

Even in the basement, I can hear my siblings. And West is always surprised when I say I can't get any studying done. This is why.

I'm slumped over my desk, my head in my hand as I read over the same paragraph ten times because it's still not sinking in.

I don't understand because digestion is simple. Mouth, esophagus, stomach, liver, intestines, bowel. There's a gall bladder in there somewhere too, I'm sure. My point is, shouldn't I be learning about what foods are good and which ones are bad? So then I can be all "Carbs good. Sugar baaad" to my future nonexistent clients because I'm going to be a hockey player no matter what.

Even if I have to play for the AHL for a while. Hell, even the ECHL. I don't care if the pay is shitty as long as I get to play.

I stare at the words again, trying to memorize the function of the liver because apparently "It gets rid of all the toxic shit you put in your body" is not an appropriate essay answer. Don't know why. Seems perfectly valid to me.

Gah. I need a break.

I close my laptop and amble my way upstairs for a drink. I'm hit with a wall of noise.

"It's eight o'clock. Time for bed," I sing.

"They haven't eaten dinner yet," West says from the kitchen where he's trying to cook … I want to say taco meat? I can't be sure.

"I can do it." I try to take over, but West nudges me out of the way.

"How's studying?"

"I can't concentrate with all the noise. I'll try again when they're all asleep."

"That's going to be a while. Why don't you go to the library at school and try to get it done? You're dangerously close to losing your spot on the team."

I scowl. "You've been checking up on me?"

"I'm your coach. Your professors have to report your grades."

Fuck that shit.

"I'll do it after the kids are fed."

"No." West raises his voice. "You'll go do it now."

I huff. "Fine. Whatever. Don't accept my help."

Emmett comes into the kitchen and opens the fridge for something to eat.

"Dinner's almost ready, Ben," West says.

I grab an apple from the fruit bowl and throw it to Emmett. "That's Em," I tell West and make my exit.

"Damn it. Sorry, Emmett."

If West doesn't learn to tell those two apart soon, teen life with them is going to be so hard.

I go back downstairs and grab everything I'll need and shove it in my bag.

Maybe being in a library will help me feel smarter, therefore I will think smarter.

The drive is only a couple of minutes, and parking is usually a bitch, but this time of night it's not too bad.

I make my way inside the three-story building and automatically head for the study rooms people usually use for group assignments. Anywhere else and I'm worried I'll get lost. Not a big shocking revelation here, but I don't know the library well. Or ... really at all.

Kole's head pops up from a table near the door as I enter, and ... *whoa*. Kole's wearing glasses. Black, square ones that frame his eyes, and all my blood flows south.

If you'd asked me two seconds ago if I had a nerd kink, the answer would have been hell no, because someone like Foster's boyfriend, Zach, would have come to mind. But this ... tall, chiseled features, and *glasses*? I've found my new weakness.

He's with a group of other people I don't recognize, but that doesn't stop the smartass from coming out of me.

I smile and wave. "I know, right? I didn't think I could step inside here without bursting into flames, but apparently a library is not like a church."

His friends don't seem amused, but at least Kole's lips twitch.

"So, this is a library, huh?"

Still nothing. Oh well.

And now this is awkward.

"I'm just gonna ..." I tip my head in the direction of a free desk and then follow through.

But like at home, I can't concentrate. Only, I can't blame the noise this time.

The words are there, I understand them fine, but it's not

sinking in. I don't have a learning disability or anything like that, but it's hard for me to retain information on things that I find mind-numbingly boring.

I read and read and read, but all my brain is doing is going "Ooh, look, shiny things" and "I want to nap." Then there's the screaming in my head like "Why are you doing this to me? Please don't make me think with the thinks. Braining is too hard."

I've barely gotten any further in the text when I sense a presence standing above me.

"You look like you're having so much fun." Kole's hazel eyes shine in amusement, even through his glasses.

"This is worse than getting punched in the face."

He takes the seat next to me. "Yes, well, as we established, you find being punched fun, so ..."

I want to argue with him that it's not so much fun, but telling him that hurting makes me feel alive is probably not that much better.

"What are you working on?" he asks.

"Digestion. Fun stuff."

"What are you struggling with?"

"All of it. Sometimes I wonder if my brain is an actual brain or if maybe it's, like, an avocado."

Kole laughs. "Want some help?"

Yes. "Nah, it's okay. Thanks though."

"Seriously, I'm premed. I could talk to you about the digestive system all day."

I bite my lip. Do I really want Kole to see how much of a dumbass I am? Then again, he saw me pick a fight for absolutely no reason, and you can't get more dumbass than that. A smarter guy would work to put distance between us, not encourage a friendship that I'm sure I'll screw up. "If you're okay with it."

"More than okay." He pulls my laptop closer. "I took this

course freshman year. I can totally help you. I probably still have all my notes too."

"You ... keep your notes?"

"If I'm going to go to med school, I need to be good at note and record keeping. Okay, where should we start?"

"I was trying to memorize all the technical terms for the functions of each organ, but I gave up on that. I can't even remember all the parts to the intestinal tract. There are three segments of the small intestine alone."

Kole nods. "Okay, and what's your problem? Is it spelling the words, remembering them, what?"

"I'm not the type of guy to look at a text and memorize it. I don't have a photographic memory."

"Neither do I. We use mnemonic devices to help remember."

"What's that?"

Kole takes my notebook and writes Intestinal Tract.

Duodenum.

Jejunum.

Ileum.

Cecum.

Appendix.

Colon.

Sigmoid colon.

A concentration line forms above his brow, and then he starts writing. "Defenseman Josi ices Crosby and chirps Sceviour. DJICACS."

"Sorry, what?"

"If you remember this sentence, you'll remember the letters the intestinal tract starts with, and then it will be easier to pull the words from your brain."

"So to recall words, I have to learn ... more words. That makes no sense."

"I tried to make it hockey related."

"All that really told me is you're a Pittsburgh fan, and that's just blasphemous."

"Let me guess, you love Boston."

"Nope. Was a huge fan of Buffalo because they drafted me, but having to turn it down kind of soured me on them."

"Why'd you turn it down?"

I eye him and think about how much to tell him. The smart answer: nothing. Keeping a layer of distance between us is a good thing. That doesn't stop my mouth from answering, "Had to."

"Oh. Because of your parents?"

I frown. "You know about that?"

"Your brother told me."

"When did you talk to my brother? Is he telling you shit about me? Let me guess, making excuses for my bad behavior …" I don't realize my voice is raised until someone nearby shushes me, but I don't like the idea of Kole and West sitting around talking about me like—

Kole's hand lands on my forearm. "Calm down. It was the other day after your fight. We were in the corridor of the rink, and he said something about your attitude only getting shittier since your parents died. The way you talked about them, I thought they were busy working all the time. I didn't know. I'm sorry."

I pull out of his hold. "Why are you sorry? You didn't kill them."

Kole's voice lowers. "Because it was a shitty thing that happened to you."

"Yep." Like whenever I talk about my dad and stepmom's accident, I'm short and to the point.

I know it comes out cold and distant, but I need to remove myself from it emotionally.

West always worries that I haven't cried since their deaths. He thinks I haven't mourned properly. But I don't see the point in crying over something I can't change. I'm more angry than sad. My ruined future isn't even a blip on why I'm so pissed.

They were happy. My siblings were happy. West and I might've been a handful, but with us gone and out of their house, they were living the dream of the perfect family. The house might be old, but they made it a home.

I don't understand why they had to die.

Instead of making me sad, it makes me want to go to Heaven, if that place even exists, and punch God in the face. They didn't deserve it, and the kids sure as fuck don't deserve me and West to be their guardians.

"Sorry. We don't have to talk about them," Kole says. "You kind of disappeared there."

Like I always do, I play it off like I don't care. "Eh. Shit happens."

His eyes narrow. "Okay. Umm, about those mnemonic devices."

I sigh. "Thanks for helping, but I don't know how much good it'll do. Do you think if I take a puck to the head repeatedly, I could get information to stick that way?"

"Uh, no. I highly don't recommend you try that."

I slump.

"Tell you what. I'll room with you at away games, and we can work on it together."

My gaze flies to his. "What?"

"You need help. I have to be at away games because I'm your bag bitch—"

"Don't use that term. It's offensive."

He rolls his eyes. "I don't have much time outside of my required hours at the rink, but I can help you. If you want. What are friends for?"

I want to take him up on his offer, I do. But it's becoming more apparent he's a really nice guy, and I'm ... not.

"Come on. It's impossible to turn down a hot guy offering to tutor you."

I know. That's the problem. Us. Alone. In a hotel room. I can't bank on me not doing something Asher-like.

"I'll take your lack of response as a yes. Besides, even if you said no, I'm the one who controls the rooming assignments anyway. You're stuck with me."

I like the sound of that. I *shouldn't*, but I do.

"Ooh, and speaking of games, are you ready for the pre-preseason game against UVM?"

"You've seen us on the ice. What do you think?"

"Things with Simms aren't any better?"

"Yeah. He came over for a sleepover, and we braided each other's hair and sang Carly Rae Jepsen. Fun times."

"You're not going to win if you guys can't gel."

"I know that, but he's a dick."

"Oh, and you're a pure ray of sunshine?"

"Exactly."

Kole pats my shoulder. "Keep thinking that, buddy."

8

KOLE

When it comes to Colchester U, there isn't a huge divide between the jocks and the rest of us mere mortals like at some other colleges my high school friends went to. For the most part. The hockey team is a totally different story.

Over the years, they've steadily grown in popularity and fan base, and then along came Foster Grant. Insanely talented, yes, but also out and proud and completely confident in who he is.

I remember the first time Dad mentioned him. Foster was only a freshman, and I was still in my ugly-duckling phase. I maybe, sort of, developed a crush, but Foster had no idea I even existed. It was around then I quit hockey and started to work out who I was beyond *Coach's kid*.

It wasn't until Foster's senior year, when CU made it to the Frozen Four, that campus literally exploded in support. More queer players came out. Beck and his boyfriend, Jacobs. Richie Cohen. The campus magazine went wild with it.

The hockey team has had more articles written about them than the football and swim teams combined.

I hated that I had to go to a *hockey school*. I hated how proud

Foster made Dad. I hated his team and their popularity and the overall arrogance that came from a dude bro wearing a Mountain Lions hockey jersey.

I thought they had it made.

But now, grudgingly, I'm starting to understand a little better.

With notoriety comes pressure.

And damn, this year's team is under pressure. The closer we get to actual preseason, the more Dad's stress levels spike.

Katey cringes from beside me as we watch the last team practice before the UVM game tomorrow. "You're right. They kinda suck."

"I didn't say *suck*. They just …"

"No, no. They suck. And at this point, you wouldn't even be mean to say it—it's fact. Are they planning to play *together* against UVM, or do they think if they confuse the other side enough, they'll be handed the win?"

I drop my head forward onto my folded arms. Katey finished classes early today, so decided to come and hang out at the arena so we could go to dinner once practice was done. She didn't believe me that the team was a mess.

Well, exhibit A.

"Oh shit. Did he actually bodycheck his own line mate?"

I don't even need to look up to know who she's talking about. Asher or Simms is my guess, and when Dad blows his whistle, screams so loud people across campus can probably hear him, and sends them *both* to the team box while he reorganizes the lines, my suspicion is confirmed.

"I know I probably shouldn't say this …" Katey starts, "but that Asher Dalton is hot as fuck. I mean, his brother is more my taste, because his authoritative tone does things to my lady bits—"

I cringe. She doesn't stop.

"But there's something about the badass big-dick energy Asher's radiating that makes me want to break my look-and-don't-touch rule."

I laugh at her. "He's hot but going through a lot. Trust me when I say it's better to steer clear."

"I don't want to date the guy." She pouts. "I just want him to spank me, Kole."

I glance over at where Asher's watching the guys on the ice with the kind of intensity that would melt me in the bedroom. "Oh, babe. Don't we all?"

Once Dad finally calls an end to the torture session, Katey helps me pack shit up. We agree to meet at her car after I tell Dad I've got a ride.

Good timing too. I doubt he's getting out of here anytime soon.

When I get to his office, he's in there with Coach Dalton and Beck, ranting about the game tomorrow.

I lean against the doorframe and lightly knock. "You need to calm down, old man. That blood pressure will get the better of you one of these days."

He opens his mouth like he's about to rip me apart when he seems to remember that, oh yeah, I'm his kid and *not* one of his players. We've had so many arguments over me wanting him to treat me like his son instead of the athlete he wishes I was. I always find it amusing the way he forces a steadying breath because it does nothing at all for his temper.

"Kole. We're in the middle—"

"I know. I'm going out with Katey, so I'll see you back at home."

He acknowledges me with a half-hearted wave, still looking the kind of stressed that makes me worried. So before I can leave,

I walk over to the minifridge in his office, grab out a Gatorade, and drop it on his desk. "Hydrate."

He waves me off but immediately reaches for the bottle.

I'm almost clear of the room when Coach Dalton calls me back.

"Wait, Kole."

My stomach drops. I know without him asking that this is going to be another Asher request, and while I *like* Asher, and I want to help him, Coach Dalton asking me to do it is starting to make me feel uncomfortable.

"We were just talking about what the team did last year to fix the issues they were having. Asher ended up making friends with one of his line mates, Cohen, and the more they hung out, the more things started to work. We need something like that with him and Simms."

I think back to the derision in Asher's voice when he mentioned them hanging out and braiding each other's hair. "You want me to invite them for a sleepover and try to get them to sing kumbaya? There's no way that'll happen. If you haven't noticed, I have no pull with any of the players."

"You do with Asher," Coach Dalton says. "He told me how you helped him study the other night."

"Kole." Dad looks me in the eye and uses the pleading tone he only brings out when he really wants something. He's tried it so many times to get me to go back to hockey. His posture, the way he holds his head down … the man is defeated. "I don't know what else to do with those two."

Even Beck's looking at me now, and for some reason, the three of them thinking I can fix this, fix *Asher*, sends a jolt of anger through me. "What happened to not taking on another pet project?" I ask Dad.

His lips quirk. "Blood pressure, kid."

"Yeah, because talking to Asher never sent anyone's blood pressure sky-high. I have to go."

I turn on my heel, yet the whole walk out to Katey's car, I want to go find Asher instead. I *want* to do what they've asked, but since they've asked me, I can't. I'm uncomfortably aware of how Asher would feel to know we were all standing around talking about him and how to make him play nice. Just look at his reaction after he found out Coach Dalton told me about his parents. He'd be pissed to know they think they can use me to get in his ear and control his decisions.

Which is laughable anyway.

Asher might think he's stupid, but he's smart enough to know when he's being manipulated into doing something he doesn't want to do.

And so am I.

Which is why I leave the arena and put today behind me.

After all, I couldn't care less if they win or lose this weekend.

X

I'M A LYING liar who lies.

I care. I care more than I ever have for one of Dad's games before. Dad's face has turned a splotchy kind of red, Asher looks like he wants to hit something, and this entire game is one big embarrassment, so yes. I care.

Damn it. I'm catching the hockey.

Beck is practically *twitching* beside me, muttering plays under his breath.

"You okay?"

He shakes his head. "You have no idea how frustrating it is to be *sitting* here. Now I know why your dad was always so angry when I went rogue out there."

"Aren't you planning on opening some kind of hockey camp?"

"Yep. But after this, I will never, *ever* watch one of my kids play. *Ever*." But even saying that, his eyes don't leave the ice. "It's all Asher and Simms."

"They're not the only two on the team."

Beck jumps to his feet as Kaplan tears past us and takes a shot on goal. Even my gut jolts as the puck flies through the air—and meets the goalie's glove. *Shit*.

"That's what I mean," Beck growls. "They won't pass to each other. They keep giving it to Kaplan, and UVM knows it. Our defense is good, but playing in UVM's attack zone all night means they're flagging."

As if to prove his point, Stalberg trips a UVM player, earning two minutes in the sin bin and giving a power play to UVM, who finds the net almost immediately.

I groan into my hands.

I really, really wish I didn't care.

"So you agree with my dad and Coach Dalton?" I finally ask Beck.

"That those two need to get along? Obviously. They're being a pair of ... ah, unprofessional players, out there."

"I'm not on the team. You can say dickheads if you want to."

Beck points at me. "I'm trying to be responsible and shit, but yes, that. That's *exactly* what they're being."

"Asher will never make the first move, and I can't see Simms putting aside their shit either."

"Well, unless we want to come dead last this season, we need to do something."

He's right. As the clock winds down, it's like the entire team gives up. Somehow Simms manages to sink one in the net, but we still lose 7-1, and the walk back to the locker room is filled with so much tension I wouldn't be surprised if the team was plotting to drown Asher and Simms in the showers.

Asher's doing that usual thing where he ignores everyone, even as Dad lists, in great detail, everything he did wrong out there.

He just takes it.

In front of the whole team.

Dad's not even yelling at me, and *I* want to cry. Asher looks so unaffected when I'm sure he wants to rage, and it makes me question what he's going to do after this to let it all out.

Go home and be pissed off? Go out and get laid? Start a fight?

This can't keep going on. I know, without a doubt, that Asher won't agree to play nice with Simms. But maybe we need to force his hand.

I grab Beck and drag him out of the locker room with me.

"I have an idea."

"About those two?"

"Yes. I don't like the idea, but I think it'll work."

Beck eyes me. "What is it?"

"At this point, I think the only way we're going to get through to them is to lock them in a room and let them have it out."

"You're joking."

"Nope."

"And what if they kill each other? Because I've got to say, it seems likely."

"Then you'll have two less players to worry about." I sound way more nonchalant than I feel, because Beck's right. They actually might.

All I know is that when Asher finally lets his guard down, it's impossible not to like him. I've only seen small glimpses, but I hope Simms will see it too.

I sneak into Dad's office and grab his keys while Beck goes and tells them Coach wants to see them.

Thankfully, Dad has gone out the front of the arena to meet Mom, so his office is free for the moment, but we need to hurry up because he definitely will not want to be part of this plan.

Asher's first to arrive. His scowl lessens slightly when he sees me, but he doesn't say anything as he throws himself into one of the chairs to wait.

"You okay?" I ask.

"Yep. Love being an absolute embarrassment. It's a good time."

I shift for a moment and contemplate whether I'm doing the right thing. "Do you think maybe you and Simms need to go out and get drunk together?"

Asher snorts. "If I get drunk with him, we will really get into a fight. Why do you care, anyway?"

"We're friends."

"You shouldn't be friends with someone like me."

"You asked."

"Yeah, but I'm the idiot. You're the one who's supposed to make the right choices."

Fine, if that's how he wants to play it.

Simms shows up before I can reply and sighs at the sight of Asher sitting there.

I stand and walk to the door. "You want me to make choices for you, Asher? You two can come out when you're friends."

I catch their confused expressions for a second before I slam the door and quickly lock it with Dad's keys.

Beck watches me with what I think is concern etched across his face. "Come on, kids, join the hockey camp with the coach who locks kids in a room together."

"It's fine," I say. "I did this. You were just … there."

"Does that make me an accessory to kidnapping? Oh, shit, *is* this kidnapping?"

"It's ... a training exercise. They have water in there. Dad's private bathroom. It'll be ... fine." I hope.

Someone tries the handle from the inside, and I hear Asher curse. "Did you just parent trap us?"

"I have nowhere to be," I point out. "Take as long as you like."

There's more swearing, and Beck shakes his head. "This better work. Because if they kill each other, your dad will kill me, and then my boyfriend will dig me up and kill me again for leaving him."

"It will work." My voice is a lot more convincing than I feel. "Probably."

Dad takes that moment to appear, and his gaze immediately flies to the door rattling right behind me. "Why do I get the feeling I don't want to know?"

"I'm helping the only way I could think how, but you might need plausible deniability on this one. You should probably keep walking."

"Okay." He slowly backs up and disappears.

I love that he doesn't even question me. Dad might be disappointed in me when it comes to hockey, but he *trusts* me.

"I hope you know what you're doing," Beck says.

Holy shit, so do I.

9

ASHER

"What the hell?" I hiss.

"Heard that," Kole sings like he doesn't have a care in the world.

I slap the door, making a loud *thwack* sound because I know punching it will only hurt my hand.

Simms doesn't seem to care. He just sighs and takes a seat at Coach's desk.

"Do you know how to pick a lock?" I ask.

"Who doesn't? Let me pull my lock-picking kit out of my ass."

"I'd offer to help with that, but I don't want to get punched in the face again."

"Are you always so …"

"The most annoyingly arrogant fuckboy in a fifty-mile radius at any one time? Yes. I polish my crown daily. Next question."

"Why are you like that?"

I look up at the roof and mutter, "I'm going to kick Kole's ass." I throw myself in the seat next to Simms. "Do you want the excuse of always having to live up to my NHL star brother or the poor orphan card? I can play either."

"I want the truth."

Eww. "What if we beat the shit out of each other and get it out of our systems?"

"Will it make you stop acting like a dick?"

"Nope."

"Then why don't we *talk*, which is what they obviously want us to do?"

"Because that sounds like a healthy way to deal with conflict."

Simms keeps his face blank. "Oh, the horror."

"Right? What if we throw crap around the room and make it *sound* like we're beating the shit out of each other? They'd have to let us out then, right?"

Simms throws his head back. "Dude. I'm exhausted. That game sucked—"

"Thanks to you."

"*And* you. I just want to go home."

I lean back in my seat. "I have all night, and they're not going to leave us in here forever. In a game of who's more stubborn, I will always win."

"Why are you like this? I've never met someone more …"

"Incorrigible, frustrating—"

"So emotionally unavailable I have to question if you're a sociopath."

"Ooh, sociopath. That's actually a new one. No one's ever called me that before." I force a smile. "I think I like it."

"Can we please find some middle ground here?" Simms is begging now, but I'm not ready to give up the fight.

"How about the middle ground that I play center and you stay in your fucking lane."

"How about the middle ground that you recognize you're not the only one on this team, and you give me some slack."

"Nah, I like my thing better."

Simms throws up his hands. "Then there's really no point to this."

"Agreed."

We both fall silent, and for about five minutes, I feel like I've won. Until another five minutes pass, and I realize I really haven't.

We haven't gotten anywhere, and I know Kole won't let us out of here until we come to some sort of truce. Even if it's superficial.

That's it—my key out of here. I can pretend to care. I'll listen to whatever Simms's sad life story is. I'll pull the sympathy card. It doesn't mean anything has to change. "Fine. We'll do it the healthy way. Just don't blame me if you grow up to be a stand-up kind of guy because of it."

Simms's mouth opens, but nothing comes out, like he's not sure if I'm being serious or not and doesn't know what to say.

"I guess we should start with what your first name is," I say.

"You don't even know my first name?" he exclaims.

"I don't know half the team's first names. All I see is what name is on the back of their jersey. And before you say it, yes, I can *read* them. Well, except Kvasnička."

"Wow. There's that great team spirit coming out again."

"My kindergarten teacher always told my dad that I don't play well with others. It stuck."

"And you chose to play hockey ..."

"Hockey chose me."

Simms grunts. "Do you turn everything into a joke?"

"That wasn't a joke. West played hockey; my dad wanted me to play too so he could drop us at the rink and disappear for a while, but I fought him so hard on it. I wanted my own thing. I didn't want to have to be compared to the great and powerful hockey prodigy."

"So what happened?"

"Let's see. I couldn't catch a football to save my life. I struck out in baseball. I even tried soccer, basketball, and lacrosse. Lacrosse stuck for a little bit."

"What changed?"

"I put on a pair of skates."

Simms nods. "Ah. And the rest was history?"

"Pretty much. Okay, your turn."

"My name, by the way, is Kieran."

I screw up my face. "You don't look like a Kieran."

"You don't look like an asshole, but then you open your mouth. So …"

"Touché."

Simms leans forward. "Okay, real talk. My parents have given me until the end of my degree to get an NHL contract. They say if it doesn't happen, I need to go to law school. I don't want to be a fucking lawyer. I've missed my chance at the draft, so I'm hoping I can get signed as a free agent, but to do that—"

"You need ice time."

"I need eyes on me. It's why I'm willing to learn to play on the left if it gets me on that first line. I'm used to playing center, and I'm not trying to screw up on the ice, but you don't make it easy."

I run a hand through my hair. "I shouldn't have to be watching my back for when my teammate might try to steal the puck from me."

"I get that, and I'm *trying*. It might go a whole lot smoother if you show some patience though."

"I don't think I was born with that gene."

"A patience gene?"

"Exactly. I need everything, and I need it now."

"In other words we're fucked. Goodbye, Frozen Four. Goodbye, NHL."

Simms has managed to hit me where I understand the most. Hockey is everything, and he desperately wants to make it. I'm worried by putting my life on hold to look after my brothers and sisters that I'll miss my chance. Simms doesn't even have that chance yet.

I sigh. "I can try. We probably just need to get comfortable with each other."

"How did you do it last year with Cohen?"

"Drank lots and flirted with his boyfriend."

Simms shakes his head. "Anyone ever tell you you're messed up?"

"More than you'd think."

"I dunno. In my head it's a lot."

"In reality, it's a lot more." Even if it's my own voice saying it.

Simms shifts in his seat. "So … his boyfriend, huh? You gay too?"

"Nope. Not *gay*." I omit the other labels I could be considered: pan, fluid, heteroflexible … I'm not getting into it with him.

"But—"

"I was hoping Cohen would punch me in the face." And when I realized that was never going to happen, I'd discovered it was fun to mess with Seth. "Since you don't have a boyfriend I can flirt with, I can either hit on your girlfriend or we can try the drinking thing if you want."

"You're not going anywhere near my girlfriend, but I'm only twenty."

"Fake ID?"

"Nope."

"Damn. I could probably—"

Simms shakes his head. "Can't risk it. If I am going to become a lawyer, I can't be busted with a fake ID."

I grin. "We'll have to make sure you don't become a lawyer, then."

I realize I actually mean that. We don't need to be besties to gel on the ice, but mutual understanding and a love for hockey will help. I know what it's like to be held back from the NHL, and I wouldn't wish that on anyone else or actively try to sabotage their chances.

I'm an asshole; I'm not sadistic.

"Is that enough to be let out of here?" I yell.

"Nope!" Kole yells back.

I'm starting to question my friendship with him. Honestly.

"Do you have any free time for one-on-one practice to try to get us to gel?" Simms asks. "I want to be like Foster, Jacobs, and Cohen were the year we won the Frozen Four. That game was magical. Everything was smooth. I only got seven minutes of ice time, but watching those three do their thing, I wanted to be like that."

"That game is why I agreed to come to this school in the first place. But ... I really don't have any extra time. I have five younger siblings at home, and West tries, but he can't handle them all. In between making sure they're fed and happy and studying—"

"Shit, man. That sucks. I have two younger siblings, and that's enough of a headache for me."

Suddenly, the door clicks open, and my brother steps through. "I'll work something out. I'll hire a nanny or—"

I want to yell at him for eavesdropping, but I get more stuck on the nanny thing because he's been so against it from the beginning. "You don't want to leave them—"

"The thought of leaving them with a stranger doesn't sit right with me, but it's clear Zoe can't handle them anymore, and she shouldn't have to. You can't sacrifice the team or your college education because of it. I'll ... find a solution."

I purse my lips. "You know I don't mind helping with them."

"I know, but they've—no, *I've* disrupted your life too much already. I'll organize more ice time for the two of you if you think it'll help."

I glance at Simms, who's looking at me like I've grown two heads. What is it? I haven't been a dick in the last two minutes? I'm tempted to prove all his preconceived notions about me correct, but I'm exhausted. Plus, with two more years on the ice together, we really do need to work out how to play nice if I'm going to see a Frozen Four.

"We need more time on the ice," I say. "With Kaplan too. And without an audience. I can sense the team anticipating when we'll fuck up next, and it's pressure none of us need."

"I'll see what I can do," West says.

"Can we go *now*?" I ask.

He steps away from the door.

Kole's standing next to Beck outside Coach's office, and I scowl at him.

Oh, he tries to put on an innocent smile, but I'm not buying it.

He steps forward and pats my cheek. "Good boy."

"Wow. Could you be any more condescending?"

"Yes, I can. Would the good boy like to go for some ice cream as a treat? I'm buying." His hazel eyes shine up at me as he waves to Beck and grabs my hand to drag me through the locker room.

"I'm not saying no, but so you know, you owe me so much more than fucking ice cream."

"I'll even throw a cherry on top." He winks, and I hate that it's that easy to make my anger at him disappear.

"I'll have a scoop of the rocky road," Kole says. "And he'll have ..." He turns to me.

"A chocolate brownie sundae with the works. Chocolate sauce, nuts, and *two* cherries." Just because I'm not mad anymore, that doesn't mean I'm not going to milk it.

"You earned it." Kole slaps my shoulder. "You used your big-boy words and not your fists. I'm so proud."

A joke about using my fist for other things is on the tip of my tongue, but I bite it back. One, because we're in a very public place. And two, I wouldn't want him to think I was serious. I might be open to a lot of things, but that's on the nope list for me.

We're given our ice cream, and we find a table in the corner of the small place. It's super late for somewhere like this to be open, but we're far from the only ones in here—probably because it's after a game and everyone is still out.

As I take a bite of gooey brownie and chocolate ice cream, I hum happily because this is what heaven tastes like.

"Does that mean I'm forgiven?" Kole asks.

"Not even close." Sauce dribbles onto my lip, and I lick it off. A weird, strained noise comes from Kole, and I can't help smiling.

He's fixated on my lip, but when he sees I've caught him staring, he averts his gaze. "You know, I did promise to tutor you. For free. That has to earn me some forgiveness."

"Oh, and that sounds like so much fun too," I say dryly. "I'm thinking ..." I decide to tease him some more because I've finally found something that makes Kole Hogan uncomfortable. Me flirting with him. Hello, future ammunition. "You could do something ... else."

He stares at me expectantly.

"Something that we'd both enjoy." I scoop another spoonful of ice cream into my mouth slowly.

Kole catches on to what I'm doing. "Not gonna happen, big guy. You aren't my type."

"Your staring would suggest otherwise."

"Oh, you're hot, and I think we've already established I know it and you know it, but geez, all you hockey players can talk about is hockey, and I get enough of that at home."

"For what I had in mind, there wouldn't be any talking at all." Shit. I don't know if this is teasing him or me because now I'm imagining doing very hot things to him.

He laughs *out loud.* I'm starting to think I should be offended.

"Do lines like that really work?" he asks.

"You tell me." I shift back in my seat and don't miss the way he eyes my long torso.

His Adam's apple bounces, and he looks away. "Like I said. Jocks aren't my type."

"What about emotionally unavailable guys who treat people like shit? Because I'm that too. Don't pigeonhole me, dude."

"Sorry, that doesn't really do it for me either."

"Shame. I'm really good at sex."

"Sure you are. Like you're super good at communicating."

"I speak words good."

Kole smiles at me, and it's both a blessing and a shame I'm not his type. It's a blessing because I won't fuck up this friendship or my spot on the team by crossing lines. But damn, it would be fun to have a few sweaty hours with him.

When he checks me out again, I can't stop the smug look from spreading across my face.

"Just to clarify, you're not into me? My eyes are up here."

"Like my best friend Katey says, I can look with my eyes, not with my hands."

I'm almost tempted to try to change his mind on that, but no. Not hooking up with the only friend I have at this school is smart.

Then again, when did I ever claim to be that?

10

KOLE

After our ice cream date, Asher's been busy with hockey and I've been busy with school, but most importantly, *I've* been busy trying to get images of us fucking out of my head.

Because it turns out, I am not immune to Asher Dalton's flirting. Which sucks because he's so ... *him*.

Every time I jerk off lately, all I can think of is messy black hair and taunting green eyes. Then I'd turn up for practice to fulfill my equipment manager obligations and witness him do some boneheaded, testosterone-induced toxic masculinity shit, and I'd be so disappointed in myself.

My standards have never exactly been at the meet-my-parents level, but this is a new low even for me.

I have to admit, he's been nicer to the team since he and Simms talked it out, but one conversation isn't going to make years of using his nonchalant attitude as a shield disappear.

I'd really been hoping to build up some kind of resistance before the team's first away game, but here we are, on the bus back to the hotel after the team managed to pull a win out of their asses, and when I glance back at Asher ...

No, no, nope.

I'm definitely, certainly, incredibly *not* thinking about the way his tongue wrapped around that ice cream spoon.

He was only flirting to get under my skin as payback, and well, it worked. It really fucking worked.

Dad's in a rare good mood with his players, even though they lost the first two preseason games. This one was more a case of them getting lucky, but it was good to see Asher, Simms, and Kaplan finally starting to look like a team. There might be hopes for the season yet. It'll be interesting to see if they can pull it off tomorrow and get back-to-back wins. Dad's already warned them that if anyone sneaks out tonight, they won't be playing.

As promised, Asher and I have a long night of studying ahead anyway.

When we get to the hotel, I hang back to make sure everyone on the team grabs their bags off the bus. It really is like babysitting a bunch of man children, but at least today, they're high from finally coming out on top.

And they're all in suits. Hot men in suits are my weakness. Wait, hot men in general are my weakness.

Dad sorts out the registration while the team fills the foyer, being loud and taking up way too much space. As a shock to no one, they're recounting the game and talking through plays and convincing each other that they have the game tomorrow in the bag.

Even Asher manages to crack a smile. It's probably a good thing smiling for him is rare because damn, he's possibly the most attractive man I've ever seen up close when he does.

I sling my bag over my shoulder and grab the room keys from Dad to start handing out. Like I told Asher, I'm in charge of rooming assignments, and if I was any kind of team player, I would have roomed Asher and Simms together.

But when it came time to write out a list for Dad, I'd convinced myself that Asher studying was more important. Besides, I can handle a little flirting. Especially when it's coming from a guy who has no follow-through. He's only doing it to make me uncomfortable.

Once all the keys are handed out except for ours, I cross the lobby toward Asher and flick him his room key. "Want to go up?"

He nods, and we leave most of the team behind who are still celebrating their win while they can. Dad will call for curfew in a bit and send them all to bed.

The doors to the elevator close with only us in it, and the space feels way too small.

"Good game today," I say to cut him off from shamelessly saying something laced with innuendo.

"We were still shit. Just got lucky that the other team was worse."

I hum because disagreeing would be a lie. "Maybe you'll get lucky again tomorrow."

"Maybe." He leans against the side of the elevator and drags a hand through his hair, pushing it back from his face. "What have you been up to? I've barely seen you."

"I'm premed. I told you I didn't have much free time."

"Not even for your best friend?" he asks playfully.

"Actually, I see Katey a fair bit."

"I was talking about me, buttmunch."

Fucking duh. "Since when are *we* best friends?"

"Since you parent trapped me. Only best friends get away with that shit." Asher shifts. "Maybe, uh, we could all hang out? You, me, and your friend."

My stomach bottoms out, and it has nothing to do with the elevator reaching our floor and jolting to a stop. I'm not sure if Asher even knows who Katey is, but as much as he'd tried to keep his tone casual, that question was anything but. Asher's already made it clear he's not picky, and Katey thinks he's hot because, well, she has *eyes*, and now all I can picture is the two of them going at it and *gross, gross, gross.*

"Yeah, maybe," I finally answer. But that maybe translates into *never, ever, never.*

Ever.

We reach our room, and Asher walks straight past me and claims the bed next to the window. "So you know, this side's always mine."

"Why?"

"Because if someone comes through the door to murder us, you'll be the first victim."

Big, bad hockey player, folks. "Makes sense. If we were about to be murdered, I wouldn't want to watch what was about to happen to me. I'd rather go first."

A flicker of uncertainty crosses his face.

"But hey, if I'm gutted, at least you'll be able to study the intestinal tract in great detail before you die."

He groans. "I'm still lost on that."

"Good thing we have all night to study."

His attention snaps back to me. "Yeah, no way am I spending the whole night doing that."

"Too late. We already agreed."

He hangs his head back. "The one time I don't have to go home after a game to look after my siblings because my parents *died* and you're going to lock me in a room to study?"

I almost laugh. Ever since Coach Dalton mentioned Asher does that, I'd been waiting for him to use it against me. "Am I supposed to give you sympathy now?"

"Worth a try."

"I'm not going to lock you in a room—again. If you want to

go, then you're a grown-up and can make your own choices. When you're kicked off the team, maybe I'll room with Simms." They might be getting along better now, but I don't think the vague rivalry between them will ever die.

"Fine." He starts pulling clothes out of his bag. "Let me get changed out of this damn monkey suit first."

I want to argue that there's no reason for him to do that. Studying in a suit is totally a thing that people do.

He passes me on the way to the bathroom, and I can't pull my eyes away.

Asher catches me checking him out, and at this point, I think we're both well aware of how attracted to him I am. "Keep looking at me like that and we'll be doing something other than studying tonight."

"It's sweet you think I'm that easy."

"It's more that I'm confident in my skills." His gaze rakes over me as he closes the bathroom door. I'm sort of surprised—and disappointed—that he didn't change in front of me since he's already proved he's not exactly shy about showing off. Then again, stripping off in a locker room is a bit different to stripping off in a hotel room in front of a guy who's basically drooling over you.

I wish he would though. It'd be so tempting to touch, but all that skin and muscle is worth teasing myself over.

While he's gone, I grab my laptop and a notebook and set up at the small desk. I slip my reading glasses on as I sign in to the computer and pull up the document with my notes inside.

I hear the bathroom door click open, and Asher comes out wearing sweats and a soft-looking cotton T-shirt. It's not until he sinks down into the chair beside me that I realize he's staring at me.

I don't take my eyes off the screen when I say, "You do that a lot."

"What?"

"Stare."

"Says the guy who was just checking me out."

"There's a difference." I meet his eyes. "You *know* why I'm staring."

"You want to know why I am?"

"Obviously."

"You wear glasses."

My eyebrows crease with confusion. "You're staring because I wear glasses? I can take them off, but then I can't read shit."

"No, no." He clears his throat, but his voice comes out rough. "Leave them on."

"Oh." I smile and lean in closer. "You're staring because you like them."

"And now you know what I look like when I'm checking *you* out."

Asher's lips are right there, all tempting and plump, asking to be nipped and—

Shit. How does he manage to get under my skin so damn easily?

Asher knows he's driving me crazy. Still taunting me with his flirting.

I try to turn our conversation back to the whole reason we're here. If Asher keeps messing with me and trying to get a reaction, there's only one way tonight is going to go, and I told myself I wouldn't give in. Even if I really, really ... *really* want to.

"Now, what should we be focusing on?" I ask.

"We're still doing the intestinal tract, which, by the way, is a whole heap of gross."

"You want to talk gross? You should see a cadaver. At least

you're dealing with people while they're alive. The human body gets nasty after death."

"I'm pretty nasty while I'm alive."

"No hope for you, then."

He clears his throat. "I learned that moomoo thing you said. You know, Defenseman Josi ices Crosby and chirps Sceviour."

"Good! And has that helped?"

"No. Because that's *literally* all I could memorize. I remember the letters, but fucked if I remember what they stand for. Oh, wait. I remember appendix. That one's easy."

"Cool, only six more to go."

He puts his head in his hands. "It's useless. I just don't care about any of this."

I'd thought relating it back to hockey would make it easier, but maybe he's not someone who learns through reading and writing things out. "There are different learning styles. Do you think if I read out the names of each part, that would help you to retain them?"

"Nope."

"Making flash cards?"

"I've read over the words a million times and still can't recall them, so I doubt it."

"You could be a kinesthetic learner."

"What is with you and all these big words?"

I bite back a laugh. "It's when you learn through *doing* something."

"And how the hell do I *do* an intestinal tract?"

Hmm ... that's a good question. If I had one of those torsos they keep in classrooms or doctor's offices, I could make Asher pull it apart and put it back together. Hey, a cadaver *would* come in handy right now.

We need some kind of way for him to physically work

through each part. Maybe he could draw a picture ... or maybe ... If he needs a live model, I'm right here.

I pick up the pen beside me, then reach for my shirt and pull it over my head, my skin already coming alive at the thought of what I'm about to suggest.

I'm not built like Asher or any of his teammates. I'm lean but have next to no muscle. Even still, there's no way for me to feel self-conscious over it when Asher's eyes drop to my torso, and his nostrils flare as he takes me in.

"I've got to say, distracting me probably isn't the best way to help this sink in."

I hand over the pen and pull up a diagram. "You're going to draw it."

"On ... you?"

I stand, but Asher remains seated. There're barely a few inches between our bodies, and his head is level with my chest and abs ... or lack thereof. The hum of tension filling the room is almost loud enough to hear. His warm breath on my skin sends goose bumps over my arms.

"Yep." I steer his hand up to hover over my diaphragm. "Get drawing."

His touch starts light, hesitant, but the more he drags the pen over my skin, the more he actually concentrates on what he's doing, and the more confident he becomes.

"Duodenum," he murmurs as he draws. "Jejunum."

One of his hands closes over my waist to steady me, and I try not to get lost in the warmth of his touch, the light calluses on his fingers that are bringing my skin alive. With his head tilted down, his eyelashes are fanned over his cheeks, and when his lips bunch with concentration, it draws my attention. They're so full and pink, and my own lips are tingling at the thought of what his might feel like.

It can't have escaped his notice that I'm breathing heavier, because he is too. His grip on my waist tightens. He drags the pen across my stomach, and this time, his fingertips lightly trail after it.

I try to hold back a shudder but can't.

Now not only is Asher torturing me, but I'm doing it to myself. Why did I think this was a good idea?

"Appendix." His husky voice sends vibrations over my skin and has my cock starting to lengthen. I'm past the point of caring if he notices. I can't drag my gaze away from him.

When Asher reaches my jeans, he drops the pen completely, and I barely hear it hit the ground.

Asher meets my eyes as his fingers lightly inch under the waistband of my briefs. It's a delicious tease, and I want to encourage him lower, but instead he trails his fingers across my hip and around to my back, pulling me closer so I'm standing between his legs. We're not touching, but I can practically feel him everywhere. "Only one part left." He watches me for a second, holds my stare, and then ... his index finger dips lower, sliding down over my tailbone and into the crease of my ass. My breath catches.

"Fuck ..." The word escapes before I can stop it. "You're, umm, a quick learner."

His heated stare has me so turned on my brain is starting to scramble. "You're a good teacher."

I need to touch him. "The best way to learn anatomy is with a hands-on approach." My body thrums in anticipation. It's begging, *Touch me, more, please.*

"I can see that," he rasps. His green eyes darken as he takes me in. They trail over the pen marks he left, but he still doesn't make a move.

He's stronger than I am.

Though his finger hovering so close to my hole really isn't helping me brain.

I swallow hard. "There's another proven learning technique we could cover."

"What's that?"

"A reward system."

His lips quirk. "And how does that work?"

"Each time you learn something new, I reward you."

"How?"

I lean over and whisper in his ear. "However you want."

Finally, he breaks, and a crack in his restraint shows. Asher shoots back in his chair and stands. "Pity I'm not your type ... right?"

"I'm prepared to make sacrifices in the name of education." The needy tinge to my words makes Asher smile, but it falls fast.

"You're fucking with me." He squeezes his hands closed by his sides and then folds them across his impressively wide chest.

I don't know how to tell him that I'm really, really not. "How does it feel? You've been doing it to me ever since I locked you in that room with Simms."

"So this is payback? All of this?" Asher waves his hand, gesturing to all the writing on my skin.

"Nope. I really am trying to help you learn." I step closer. "This way could be a good idea."

"Hooking up is a terrible idea."

"But what if it works?"

"Do you really think a reward system will?" he asks.

"The mess on my stomach proves it does."

Asher's tongue darts out to wet his lips. "We wouldn't want to wreck our friendship though, would we?"

We're only inches away now. I can feel his warmth. Could

reach out and touch him. "It would just be adding another way for us to be friendly."

With hockey-like reflexes, Asher's arm curls around my back and crushes me to him. I let out a little unintentional squeak as he presses his hard cock against my thigh. Damn, he feels good.

"This could be dangerous. You're Coach's son."

"No one has to know."

He still hesitates, bottom lip caught in his teeth, and I have to admit, he's proving he does actually have impulse control. He just never uses it.

"I didn't think it would take this much convincing. I must be losing my touch."

He lets out a loud breath. "You have no idea how much I want to take you up on this. But … it's not a good idea. I'm not good for you. I don't want … *feeling*s to get involved. That's when things get messy."

I snort, because the idea of falling for Asher is actually ridiculous. "Guys with the emotional range of a trash can really *are* hard to resist."

"I'm a total catch." He cups my jaw. "We're basically playing with fire here."

"What if I promise not to fall in love with you? Then will you let me suck your dick?"

Apparently, those are the magic words. All hesitance leaves him as his mouth crashes against mine. His grip on my jaw is firm, his mouth strong and domineering. I immediately part my lips, letting his tongue in, and Asher fucking *owns* me with his kiss.

Tingles break across my skin as I try to match the force he's kissing me with, but he easily overpowers me. He bites down on my bottom lip, nipping … teasing … Then suddenly, he backs up, and I'm not ready for it. I stumble forward, but his large hand on my shoulder steadies me before he pushes me to my knees. He shoves his sweats down his thighs.

He's hard, and there's already a little dot of precum hovering on the tip of his cock. And *of course* Asher has a sexy cock. A bit bigger than average and thick. So thick it makes my mouth water as I anticipate wrapping my lips around it.

I reach up to remove my glasses when Asher catches my hand. "Leave them."

Nrgh. Gladly. With a slow smile, I lean forward and drag my tongue from base all the way to tip. I'm the type of guy who loves giving head. I could do it all day ... or until my jaw aches, at least. The power dynamic of being in a submissive position while holding all the cards really does it for me. I could pull away, I could stop, or I could go all in if I wanted to, and he doesn't get a say. All he can do is stand there at my mercy.

I go slow and love every tortured sound that leaves him. His heavy breaths spur me on.

"Don't tease me, Kole." His hand finds my hair and grips it painfully. "I want to fuck that pretty mouth."

Compliments will get you everywhere.

As tempting as it is to draw this out and drive him crazy, I'm just as eager as Asher is. I wrap my lips around him and suck him down until the head of his cock breaches my throat.

Then, I swallow.

The strangled groan that leaves Asher has me whimpering. I almost tear the button from my pants as I scramble to free myself, but before I can get my dick out, Asher swats my hand away.

"Don't you dare. That's mine."

His sexy, deep growl is the only thing that stops me from touching myself, but the throbbing between my legs has me so desperate to disobey that I know I need to do something else with my hands.

I slide them up his thighs until his full ass fills my palms, and then I coax him to pick up the pace. I suck him off like my life depends on it, accepting every thrust of his hips. I'm in a hurry to get him off because *shit*, I need him touching me before I come in my fucking pants.

I'm struggling to breathe through my nose with the unrelenting way he's using my mouth. The smell of his skin, his grunts, the tight grip he has on my hair ... I'm running out of oxygen, which only heightens my arousal.

I need this.

"Kole, I'm gonna ..."

Hearing my name drenched in lust makes me weak, and I gladly accept his final thrust, trying not to struggle as he forces himself deep. He comes down my throat, and when I finally open my eyes and glance up at him, he's already looking down at me.

His thumb brushes my cheek, just once, before he loosens his hold and lets me pull back.

I gasp down a deep breath as he hauls me to my feet.

"Holy fuck. I might have found a new favorite way to study."

ASHER

As soon as I have Kole to his feet, I spin him around and push him down on my bed. I have every intention of returning the favor because holy shit, my reward deserves a reward. Kole Hogan knows how to suck a dick.

My knee lands on the bed, and I reach for Kole's pants, but he grips my hands.

"Not so fast."

"What's wrong?"

"Nothing. But you need to earn it."

"My mouth on your cock is a reward for *you*, not for me."

"Access to my body is a privilege. You'll do well to remember that." A sly look crosses his face, and damn it, he's right.

I want to suck him dry, I want to make him come, and I'll do anything to make it happen. "What do you need?"

He points to the first marking I drew between his stomach and his belly button. "What is the function of the duodenum?"

"You *have* to work on your sex talk."

"I am nothing but a professional tutor."

This is anything but professional. At least I'm not paying him. That would make this all kinds of weird.

"You don't get any more unless you give me the right answers," Kole says.

I both hate him and appreciate him for doing this, but I have to wonder if he could hold out longer than I could. I've already come. I could be totally selfish and go to sleep. But then I look at Kole's face, and his hazel eyes look at me like I'm a better person than I really am, and for some fucked-up reason, I want to prove to him I could be the guy he thinks I am.

I look at where he's pointing and try with all my effort to remember the text.

"It produces hormones and receives all the gross stuff from the liver and pancreas to facilitate chemical digestion and to neutralize the acidity coming from the stomach."

"Close enough." Kole undoes his jeans but only shuffles them to under his ass. The tip of his hard cock is visible through his boxers where there's a wet spot of precum on the light blue underwear.

My mouth waters.

"Next question," Kole says. "What does this do?" He moves his finger to where I labeled his liver.

Remembering back to my unacceptable answer of "gets rid of all the toxic shit," I try to recall the proper functions. "Produces and excretes bile. Stores vitamins, minerals, and …" I close my eyes. "Shit, that other word. Starts with a *G*."

"Gly …"

"Glycogen!"

"What else?"

Kole moves his hand down his chest and rubs his cock over his underwear. *Fuck, fuck, fuck, think, Asher, think.*

"Blood detoxification and purification."

"Mm, good." He moves his pants down a tiny bit more.

"Enzyme activation."

Kole smiles, and even though I'm still thoroughly wrung out, my cock twitches.

"Ooh, excretion of cholesterol and hormones and shit."

"Nope, wrong organ for shit."

"I can't think of the other ones," I whine.

"Hey, you got more than I was expecting. I guess you've earned a little taste." He pulls his jeans down the rest of the way, letting them pool at his ankles. Then he exposes his cock, but he doesn't take off his underwear.

With his free hand, he crooks his finger for me to come to him.

I dip my head, and he grips the back of my hair, guiding me to his cock. When he said I could have a taste, I'm expecting more than a light lick. He doesn't even let me close my mouth over him.

He pulls my head back. "Next." His voice comes out deeper. "Which part of the small intestine absorbs sugars?"

Damn it. I groan and drop my head to his hip. I'm surprised he lets me. He still grips my hair tight, and now my head is right next to his cock. I want to suck him so bad.

"I'm waiting for an answer."

Come on, brain.

"The ... jejunum."

"Good job."

I lift my head, determined to swallow his cock.

"Uh-huh. This is a two-part question."

"I fucking hate you."

He chuckles. "What else does the jejunum absorb?"

"Amino acids and fatty acids."

He releases my hair, and finally—finally—he allows me to

swallow his dick. Worried he'll take it away again, I dive right in, sucking him to the root.

His hips buck off the bed. "*Nrgh.*"

I want to quip, "*Still got questions for me?*" but I'm scared he'll say *yes*.

"Whoa, whoa, whoa." He tries to get me to slow down, but that's so not going to happen. I'm bringing my A game at double the pace. "If you keep ... Oh, shit. I'm gonna ... No, wait, I had more questions." He gasps. "Fuck. No. Ignore me. Keep going."

I want to laugh, but I can't with his pulsing dick in my mouth.

Kole tenses and lets out a curse, and as the first spurts of cum hit my tongue, I moan around him and swallow it down.

I wait for the gross shame that usually washes over me after sex, but it doesn't come. Usually, I'm hooking up with someone to piss someone else off or to get back at someone or to just mask the constant hurt I carry around with me.

This was different but still wrong. Yet, the shame continues to stay away while I lick him clean, when Kole taps my shoulder to get me to release him, and even when he pulls me to him and kisses me deeply.

Which is weird because after everything we did, the kissing should make me uncomfortable. It's not that I don't kiss my hookups, but it's foreplay. Once we've both gotten off, there's no point.

Kole's mouth becomes soft and lazy, and when I pull away, he follows and finishes with one last, sweet kiss.

I wish I could say I hate it, but I don't. It does a weird flippy thing in my gut.

He stares up at me with concern in his hazel eyes. "You okay?"

Nope. Not at all.

That was ...

Blowjobs, Asher. It was just blowjobs.

"I'm kind of terrified." Wait, what? That did not fucking fall from my lips.

"You don't need to worry. We didn't mess anything up. I promise I'm not in looooove. Good way to blow off some steam though, huh? Get it? *Blow* off steam?" He waggles his eyebrows.

I shake my head and squash down the weird feeling in my stomach. Finding the snark is hard, but I manage. "It's not that. I'm terrified in class on Monday I'll pop a boner when the professor asks about digestion or liver function."

Kole bursts out laughing. "It worked though, didn't it? Quick, tell me everything you were able to memorize just now."

Surprisingly, I find it easy to pull the information from my subconscious.

Kole smiles at me. "See? We'll turn you into a grade A student yet."

"Any chance you're good at numbers? I'm also flunking math."

"Why are you taking a math course for a degree in nutrition?" He looks confused for a moment but then must remember something. "Oh, right, science core subject. Everyone doing a science degree has to take it."

"Yep. I suck at math."

"Hmm, well, I'm not so sure about the math part, but you definitely have the *suck* part down."

I nudge him playfully.

"All right. Well, we didn't get everything I wanted to cover done, but I think we made progress." He wriggles his way to the end of the bed and stands, pulling up his boxer briefs but stepping out of the pants that were still around his ankles. "After that, I'm ready for sleep."

He gets his phone and immediately crawls into his own bed

while I remain on mine, kind of stunned. I was expecting ... Well, I don't kiss hookups after the fact, but I've nearly always shared a bed with them. That cheap discomfort I'd been expecting earlier finally kicks in, but it's different this time.

"Hey, Kole?"

He glances over at me. "Don't worry, I'm not live tweeting about hooking up with the hotshot forward for the CU Mountain Lions."

That wasn't even on my mind until this second. "Good. Because West would kill me. And your dad." Oh fuck, I blew Coach Hogan's son. "I kind of want to live to be twenty-two years old."

Kole chuckles. "We're just studying. There's nothing to tell *anyone*. My dad told me to stay away from you."

"Why?" I deflate. "Oh, wait, yeah, you don't need to answer that. I'm not exactly model boyfriend material. I'm definitely not going to be a doctor or anything like you."

"I don't think it was that," Kole says. "Dad knows you're going through a lot, and when I see someone hurting, I want to fix them. It's why I'm becoming a doctor. He's worried you'll distract me from my goal."

Great, now I'm worried too. "If you don't have time to tutor me—"

"I do. Especially at away games."

"All right, we leave it at that, then. This only happens at away games?" I think I can live with that.

"Sounds good to me."

I nod. "Okay."

"You should try to get some sleep. You have another game tomorrow."

"What time's morning skate?"

"Eight. Then you have a few hours free if you want to study more."

Hell yes, I want to study more. I've never been so excited to study in my whole damn life.

Okay, I'm a fucking fuckup and never learn from my mistakes.

Clearly.

Using sex as an outlet is perfect ... when it's with someone who's not Coach's son.

Did that stop me from going there again Saturday morning? Nope. Did it stop me from climbing into the shower with him and jerking him off while murmuring about organ function on Sunday morning before the bus ride back to CU? Nope.

But now, as the sun rises on Monday morning and I make my way to the gym for weight training with the team, I realize what a dumbass move hooking up with Kole was.

Not just because he's Coach's son, but because we were beginning to become friends. Good friends. What if I've gone and messed that all up now?

Will it be worth it in the end?

I flash back to him on his knees, that sexy mouth wrapped around my dick, and okay, I'll relent, the blowjobs were spectacular, but what now? Kole says it's not going to be weird, but that's easier said than done.

I shouldn't care. The Asher from last year wouldn't have. But ... ever since I slept with West's best friend, I've been trying to make better decisions—especially when it comes to who I have in my bed.

Kole is not a smart decision. When I think of the person with the most self-destructive outcome I could stick my dick in, it would be him. Then again, he did get me to memorize the intestinal tract, so that has to count for something, right?

Right?

I'm asking for that little inner voice who tries to get me to make good choices, and now it shuts up?

Ugh.

Stupid fuckboy did a fuckboy thing. Am I really surprised at myself?

The question is, where do we go from here? We should pretend it never happened. I'm good at forgetting my sins—I've had enough practice, but I don't know how Kole will take that.

The way we left it, I think we both kind of agreed to a regular thing. At away games and for studying purposes. But as I step through the doors to the team gym, with the harsh light of *what have I done* blinding me, I'm not sure how practical a fuck-buddy-type situation will be.

We still have to see each other outside of those hookups, and we have to act as if we didn't make each other come countless times over the weekend.

I should offer him a five-day change-of-mind policy like insurance companies do … Because that's so sexy.

I bury my face in my hand and let out a pathetic noise.

"You better not be hungover or Dad will kill you."

I freeze and peek through my fingers to find Kole smiling up at me with a green smoothie in his hand.

I lift my head and try not to remember what talented things those lips of his can do. His dirty-blond hair falls in front of his eyes, and I resist the urge to reach and push it back for him.

What the fucking fuck?

"What are you doing here today?" I croak.

His smile widens. "Dad wanted you all to have a protein

shake, so I put my domestic goddess hat on and made you all some." He holds it out to me.

"*You* made this?"

"Mmhmm."

"Thanks." I take a sip and can't help screwing up my face. "What the fuck? That tastes like—"

"I put extra kale in it. Just for you." Kole leaves with an extra spring in his step.

And okay, that wasn't weird. He's acting like his usual self. He's a dick for giving me this shake that tastes like ass—no wait, worse than ass—but ... maybe I'm overthinking this?

I guess I'll play it cool and see what happens in two weeks when we have another away game.

Maybe we've both come to the same conclusion, and we'll pretend nothing ever happened, and then we won't even have to talk about it at all.

Ooh, I like that plan.

12

KOLE

It's been a long two weeks. Classes all day, hockey duties, then classwork. And the classwork is a thousand times less fun than the study session I had with Asher. I was low-key worried things would be weird after we hooked up, but being around him at practice has been the same. He's still his usual closed-off self, but not as bad as he once was, and he has even managed to throw a smile or two my way.

Thankfully, tomorrow is the next away game, and with any luck, we'll be able to work in some more fun after another tutoring session—or even during it.

I want a repeat. It's long overdue. I can't see the study lasting long before I tell him he's doing great and oh yeah, he should be naked already.

I am *thirsty* for the guy.

Once I've made sure the storage shed is packed and locked up, I head for the locker room to see what mess those Neanderthals have left for me. Hopefully it's not too bad because I told Dad I wanted to leave early today to get a walk in for Hades, so he should be wrapping up any minute.

But when I walk into the locker room, it's not a mess waiting for me.

It's Asher.

"I know your teammates didn't pick up their own shit."

He shrugs. "There may have been some threats involved."

"Feel free to threaten them every day, then." I cross to the showers to make sure all is right in there too, and he trails after me. "What are you still doing here?"

"I, uh, wanted to tell you our study date was a success. I remembered everything and passed my midterm."

"That's amazing." When I turn to look back at him, I find his cheeks a little red.

"Yeah, thanks. I guess."

I pretend to cringe. "That sounded painful. Was it painful?"

"I might need first aid."

"Or ..." A thought starts to come to me that's both delicious and risky. "Maybe a reward?"

"What?"

"We've established a reward system works well for you. You passed your test. So ..."

He stares at me for a moment. "Like, tomorrow? At the away game?"

I step forward and hook my fingers into the waistband of his jeans. "I'm thinking right now. Shouldn't delay gratification and all that."

"*Now?*" I swear his voice jumps up a register as he shoots a look at the door. We're standing in between the locker room where the cubbies are and the tiled shower and bathroom area with a direct line of sight from the entry.

"Scared, Asher?"

"Of your dad? Very."

"We don't have to …" I pull him around the corner into the bathroom and step closer, pushing him against the wall.

"Umm—"

I lean in and run my nose over his neck. There's no reason why we can't wait until the safety of the hotel room tomorrow, but the thought of doing it here, maybe being caught, is hot as hell. And I'm going to take any chance I get to touch Asher again. My fingers dip down into his jeans until they run through his pubes. "Tell me to stop."

He whines. Actually whines. He tries to look around the corner toward the door again, but he can't from where he is.

"No one's there," I reassure him.

He catches my free hand and presses it against the bulge in his pants. "I *have* been a very good student."

"You have. Don't you deserve a reward for your efforts?"

He finally meets my eyes, and the conflict in his expression is such a turn-on. He wants this bad, but he's afraid of being caught, and yeah, I can't blame him. The last thing I want is my dad catching me jerking off one of his players.

"Don't mean to pressure you, but we don't exactly have the luxury of time here," I point out.

"Screw it." Asher releases me and quickly undoes his pants. "Just do it."

He doesn't need to give me more direction than that. As soon as his jeans are loose, I spit in my hand, then wrap my fingers around him. His dick is hot and heavy in my palm, and I wish we had the time for me to tease him and draw this out, but the urgency is sort of fun.

I keep my ears strained for noise, knowing Dad could come looking for me at any minute.

A small moan comes from the back of Asher's throat, seeming

loud in the still room, so I quickly cover his mouth with my free hand as I squeeze his dick tighter.

"Fuck you're hard," I breathe against his ear. "Bet you're so close, aren't you? Bet you love this, the thought of being caught."

His groan hits my palm as I increase the pace.

"Anyone could walk in and see this. See how hard you are for me." I press my erection into his thigh. "Better make it fast, Asher. I want to see you come for me."

My hand eats his words as he starts to thrust into my fist. His eyes are half-mast, and he looks so out of it my dick throbs, making me wish I had time to take care of myself as well.

I jerk him as fast as I can, and it only takes a few more seconds before he stiffens and his cock pulses in my hand. Cum coats my fingers, and I do my best to catch it all. I'm a gentleman like that.

He's still, panting hard for a moment, before he sags back against the wall. He reaches dumbly for my hips and pulls me against him.

"That was …"

"Fun?" I grin, and he laughs weakly.

"Terrifying. And so fucking good."

I hold his stare as I lick his load from my fingers.

"Shit …" he whispers. "So, this whole hookup thing. We're still doing this, then?"

"I'm up for it if you are."

"Yeah." He swallows. "Definitely."

Asher reaches for my jeans, but I quickly step back away from him. "You can show me what a good teacher I am tomorrow."

"You don't want me to get you off now?"

"No time."

And as though I've summoned him, Dad's voice sounds down the hall. "You ready to go, Kole?"

"Coming, Dad." I drop my voice. "Or I will be tomorrow night."

"Jesus." Asher drops his head back against the wall. "I'm a dead man. Coach is going to kill me."

"Probably. So you might as well make sure it's worth it." To completely drive him wild, I lean down, lift his shirt, and suck the leftover cum off his dick. "Better put that thing away before Dad sees it."

Then I leave, praying my cock deflates in the time it takes me to get to Dad's car.

KATEY'S MEETING me at Bean There during one of our rare overlapping breaks. I slide into the booth opposite her, but she doesn't even acknowledge me. She's studying the menu like she hasn't memorized what they serve, and she's obviously had a big weekend given she's wearing her sunglasses *inside*.

I had a different kind of big weekend. The kind where I'm wondering whether Asher's reward system is such a good idea. That maybe hooking up again … and again is playing with fire.

In my defense, he's really pretty when he's not scowling, and —oh, who am I kidding, he's hot when he scowls too. But more importantly … his dick. Yes, that's the most important part of this whole thing.

Nothing changed between us after the first time. Our friendship was still solid. There was no weirdness. But I wanted it again badly, hence the hurried handjob in the locker room.

I'm starting to wonder if we should hold off on doing it again. The locker room was a lapse in judgment. A hot one. But it was a mistake I shouldn't have made because there wasn't a whole lot of studying going on. None, in fact. And that's against the rules.

Maybe hooking up can be one giant reward at the end of the semester when he doesn't get kicked off the team. This is supposed to be about that.

The thought of not having his mouth on mine again though ...

Katey snaps her fingers in front of my eyes. "Hello? Anyone home?"

I blink out of my trance. "You look ridiculous." I point to her sunglasses.

"Voice ... volume ... down."

She should know by now that only encourages me.

I pitch my voice a little louder. "*So* how was the weekend?"

"Probably better than yours. You missed that Halloween frat party that we do every year."

"Halloween is next week."

She frowns. "Then why were people in costumes? Either way, you missed a good night."

"From the looks of you, that's probably for the best."

She finally takes off her sunglasses, glaring against the light. "I didn't get home until Sunday afternoon."

"Wow. A *very* good night. And day, apparently. Did you sleep with a frat bro?"

Katey scoffs. We both have the same opinions when it comes to frat guys and jocks. They're too painful to deal with. Well, actually, no. Asher *is* painful to deal with, but I ... like it? Yeah, tabling that thought for a future psychiatrist.

"Of course I didn't hook up with a bro. Technically, it could have been because I didn't see under the mask until later. He was dressed as Batman, but under the clothes, it ended up being that French guy in bioengineering. With the manbun?"

"I will never understand your fascina—"

"*And* his girlfriend. She was Catwoman. It was eighteen hours of some weird DC fetish cosplay thing. But it was hot."

That sounds exactly like her. Katey's never really been interested in people romantically, and I don't know if she's aromantic or focused on having fun, but when it comes to sex, for her it's the more people, the better.

I love how open she is. And maybe I'll do the whole threesome thing one day, but for me, I like to give whoever I'm with my full attention. Sex is intimate and intense, and I'm not sure I'd get the same high if I was trying to multitask.

"So this threesome went okay, then? No jealousy?"

"Yeah, Frenchie was cool about it. Unlike the last guy." She rolls her eyes.

"Still don't know his name, huh?"

"I *know* what it is, I just can't pronounce it."

She looks sleepy, so I go up and order our usuals before carrying everything back to the table. As soon as she catches sight of her toast, muffin, and coffee, some of the moping lessens.

"I love you, Kole. I really, really love you."

"You're only human."

It's not until she's halfway through her coffee that she finally speaks again. "So how was your weekend? The hockey kids play nice?"

"Actually, they won both games." It was on purpose and everything. I finally saw some of that talent that's made Asher so damn cocky.

"Well, that's a surprise."

"Even to my dad. He took me and Mom out to dinner last night and couldn't. Stop. Talking. About it."

"Ouch."

"Hmm." Surprisingly though, it didn't grate on me as much as it usually does.

"Does your dad at least let you have your own room at away games?"

"You'd think so with the hockey budget this school has. But no, I shared." I purposely leave out with who, but my voice must do a thing. When I look up, Katey's staring at me more intently than she has since I got here.

"Shared with …"

"Asher Dalton." I try to play it down. "I've been helping him study. It was a *wild* weekend."

She doesn't need to know I'm not being sarcastic.

"Well, that Tray guy was asking about you at the party."

I try to picture who the hell Tray is, and with a douchey name like that, I'd usually remember.

"From one of the graduation parties last year," she prompts.

The vague memory of a flannel-wearing hipster comes to me. "Huh. Okay."

"He was really annoying and wouldn't stop talking about you, so I told him to text."

"*Why* would you do that?"

"*You're* the one who gave him your number last year," she shoots back.

Fair point. "I was drunk."

"Well, so was I. Drunk and not interested in him. You really do know how to pick the most *boring* people to hook up with."

"It's not like I keep them around for the conversation."

I usually don't keep them around at all. My schedule tends to get in the way. Or, at least, that's the excuse I use. I've never had a regular fuck buddy before, and I don't know if that's what this thing with Asher and me is.

Blowing him definitely isn't a hardship.

And as though I've willed him into existence, I look up as a wall of navy-and-silver Mountain Lion jackets walk in, and there he is. His dark hair is all floppy and sexy, and it instantly makes me think of how it looks gripped between my fingers.

Okay, definitely not suggesting waiting until the end of the semester. No fucking way.

There are only two weeks until the next away game ... not that I'm counting.

The surprising thing is, though, Asher is with some of his teammates *talking*. His usual snarl is missing, and he might even be *smiling* slightly. Holy shit, hell has frozen over.

"Aww," I can't help saying. "He's making friends."

Katey turns to see where I'm looking. "Who are you—oh, Asher, you mean?"

I nod. "Look at him. Being all social and making an effort. I'm so proud." And I am. Even though I try to make it sound like I'm being patronizing, seeing Asher with *actual live people* makes me happy.

And maybe I'm smiling too much because—

Katey gasps. "You slept with him!"

Oh shit. "Don't know what you mean."

She throws a sugar packet at me. "What happened, then? You *slipped* onto his dick?"

I start to laugh. "*Fine*. But for the love of my face and wanting to keep it intact, keep your voice down." The people at the table closest to us aren't hiding their stares.

"How was he?" She takes a slow sip from her mug. "Good enough to throw *all* your morals out the window?"

"And then some."

"Dick?"

"Perfect."

"Did you fuck?"

I mime locking my lips.

"At least tell me if he spanked you. He looks like the punishment type."

If anything, I was the one doing the punishing.

"*Who's* the punishment type?" That deep rumbly voice goes straight to my groin.

I jerk around to see Asher casually leaning against the side of the booth, and fuck, fuck, *fuck*, I have no idea how long he's been there. Katey's face rapidly turns bright red.

Luckily, I'm harder to embarrass than that. "Just a guy from my biology class. Labrat, hunchback but in a cute way. Totally my type."

Asher takes the liberty of sliding in next to Katey. He leans close, pretending to whisper to her while not taking his eyes off me. "Why do I feel like he's lying?"

"Ah, no. Bio guy. Scrawny and short. The opposite of a jock. Yeah, totally. So his type." She's hopeless. And completely tongue-tied with Asher sitting next to her.

"Thanks for the save," I deadpan.

Katey checks Asher out, and something in my gut twists. We've never cared about sleeping with people the other has if the guy swings both ways, but with Asher … Yeah, the thought makes me feel weird.

Asher kicks my foot under the table. "I thought you weren't going to tell anyone?"

"Technically, I didn't."

"If my brother finds out. Or your dad …"

"Oh, honey," Katey says. "As if I'm going to spill. Besides, there's no way Kole could keep this a secret from me. He didn't even tell me. His face said it all. I have a nose for these things."

"That's creepy." Asher shakes his head. "And it's only to help me study anyway."

She looks confused. "What is?"

"Hooking up."

I silently try to convey to him not to say anything else, but apparently, I'm not telepathic.

"Reward system, right?" Asher glances at me.

"Wait ..." Katey smacks her hand on the table. "It's happened more than once?"

I give her the sweetest smile I can manage. "Ah, for educational purposes?"

"What's the problem?" Asher asks.

"Kole! Did you take a hit to the head, sweetie?"

"Should I be offended?" Asher's voice is dry.

Katey turns to him. "You are hot. *So* hottie, hot, hot. I can forgive Kole for a slipup because let's face it—" She gestures at Asher. "—*hot*. But I never, ever thought I'd see the day my boo did the jock thing. Isn't that what high school is for?"

"High school was definitely not like that for me, and you know why."

Asher leans forward. "I don't. Why?"

Katey turns to him. "Kole here is what you might call a late bloomer."

"Katey," I growl.

She pins me with her stare and holds up a hand. "I will bless this union of bodies because sex is an art form, but if you come at me talking feelings, I'm going to have to stab out both your eyes."

"Deal."

Asher looks at us like we're both speaking another language, but I'm saved from explaining when Asher's teammates approach, and the three of us hurry to shut our mouths.

"You owe me." Simms places a takeout cup in front of Asher and gives me an up-nod. "Hey, Kole, what's up?"

"Not much."

We chat a bit before they leave, and as Asher slides out of the booth, his eyes lock on mine. It's only for a second, but the look is heated enough to make me shift in my seat. He's so attractive it should be illegal.

I swear the more I see him, the hotter he gets.

"Stop staring at his ass." Katey giggles.

"There isn't a single part of me that wants to stop doing that."

And as though Asher can sense it, or knows me well enough by now, when he reaches the door to leave, he turns enough to give me a subtle wink.

The next away game can't get here fast enough.

13

ASHER

Sundays are supposed to be the one day off the hockey team has, but they're the only day West has been able to organize extra time for Simms, Kaplan, and me to get our shit together.

After a few sessions, we're really clicking. I have no doubt our improvement during our games is because we've been doing these extra practices. But, the thing is, I'm not sure how much more we can grow as a line when there's no one challenging us.

We fly down the ice in sync, our passes are smooth, and our shots on an empty goal are always on target. Not that it's hard when there's no goalie.

When I sink one, Kole mockingly whistles and cheers from the stands. Beck has been supervising the last couple of Sunday practices, but he's in Dorset this weekend with Jacobs and his family, so Coach Hogan gave Kole the responsibility of letting us in and out of the hockey facilities. Apparently, we're untrustworthy with the keys. Either that, or he still doesn't trust Simms and I won't kill each other.

Ever since Simms and I came to a mutual understanding—

hockey is everything—I don't have a problem with the guy. I'm more patient on the ice, although sometimes I want to strangle him for making stupid penalties during games, but we're getting there.

We're ... friendly.

I don't think that makes us friends, but at least we're not fighting anymore.

We've only been on the ice for an hour, and I don't really know how much longer we can keep messing around just passing the puck back and forth to each other. It might be bonding, but it's not building our skill as a team.

As if reading my mind, Kole closes his laptop and approaches the side of the rink. "You need to learn how to work as a team when you have obstacles in front of you."

"You want us to put down cones or something?"

He taps the railing. "I have a better idea. I'll be right back."

Simms skates up to me. "Do you think he's as sadistic as his dad? Should we be scared?"

"Please. Kole is a kitten." A sexy kitten. No, wait, that's weird. I watch him the whole way down the chute.

Kaplan joins us. "I kind of had a crazy idea for a play."

We turn to him.

"We're listening," I say.

He goes into way too much excited detail, drawing on the ice with his stick, and it doesn't take long for him to lose me.

He's still rambling when Kole reappears wearing hockey gear and one of the team's practice jerseys.

My mouth drops, and I go to say something, but Kole points his stick at me.

"Not a word. I'm doing this to help."

"Can you even skate?" Simms asks.

Kole lifts his chin. "It's been a while, but it's like riding a bike, right?"

"This should be fun," I say.

I watch as Kole wobbles his way out onto the ice. Right before he reaches us, his eyes widen, and I know where this is going. He's forgotten how to stop.

With quick reflexes, I wrap my arm around his back and pull him against me. Just being near him now has my body warming and my cock taking interest. *Down, boy*. This is not sexual, damn it. "You good?"

"Give me a few minutes."

He takes off, starting slow, but before I know it, he's doing crossovers, jumps, lunges, and switching between skating forward and backward. He sends a smug smile in our direction.

He remembers how to stop now apparently too, doing a hard stop and shaving ice all over us. "Two on two. Asher and Simms against me and Kaplan."

Kole's eyes shine with confidence, but he's so going down.

"You're on." I face off with him and immediately pass to Simms.

Kole tries to shove me out of his way, and I want to pat him on his head and coo that he's a big bad enforcer, but I don't get the chance because he's too fast. And he's got moves.

He bodychecks Simms and steals the puck, but when he goes to pass to Kaplan, I intercept it and take it back.

Kole was right. This is what we needed.

I shoot to Simms, but he's not where I expect him to be. Kaplan digs the puck out from the boards and flies down the ice where Kole's waiting to put it in the net.

"Damn, the future doc has *skills*," I call out.

"I could skate circles around you, hotshot," Kole taunts.

We continue our two-on-two scrimmage, and it's the first time it feels like our work is paying off because Simms and I start clicking.

When we've sunk five goals against Kaplan and Kole, Kole switches us up. "Okay, Kaplan with Asher now."

"Aww, you don't want to play on my team?" I taunt.

"Nope. I'd rather kick your ass."

"Ooh, challenge thrown." And I love it.

It's the first time since last season when Cohen and I raced each other to score a hat trick that I've truly had fun on the ice.

Hockey is good for me. It's a healthy outlet for my aggression and energy. I love it. But yeah, it's been a while since I found it *fun*.

And even when Simms manages to get by Kaplan and me and passes to Kole, who's next to the net, I can't stop smiling when Kole scores again.

The last rearrangement has the three of us against Kole, and even though it's a lot easier to get around only one obstacle, having him there helps us find a groove.

We finally call it when Kole's phone alarm starts blaring through the space.

"Three hours. Time's up," Kole says. "Dad didn't want you guys to wreck yourselves."

"Says the guy who waits until someone throws up first practice every year," I point out.

But yeah, three hours is longer than most of our practices.

We leave the ice, Simms and Kaplan ahead of us, and I grab the jersey Kole's wearing and pull him back. "You know, if you practiced—"

"I'd still hate hockey as much as I always have."

I pause. "Really? You can't tell me you hated it out there. That was the most fun I've had in a long time."

Kole mockingly gasps and then lowers his voice. "My blowjob skills take offense."

"The most fun I've had *on the ice*."

"That's better. But that was just helping you guys. It wasn't as horrible or grueling as what Dad used to put me through, but sports aren't my thing."

"Pity. You look hot in a jersey."

"I probably should've kept my ass in the seat and studied for this massive midterm coming up. I decided helping you guys was more important."

It's already happening. Kole is prioritizing helping me instead of his studies.

"You should take the rest of the day to study."

"I will. I just have to resurface the ice first. I promised Dad—"

"I can do that."

Kole laughs. "He told me I had to do it because he didn't trust any of you three with the Zamboni."

"Oh, true. He doesn't let anyone on the team near that thing even though I've driven a million of them."

"Have you got any study plans for after this?" he asks as we enter the locker room. The other two are already in the showers, and it's only now I become keenly aware that Kole is about to join them.

Naked.

With me.

I face my cubby, take a deep breath, and tell my already hardening cock to calm down. I've seen Kole naked before. I've had his dick in my mouth, so this is no big deal. But damn if I haven't been thinking about it. Repeatedly.

I look at him over my shoulder. He's already stripping down.

Oh God, there's his long torso that I drew all over. The ink may be gone now, but I'll never be able to see him shirtless without thinking about that night.

"I didn't think it was that hard a question," Kole says.

I shake my head. "What?"

"After this? Any coursework you need help with?"

More images of his naked body fill my head. "You offering?"

Gah, no, he can't be. He has his own studying to do. And, like, *actual* studying. Not euphemism studying.

He drops his hockey pants to the ground, and I swallow hard.

"Dad took Mom out for the day, so my house is free."

"I could … study."

Remember the rules, Asher. *Only as a reward.* I cannot hook up with him right here and now.

Though … we've already broken the *only at away games* rule.

No. No hooking up in the locker room. Uh, again. And definitely not with Kaplan and Simms here.

Even if I'm getting along with them better, I don't trust them not to run their mouths if they saw anything.

Good thing they're in here with us then.

But that's the problem. As soon as Kole and I both strip down and join the showers, they're finishing theirs.

I'm not going to look.

I'm definitely not going to turn my head and check out his round ass.

I'm not doing it. Nope.

Damn, that's a biteable ass.

Shit, I need to hurry up and get all the sweat off me so I can get out of here and put clothes on. No, I need Kole to hurry up and put clothes on. He's taking his sweet-ass time though.

I rush through my shower and dressing. I move so fast, I'm

still damp, but I even beat Simms and Kaplan to getting fully dressed.

And while I sit on the bench by my cubby, doubt tries to creep in. I could say I want to go to Kole's because I really need to study—which is true. I really, really need to study. But the truth is, I'm going over there for the sex.

I should leave Kole to do what he needs to. I should not be selfish for once in my life.

Kole enters the locker room with a towel slung low around his hips with drops of water running down his chest. He knew what he was offering with that invite, and he knows what he's doing right now.

Oh, I am so going to be selfish.

Simms throws his bag over his shoulder and faces me. "Are you coming? We're going to the dining hall for lunch."

I wave him off. "I'm good. I need to get home to my siblings."

When Simms and Kaplan leave, I can't help myself. I stand and make my way over to Kole until I've boxed him in against the cubby.

"If you need to get home, we could—"

"I lied," I say. "West is with the kids."

The smile that spreads across Kole's face is breathtaking. No, not breathtaking. It's hot. Sexy. Something not so … mushy. It makes me want to kiss it off his gorgeous face. No.

Fuck.

"I'll get dressed and then resurface the ice."

"I can do it."

"Dad will kill us."

I can't resist. My hand goes to his hip, and I lean in, putting my lips near his ear. "We're already doing things that could get us killed by that man."

Kole shivers and drops his head forward.

I get the feeling he's trying to hold back as much as I am.

He shoves me off him. "You need patience."

"Or a way to get to your house faster." I step away, backing up toward the door. "And I know exactly how."

"Asher," he warns and tries to pull up his jeans.

I turn on my heel and hightail it out of the locker room. I rush out to the ice and open the doors to the storage area where the Zamboni is. I jump in the seat and turn it on with the key that's been left in it.

The Zamboni purrs to life, and I shove it in gear, but no sooner have I gotten it out onto the ice than Kole jumps up onto the footstep next to me. "Get off."

I wink. "Later. I'm *helping* you."

Before I know what he's doing, Kole sits on my lap. "My job."

I shift in my seat, his ass rubbing against my hardening cock. "Ooh, one of my hottest fantasies is about to come true."

Kole grabs the steering wheel. "Crashing a Zamboni and damaging school property is one of your fantasies?"

"No, but Zam*boning* on ice is." I rotate my hips a little. "Road Head On Ice? The next Disney show?"

"You're ridiculous. This will go a whole lot faster if you just let me do it."

"That's what she said."

"You're such a man child."

I take my foot off the gas and come to a stop. "Fine, but can you please hurry up? I really need to *study*. Like, my brain is so hard for you."

"We both know you're not talking about your brain."

"And now you're thinking about my dick." I'm tempted to grab it as I climb down onto the ice, but I resist because I'm a classy fucker. "My work here is done. Hurry up so we can get out of here."

He takes off, mumbling something like who knew petulance could be a turn-on.

"It's a talent!" I call after him.

KOLE

WHAT IS WRONG WITH ME? MOODY BASTARDS HAVE NEVER BEEN my thing, but all I've been able to think of all day—hell, since Asher sucked my dick—is how to get back in his pants.

And as soon as we get to my place, whatever I've done has clearly worked. He parks his car across the street and rushes to catch up to me.

It snowed last night, the type that sticks to the ground, and Asher almost slips on some black ice, but the need to get off apparently doesn't affect his reflexes as he rights himself and meets me at the door.

We've barely crossed the threshold when Asher slams me into the wall opposite and his body covers mine. His erection presses into my hip as my bag digs into my side, and he lowers his mouth to mine.

It's all tongues and greedy mouths devouring one another.

Damn, he can kiss.

We fight for control, for dominance, and it's such a fucking turn-on when he reaches up to lock my face where he wants it that my dick goes from half-mast *this-is-hot-but-bearable* to *Houston-we-have-a-problem.*

I tear my mouth away from his, and Asher tries to follow until I gasp out, "Wait. Wait, wait … wait."

For …? Words, Kole.

"I need to check my parents aren't home."

Asher pauses. "You said they were out."

"They're *supposed* to be. But we wouldn't want to get busted and out ourselves, would we?"

He hurries to shake his head.

I take a deep breath and yell, "Mom, Dad, I'm home!"

Then we both fall silent, straining our ears to pick out any sounds over our heavy breathing.

After a minute of deep quiet, Asher relaxes, and his stare immediately drops to my lips. "Where were we?"

I scramble out of his hold before he kisses me and sends me brain-dead again. "Studying. Lots and lots of studying."

"That better be a fucking euphemism," Asher growls. I take his hand and drag him after me, leading the way upstairs.

I need to stay strong and make sure he gets some studying in first, and I have approximately ten seconds before we reach my room to find my restraint.

Which is nearly impossible when I pause for point three of a second to open my door and Asher presses up behind me. Hot breath tickles my neck as he shoves us inside and kicks the door closed, but before things can escalate, I turn the tables.

I spin in Asher's arms and back him up to my bed before pushing him down on the mattress. He lands with a thump, and I run my hands up his spread thighs, stopping before I reach the straining bulge in his pants.

Asher's hips buck off the bed in encouragement, but I

smoothly step back, ignoring the begging my own cock is doing, and flop into my desk chair instead.

"You. Are. A dick."

"No, you want to see my dick." I grin. "There's a difference."

And then, because I'm enjoying myself, I drop my bag to the ground and reach in to pull out my glasses.

His jaw ticks. "Now you're being cruel."

"What do you need help with this time?" I try to keep my voice level, but Asher chooses that moment to crawl off the bed and approach with slow, stalking strides that make me shiver.

"Lymphatic system."

"Let's start there, then."

"Or …" He sinks to his knees and buries his face into my crotch, and well, mm …

"Fair argument." But I can't let him think it's that easy. I wind my fingers through his hair in the way I love. Then I give his head a sharp tug backward.

Lust-drenched green eyes flick up to meet mine, and I have to tighten my grip on him, both to keep him in place and to stop myself from doing something dumb like kissing him.

"We need to—"

"Reward me."

"You haven't done anything to deserve it yet."

When he leans forward, I let him. And there's that counterargument again that I just can't dispute. He pushes his face against my aching cock and nips the inside of my thigh. "Don't I deserve a reward? I've been so good."

"Well …"

"Let me show my teacher how much I appreciate his help."

"Asher …"

"Please, teach?" He mouths at the bulge in my pants. "*Please?*"

I swallow thickly as Asher looks up and spears me with that intense stare. He knows he's got me.

So instead of fighting him, I order him to strip.

Inches of smooth, warm skin are exposed, and I greedily drink him in. There's no one on earth who could fault me for being weak when the man looks like that. I want to bite his pec and drag my tongue over his abs and ... He drops his pants, and his dick bobs up hard and eager.

That.

I want that.

Asher grabs my hand and pulls me to my feet, then slowly peels my T-shirt off me. His lips find my neck, and I automatically arch back, giving him all the access he needs and letting him take whatever he wants. And the thought that Asher wants *me* has me dizzy.

He pops the button on my jeans, then slips both hands down over my ass as he pushes my pants from my hips.

"What do you want?" he asks in a sexy rasp.

"This is your reward. I'll give you free rein."

His hands clench tight over my ass cheeks. "This. I want this."

Fuck yes. "I thought you'd never ask."

"Do you have a ..."

My gut sinks. "Condom? Shit, no. I haven't bought any since summer break. Don't you?"

He pulls back, and the lust seems to clear a little. "I don't have my wallet on me. I left it in the car."

"Maybe ..." I'm supposed to be the smart one, and I can barely even think with his hands on me like that. "I could see if Da—"

His hand slaps over my mouth. "If you want me to stay hard, you won't finish that sentence."

"I mean, because ever since I hit puberty, I swear he stashed those things around the house so I'd never have this problem."

"Finding one will take too long, but don't worry. Hockey players are good at thinking on their feet." He shoves me toward the bed and presses his hand between my shoulder blades, guiding me down to lie on my front. His lips find my back, and I shiver as he drags a line of kisses all the way down my spine until he reaches my underwear. "God your ass is sexy," he mutters. "I couldn't keep my eyes off it in the showers."

He shoves my briefs down over my thighs.

"Probably why you didn't notice me staring right back," I say.

Because if we want to talk asses, Asher's is divine. The thought of sliding my cock between those big, round cheeks makes my head spin.

"Tell me you have lube."

I point vaguely toward my nightstand, and he disappears for a moment before he's back, body covering mine. His hand works his cock between us, and a tiny prickle of discomfort hits.

"We're not fucking without a condom."

He chuckles against the back of my ear. "*Trust*."

I barely manage to hold back my moan as he slides his slick cock between my ass cheeks, then dips his hand lower and smears lube over my taint and thighs before squeezing my balls.

As soon as I know where this is headed, I relax under his weight.

I'm borderline disappointed he's not about to fuck me, but then he tilts my hips up off the bed, straddles my legs, and positions his cock between my thighs.

I shove a pillow under my stomach, then close my legs around him, squeezing as tight as I'm able, and his first thrust against my taint has me desperately gripping the comforter.

"Fuck yes," he breathes as he leans forward again. He presses his full weight against me as he grips my hip on one side and reaches around to close his lubed-covered hand over my cock.

Each of his thrusts hits my balls and forces me into his fist. He's so heavy and warm at my back, and his panting is driving me crazy to the point I can't contain the small grunts coming out of me.

Maybe this should feel weird, being so exposed to someone I know, but being friends outside of the bedroom seems to make it that much better. The pleasure is heightened, each touch is more confident, and the constant teasing and sexual tension makes it explosive when we finally move as one.

I'm desperate to kiss him, and he must have the same idea, because as soon as I turn my head, seeking him out, he's there.

It's all lips and tongues and hot bursts of air, and the sweat building between us makes each glide of his skin against mine extra sensitive.

Asher drops his face to my neck as he picks up the pace. All I can think is *harder, tighter* as I cross my legs over and clench my thighs.

"*Nrgh*, Kole ... Kole, I'm gonna ..."

I thrust back to meet him as his whole body goes stiff, and I feel his cum start to coat my legs and the bed beneath me. Each noise that leaves him increases the tingling in my balls, and when he sags against me again, he gathers up his cum and wraps his hand back around my cock.

He jerks me fast, nuzzling my neck, sending vibrations racing across my skin ... I swear my eyes roll back into my fucking head.

I have barely a second of notice before my orgasm hits, tipping me right over into a land of *goddamn ecstasy*.

I'd never have imagined something could be hotter than Asher Dalton swallowing my dick, but that was ... that was ...

Shit, I can't even think.

Asher rolls off me, and I'm able to roll out of the puddle of cum we've left on my sheets.

He stares at the wet patch. "Think your parents will ask questions?"

"I've been doing my own laundry for long enough ..." It's all the words I can manage because my dumb brain is still feeling dumb.

The front door slams shut, and I frown. "Did we close the—"

"*Kole!*"

My name being yelled from downstairs makes me jerk upright.

"Holy shit, is that ..." Asher can't even finish his sentence.

It's not until I hear footsteps on the stairs that I finally launch into motion.

I shove Asher off the other side of the bed, and a second later I hear the telltale signs of him scrambling to crawl under it. My heart pounds madly as I duck into my bathroom, flick on the shower, and pull a towel around my waist just before the knock sounds at my door.

As I cross back to it, I try to calm my breathing. The room reeks of sex, and our clothes are everywhere, and I quickly kick Asher's shoes out of the way. I have no goddamn clue how I look, but when I crack the door open, I try to play it cool.

"Hey."

Dad's relaxed expression instantly switches to suspicion. "Hey. I wanted to let you know we're back, and we bought lunch if you want it."

"Yeah, thanks."

"You know ..." He eyes me. "Because you've been at the rink all morning and then studying hard."

Holy shit my dad cannot say the word "studying" ever again.

If he knew how *hard* we'd been *studying*, he'd probably explode.

"Thanks. Just let me shower and I'll be right down."

"O ... Kay. How did today go, anyway? No dramas?"

He clearly knows something's up, and I swear it's the first time I've ever actually hoped Dad assumes I've been jerking off.

"Yep," I squeak. "All good. They're really ... clicking. I think the private practice time is good for them."

"Good, good. You can tell me all about it at lunch."

"Umm ... K, bye." I hurry to close *and lock* the door before dropping my head against it.

Way. Too. Close.

ASHER

Not shockingly, this isn't the first time I've had to hide after sex. It is the first time I've feared the actual consequences of being found.

There's really not enough room for me under Kole's bed, and there are dust bunnies and a mess down here too.

If Coach catches me in his son's room, I'm worse than dead. I'll be off the team.

Priorities.

"Asher," Kole whispers.

Ooh, condom. I pick it up and wave around the foil packet. "Found a condom."

"A little too late for that."

"No shit."

I inch my way out from under his bed. Now I'm naked and covered in dust and sweat. "How do I get out of here?"

"Putting on clothes might be a good start."

"Can I steal your shower?"

"As long as you bring it back."

I make a drum noise. "Ba dum tshhh."

"Just hurry up. Whatever you're going to do, we don't have much time before they'll come up to check I haven't fallen and hit my head."

I swallow down the unexpected hurt that hits me in the chest and force a small laugh. "That sounds exactly like the type of thing my stepmom would do."

I don't mean to bring her up. The thought flies from my mouth, and I regret it immediately.

Kole's eyes soften in sympathy, and yuck. It's genuine as opposed to all the fake sympathy people give me when I make them feel uncomfortable by purposefully bringing up my dead parents.

Not that I ever saw my stepmom as my parent. She was a nice woman, and she and Dad loved each other a lot, but I always got the distinct impression West and I were Dad's kids. Our siblings were theirs. I also wonder how she'd feel with West and me being the ones in charge of her kids. She'd be well within her rights to worry. Growing up, we didn't make it easy on her. At all.

From the preteen drama of accusing her of trying to replace our mom to acting out when our siblings came along because we felt we weren't really paid attention to when shinier, newer kids were there.

She took our attitudes in stride, and honestly, I think I only acted that way because my big brother was. I remember June more than I remember my own mother, and until Zoe came along, I did see her as my mom. After that, I was a jealous little shithead that only got worse as I got older and more siblings came along.

"Were you close?" Kole asks.

And this is exactly why I don't bring them up in passing. People want to talk about it instead of silently beg to move on.

I pick up my clothes from the floor. "As much as I'd love to talk about this, and I so do," I say dryly, "I should get out of here."

"Weren't you going to shower?"

I was, but now I suddenly need to get out. "I'll shower at home. Less chance of getting caught. How do I escape?" I shove my boxer briefs on.

Kole crosses the room, still only wearing a towel. "My window opens to the roof of the porch. It's one floor. You can jump it. Just, you know, don't break anything important."

"Like my dick?"

"I was going to go with something more like your ankle or your leg. You know, something you wouldn't have to explain to Dad by saying, 'Yeah, I jumped off your roof, and now I can't play the rest of the season.'"

"Can't you distract them, and I'll sneak out the front door?"

"You want to risk that?" Kole's voice goes high-pitched.

Apparently being caught with me isn't something he's keen on either. "Okay. No."

"It's not that far to the ground. Maybe you can shimmy down one of the pillars."

"Do I look like a shimmying kind of guy?"

"No, but you do look like someone who's gotten themselves out of this type of situation before." Kole's having way too much fun with this.

"You're going to film it, aren't you?"

"I'm making a collage. Top ten walks of shame from my room." He slaps my shoulder. "You could take out top spot, but it has to be impressive."

"I'm starting to forget why I like you."

"Because I'm your friend, I help you study, and I put you in really awkward situations like this one."

"You're the bestest friend ever."

The telltale sound of footsteps on the stairs echoes up through the hallway, and we both freeze.

"Quick, go," Kole hisses.

"I'm half-naked!" I shove my foot into my jeans and almost trip over.

"Kole! Your lunch is going cold," Coach Hogan yells.

Fuck it. I grab the pile of clothes at my feet and practically dive through the window. The cold November air hits me, and I have to bite back a curse.

"Be right there, Dad." Kole disappears into the bathroom, leaving me out here on the ledge by myself.

Okay, I can do this.

I peer over the edge of the patio roof. It's not actually that big of a drop. With a deep breath, I throw my things to the ground, and they hit the snow with a soft thump.

This will be easy. Totally easy.

I'm not going to break my neck.

I move to the edge and sit, the cold-as-fuck roof probably giving me frostbite on my ass.

Oh God, I'm so going to face-plant.

Then I get an idea. Pull-ups are part of a hockey player's gym routine. If I turn around, I can hold on to the roof gutter and lower myself as far as possible before letting go.

As I turn and make my way down slowly, I can't help thinking as much as the sex with Kole is smoking hot, it might not be worth this much.

A flash of his body splayed out before me, his hole right there wanting me to fill it … okay, it's worth it. Or, it will be. What we just did was amazing, but I can't wait to be inside him properly. I'm going to fuck his—

The gutter snaps, and I fall to the ground. My feet hit first, and then my back. The snow breaks my fall, but I'm instantly frozen.

Fuck!

A quick check of my legs and feet reveals no pain or injury, so I scramble to collect my things and get the hell out of here.

I run across the street to my car, still only wearing my boxer briefs because to shove all my clothes on would mean standing out here where there's more chance of being caught.

I beg the universe that Coach Hogan isn't watching me from his front window.

As soon as I find my keys in my jeans pocket, I jump in the car and crank the heat while I shove all my belongings on the passenger seat beside me and get the hell out of here.

I don't anticipate Rhys being out the front of our house when I get home, though.

His entire face lights up when he sees me climbing out of the car.

"Don't say one fucking word," I grumble.

"Let me go see Charlotte, and my lips are sealed."

I think about that. "Tell you what. You can go see her from three p.m. until five—"

"Yes!"

"If," I continue, "you help me with my math class."

Seeing as I already got the perks of studying, I figure I better actually put in some time learning, and Rhys is a math whiz. He's in all the advanced classes at school. He kinda sucks at every other subject, which is a shame, but at least he has direction.

Rhys smiles at me. "Deal."

"Okay. I'm going to go have a really hot shower. Meet me in my room in ten minutes. Oh, and bring food. I'm starving." I go to move past him.

"I've heard sex works up your appetite," Rhys mumbles.

I turn. "Who are you talking to about sex?"

He shrugs. "Guys at school."

"If they tell you they've done it, they're lying. You're thirteen."

"When did you first …"

Mother of fuck, we are so not ready for this conversation, right? Also, do I lie here or tell the truth?

"I'm a virgin." Lying it is!

He looks down at the clothes in my hands and cocks an eyebrow at me.

"Fine, I was sixteen. And I know this is totally contradictory, but you can't until you're eighteen."

Rhys laughs. "I think you're getting the hang of this parenting thing."

I shudder. "Eww, dude. I'm not and never will be your parent."

My brother's face falls slightly, and he looks disappointed.

"I mean that because you're my kid brother, and I love you. I don't want to be your parent. I'd rather be the guy you come to if you're ever in trouble, and I want you to trust me, okay? Would you have ever asked Dad that question about his virginity?"

"Hell no."

"Exactly."

Silence fills the small space between us.

"We good?" I ask.

"Yeah, we're good."

"Awesome. Now I really do need a hot shower, or my toes might fall off from frostbite." I sneak around the side of the house to use the external entry to the basement instead of having to walk past all my other brothers and sisters undressed like this.

☒

Even though Rhys tutors me in math, and he tutors me well,

when we're given a pop quiz in my next class, I fail, and I fail hard.

"Mr. Dalton, can I have a word with you?" Professor Fuckstain asks. His name is Eckstein, but that's hard to remember. Fuckstain suits him more. And his personality. It's a shame because he's pretty hot for someone in his thirties. He looks ripped underneath his tweed jacket, a contrast of hunky covered in nerdy clothing.

As the class disperses, I approach the professor.

"You're failing this class already, and it's only November."

"I know. I've been studying, I promise."

"I know this is a core subject, so everyone thinks it's a waste of time and a flyby class where you get an automatic C by turning up, but if you wanted that type of education, you should've signed up to someone else's class."

I'm tempted to ask whose so I can do just that, but he keeps talking.

"You need to make the effort if you want to keep your minimum C to stay on the hockey team." His face screws up when he says hockey, and I get the feeling he's singling me out for a reason.

It's not because I suck at math. It's because I'm an athlete. He's not the first professor to stare me down like he is now. Like I'm the dumbest of the dumb, and it's unfair I get a free education because I'm good at sports when he probably couldn't even stand upright in a pair of skates.

"What can I do?" I ask.

"I'd suggest you drop the class. The last day to do so is tomorrow."

"If I do that, I'll need to pick up an extra class next semester, and I don't have the time for that. Last year, my classes let me do extra-credit work over the summer. Is that an option? I have extenuating circumstances—"

"Sports is not an extenuating circumstance."

"No, my parents—"

"I don't care if you're not meeting your parents' expectations. You're not a good fit for this class."

He's pissing me off, and I want to tell him to get fucked so bad, but I need this class. Look at me being all mature and responsible.

"In other words there's no extra credit on the table," I say, not ask.

"Nope. You do the work like everyone else in my class. No special treatment for …"

"For?" Go on. Say it. For *jocks*.

"For anyone."

"Got it."

I exit the class, wanting to punch something, and I guess I should be glad I'm heading for practice where I can skate all this excess energy out. It's a shame Simms and I are getting along now, because I don't want to wreck the good thing we've started, so I can't even get in his face and beg him to punch me.

I want to fight.

I want to fuck.

I just want—

Oof. I run into someone and jam my shoulder.

"Motherfucker, watch where you're—" My eyes meet Kole's.

He rubs his own shoulder. "Dude, I thought you saw me. Where's the fire? Practice doesn't start for another five minutes."

All that anger building, the tension, that urge to go and fuck shit up, dissipates immediately. What the hell is up with that? "Sorry, did I hurt you?" I step forward, trying to assess any damage I might have caused.

"You're a wall of muscle. Of course you hurt me."

"S-sorry," I stammer.

"What's wrong?"

I shake my head. "Nothing. I was distracted. Heading to the rink?"

"If I walk with you, will you bodycheck me again?"

"No. You're safe."

"Good."

But when we reach the locker room, West is there because, well, duh, he is the assistant coach, and as soon as he sees me, he knows something's wrong. Or, he's assuming there is because for the last year or so, he's always on us about our *feelings* and trying to fix what he can't.

He's at my side in an instant. "What happened?"

"Nothing."

"Tell that to my shoulder," Kole mumbles.

"What?" West asks.

I sigh. "It's one of my professors, okay? I'm failing math already, and he wants me to drop it, even though Rhys spent nearly all of Sunday afternoon showing me how to do the equations, and I thought I understood it, but apparently, I don't."

"Who's your professor?" West growls.

"Why? You can't storm in there and do the commanding big-brother thing. It won't work. The guy hates jocks and sports and anyone who has to do with either."

"Oh, you got Eckstein?" Kole asks. "Damn."

The fact Kole knows off the top of his head says everything I already suspected.

"I don't think I'm acing the class—I know I suck—but he's unwilling to give me any leeway. I'm putting in the work. I'll do extra credit. But he won't hear any of it."

"Right," West says. "Eckstein. I'll be right back."

I look Kole in the eyes. "You have no idea what you've just done."

"Hmm, I might have gotten your big brother to talk to your professor for you."

"I hate when he does that. He always feels like he needs to get involved, and it pisses me the hell off."

"Can you blame him when you no doubt grunted at Eckstein and told him to fuck off?"

A year ago, that's exactly what I would've done.

"I showed restraint, thank you very much. But yes, I *wanted* to tell him to fuck off. And there might have been some grunting. Why can't West trust me to handle my own shit occasionally?"

"I can help you with math too if you like? It's not my best subject, but I got a B when I took his class."

I laugh. "If a B is the worst you've ever received, I don't think we can be friends anymore. Can you take all my tests for me?"

"That's called cheating."

"Fine. If we're going to do this study thing, maybe we should go to the library for the study part and then—" I glance around the filling locker room and lower my voice. "—find somewhere to hook up. Somewhere without second-story windows or hormonal teens and preteens."

Kole nods. "We need to prioritize, I agree."

"Okay, library?" I ask.

"Tonight?"

"Yeah, is after practice fine? Tomorrow's the last day to drop the class, and if you tell me there's no hope, then maybe I should do it. At least I'll get to stay on the team then, even if it means a busier schedule next semester when I have to pick up an extra class."

Kole touches my arm. "I'll teach you. It will be okay."

Will it though?

I'm starting to think this whole college education thing is a waste of time. But without it, I'll no longer have hockey.

I can't leave West and the kids yet. Not until they're all a bit older.

To play the game I love, I have to do something I hate.

That's just another shitty reality in life.

Love is never easy.

16

KOLE

I purposely don't sit next to Asher on the bus to his next away game, because I don't trust myself to keep my hands off. After how close we came to being caught by Dad, we need to play it a little smarter if we're going to keep things under wraps.

Studying all week has been painful. Do you know how hard it is to use your brain when it isn't getting enough blood flow?

After convincing Asher he knows enough of the material to pass Eckstein's class the other night after practice, the exchanged blowjobs in the back of Asher's car were nowhere near satisfying enough.

I glance behind me at the same moment Asher looks up from his phone, and the second our eyes meet, heat bursts through me.

Yep. Actual *burning up my cheeks I can't wait to be alone* type of heat. I have to bite the inside of my cheek to stop myself from making a noise.

Tonight, he's going to fuck me. And who knows? Maybe after, he'll let me fuck him.

The thought sends a shiver through me right as my phone lights up.

Asher: *Did the equipment manager remember all the equipment this time?*

I almost laugh, then remember Dad is sitting beside me. The message is innocent—seemingly—but he's still going to want to know what Asher is doing texting me if he sees it.

Me: *A whole box. I'm prepared to study all night if we need to.*

Asher: *You think you can compete with an athlete's stamina?*

Me: *You're about to find out.*

I quickly put my phone away because the last thing I need is to pop a boner while I'm sitting next to Dad. And when he starts to talk me through what he needs when we reach the arena, it's enough to kill off any thoughts of what Asher and I have planned for later.

This time, I didn't even bring my notes with me.

I'm more than prepared to keep *incentivizing* his studying, but tonight is all about sex. Only sex.

My dick tries to take interest at that thought, but then Dad mentions something about the New Hampshire facilities, and I quickly turn my thoughts to gross gym socks in an attempt to make it go down.

Only a few hours to go.

Until Asher is inside me.

Goddamn it, where's a cold shower when you need one?

***

THE GAME against New Hampshire is intense. They're stuck at two for two from the first period right through to the third. Both teams are getting tired and sloppy, but there's only *one goal* in it.

I'm totally not holding my breath. Or invested.

Nope.

But I can't tear my eyes away from Asher. He and Simms are flying down the ice, passing the puck back and forth so quickly the New Hampshire players can't keep up, and then …

Asher passes to Simms, and Simms takes a shot on goal. It happens so fast. The puck flies past the goalie, landing in the net, and everyone's on their feet.

Everyone except for Asher.

I know this because even though everyone's focus was on the goal, mine was on him. One of the New Hampshire players body-checked Asher hard, and he fell like a lead balloon. He didn't even have time to get his hands down and crashed headfirst on the ice.

And he hasn't gotten back up.

"*Shit.*"

Dad's straight out there when he realizes something's wrong. I'm desperate to follow, but I keep my feet rooted to the ground, barely breathing, reminding myself that showing any more concern than I would for any other player would be suspicious as fuck.

Asher wouldn't like that.

So instead, I grip the barrier and pretend like I'm not feeling sick right now.

Like there isn't an enormous lump in my goddamn throat.

Dad shifts, and when I see that Asher is conscious and moving, I almost sag in relief.

But then Dad walks him off and sends Rossi out instead. I realize Asher's not going back out there, and my relief is short-lived.

Asher's walking fine on his own with his head held high. That's a good sign, at least.

The team trainer is waiting, so I don't even get a second to chat to Asher before they're walking with him down the chute.

Keeping my voice as even as I can, I hook my thumb over my shoulder. "Want me to go with?" I ask Dad.

"Yeah, you better. Make sure he's okay. I'll come check on him once this is over."

He's barely finished his sentence before I leave.

I find Asher, Beck, and the trainer in the locker room. I hang back at the doors, waiting for them to finish examining him.

"His responses look good," the trainer says. "He didn't lose consciousness, he's showing no signs of concussion, but he did hit his head. That means—"

"Mandatory concussion protocols," Beck finishes.

Asher slumps. "Are you shitting me? I'm fine."

"Probably," Beck says. "You're still out until at least tomorrow, and then we'll reassess."

"We'll lose if I don't play!"

"Then you better come back strong next week. And stay on your damn skates."

There's more low conversation that I can't hear, but I figure the important part is over, so I join them.

"How is he?" I ask, like I haven't heard everything.

"Unfortunately, he's still an asshole, so I think he'll be fine," Beck says.

Asher flips Beck the bird as the trainer leaves.

"That's a flippant attitude for someone on concussion watch," I say sweetly.

"You room with him, don't you?" Beck suddenly asks.

"Yep."

"Do you want me to switch out with you so you're not babysitting him all night?"

"Nope." I somehow pull off a casual tone. "We've covered some stuff on brain injuries in class."

"Have you met Asher? He's a handful."

"You're talking as if I'm not right here," Asher complains.

I ignore him. "I'll keep him in line."

Beck assesses me for a second, and for one wild moment, I think I've given away too much, but it's not like there's much to give away. We've made each other come a few times, no biggie.

And when Beck starts listing off what Asher needs, I figure that look was all in my head. Besides, I have more pressing things to worry about—

"If he vomits, complains of a headache, dizziness, or ringing ears, let your dad know, and we'll get him checked out at the hospital."

"I don't need a fucking hospital."

Beck continues. "Back in the hotel room, there should be no bright lights, so he can't be on his phone. No watching TV. And … no physical activity."

Physical activity?

My gaze flies to Asher, and he smirks like *yeah, not a smartass now.*

"So when you say physical …"

"He needs to rest. No game tomorrow, no practice …" Beck eyes me. "And no sex."

"What?"

"What?" he asks innocently. "I know what happens at these away games. I was a player too, remember?"

Okay, has he guessed, or is he just being a douche?

I force a smile. "I'll make sure there's no sneaking out."

We bus it back to the hotel after the team narrowly pulls off the win, and I know that them winning without him doesn't put Asher in any better of a mood. If I thought he was painful to deal with on a regular basis, I clearly underestimated injured Asher.

The second the hotel door clicks closed behind us, Asher pushes me up against a wall and kisses me. It's tempting, so, so tempting to go with it, fuck the consequences, but as a future doctor and ex-athlete, I'm well aware of how easy it is to underestimate head injuries.

I ease him off me. "Nice try."

"Come on, Kole. I'm fine."

"Your brain needs rest."

"No, my brain is definitely telling me differently." He grinds his hard cock into my hip.

Whyyy? Why, why, why is this world so cruel? Maybe I should have taken Beck up on his offer to switch, because tonight is going to be torture.

But I'll hold strong anyway.

"Concussion protocol."

"Screw concussion protocol."

"There you go with your winning maturity again, but I have a feeling once we've fucked, I'm going to be greedy and want to do it again. So you're going to get that sexy ass in bed and do as you're told tonight." I lean in and nip his ear. "If you do, you know I'll reward you."

He groans in complaint but doesn't fight me as I lead him over to the bed. We both strip out of our clothes, and I toss Asher a pair of my sleep shorts.

"Yeah, no, I sleep naked."

"I've noticed." *How could I not?* "But I need to be able to control myself tonight, and I can't do that if you're lying around naked."

He reaches down slowly and gives his still-interested dick a long, teasing stroke.

"Put on the fucking shorts!"

Asher starts to laugh. "Fine."

"There's nothing *fine* about getting injured. I want to joke about killing you for wrecking tonight, but I feel like that's in poor taste, given ..."

"I'm not injured. Look." He throws himself onto his bed without any finesse, and even though I agree with him—he's showing absolutely no signs of a concussion—I have to take the protocol seriously. Concussions are no joke. Schools have finally started taking seriously how dangerous they are and won't take any chances if there's even the slightest possibility of one.

Once I've changed, I pull down the covers on his bed and join him.

"Wha—what are you doing?" Asher asks.

I flick off the lamp and roll to face him in the dark. It takes a minute, but he slowly comes into focus. "This is the easiest way for me to keep an eye on you. You're lucky the whole *wake every two hours and try to keep you up* rule is no longer considered beneficial for concussions. You're cranky when you're woken up."

"I'm cranky always. I don't understand why you sleeping in the same bed as me will help."

He's still looking at me weird, so I poke his ribs. "What? You can suck my dick, but sharing a bed is too much?" That thought sort of annoys me. "Right next to you, I can feel your breathing. I want to look after you."

He screws up his face. "That's ... weird."

"Why?"

"Because I can't remember the last time someone *wanted* that."

"To be fair, it's so I don't become a doctor and have to tell everyone I work with 'Oh, I killed a guy once because I didn't take his concussion seriously.'"

"Joke's on you, I'm a terrible patient."

"It'll be good practice for when I'm a doctor then."

"Pretty sure sleeping in bed with a patient comes under some kind of malpractice."

"Then I'll keep this honor all for you."

"Blue balls. What a privilege."

I hum. "So since there's nothing else we can do, I guess we can either talk or sleep."

"I'm not tired."

"That's a good sign."

"That's because I don't have a concussion."

"Okay then, tell me something about you." I already know the surface-level stuff—like he has a major wall up. My guess is because he's experienced the type of loss people don't usually experience until later in life, and he has some form of abandonment issues. But Asher Dalton is the kind of guy who seems deeper than that.

"I'm horny."

Okay, maybe not. "Something real."

"Okay, I'm *really* horny."

"Has anyone ever told you that you're impossible to like?"

"Daily, actually. I've been waiting for you to catch on."

"It's lucky for you I don't scare easily."

"*Lucky*, you say." Asher nudges me. "You're a pain in my ass."

"I will be." I bounce my eyebrows, and it makes him laugh. He also doesn't deny it which is interesting.

Asher puts on a mocking voice. "*Has anyone ever told you that you're impossible to like?*"

"You really are *such* a charmer. I will never understand why you're still single."

There's a slight pause before he says, "I've been wondering the same thing about you."

Something in the way he drops the snark from his tone makes me fluttery inside.

"High standards."

"So this is you slumming it?"

This ... I actually don't know *what* this is.

Sex, obviously, Kole.

It's just really hot sex.

So I don't know why I'm tempted to ask him what's been on my mind for a while.

Even though we're not lying particularly close, the way he's studying me makes prickles creep along my skin. I want to move closer, but I know that's tempting fate a step too far.

"Can I ask you something?" I finally dare say.

"Obviously, but it doesn't mean I have to answer."

I'm worried bringing this up now will stress him, but I may not get another chance. "Your brother maybe mentioned that you never, umm, got sad. Over your parents."

Asher grunts.

"We don't have to talk about it."

He stays silent.

"I just want you to know, it's okay. My nan died last year, and I swear I cried for a week. It's not the same thing, I get it. But losing people leaves these little holes, like the gross, rock-hard cookies she'd bake and bring over every Sunday. I used to hate forcing them down, or wearing the ugly beanies she knitted me, or hugging her and getting a nose full of whatever strong perfume she used. I miss it now though ..."

I let the conversation die between us, and I swear the silence stretches on so long Asher's going to ignore it completely.

When he finally does talk again, it's so soft I can barely hear him. "Before I left for the juniors ... Dad and I got up early every morning. We ate breakfast together, didn't even talk half the time because he was reading his paper and I was playing on my phone." Asher pauses for a moment, and I hear him swallow. "After it ... *happened*, I was at that table, eating breakfast and scrolling through my phone, and I saw an article on Gretzky and leaned over to show it to Dad, but ... he wasn't there." Asher shifts, pulling his arms tight against his chest, and I watch as the brief hurt on his face quickly clears. "Anyway, it is what it is. Life's shitty. Look at tonight. We should be fucking, and instead we're talking about ghosts. Fun times."

I really wish he wouldn't do that, but I get the feeling passing it off as nothing is Asher's way of coping. It's not healthy, and I'm sure it can't last forever, but instead of making him see it, I lean in a little and brush my lips softly over his. "Thank you for telling me."

When I pull back, he looks a little freaked-out. "Whatever. It's nothing."

"Of course." It isn't nothing. "So tell me more nothing. What's your favorite color?"

"You've got to be kidding me."

"Mine's gold."

"That's not a color."

"Technically, it is."

"Fine. Mine's black like my soul."

I laugh. "Uh-huh. Totally big and scary and empty."

"What was it you called me? An emotionless trash can?"

"Close enough."

"Well, we can't all have sunshine radiating out of our asses."

"So *that's* why you're obsessed with my ass?"

He looks way more like himself as he reaches over and grabs me. His hand squeezes tight over my ass cheek, and he drags me a little closer.

I pull back. "Answer's still no."

"But I think I hurt my dick out there." He pretends to pout. "It needs to be kissed better."

"No blowing your load or you might blow your brain."

He sniggers. "Aren't you supposed to be a doctor?"

For some reason seeing him smile makes me smile. I drop a quick kiss on his nose this time. "Shut up and go to sleep."

He reluctantly lets go of me and rolls onto his back. "I hate you."

"Keep telling yourself that."

ASHER

Like I knew I would be, I'm cleared to play the next day, and we kick ass. There's no stopping us. We walk away with a 7-2 win, and it's the first time all season we actually win with a substantial lead. The bus ride back to Colchester immediately afterward was full of overexcited hockey players on a high from the W, but the whole time, my gaze kept falling to Kole's.

Was it frustrating our sex plans went to shit because of a stupid nonexistent head injury? Yes. But at the same time, the way he slept next to me … took care of me … my chest warms, and I know I should hate that feeling, but I strangely don't.

The following weekend, the team walks away with back-to-back home game wins.

We hope to keep it going, but if I don't start acing some tests soon, they're going to have to do it without me. No pressure or anything.

As I wait anxiously in my seat next to Kole in the library and watch him go over the answers of the mock test he gave me, I bite my lip and picture what my life will look like without hockey or what my job prospects will be without a college degree.

Maybe I should learn the phrase "Would you like fries with that?"

Not that there's anything wrong with food service jobs, but could I imagine myself being pleasant enough to live off tips? Hell fucking no. I'm pretty sure my face would speak for itself. Underpaid, overworked asshole at your service.

Kole smiles at me. I can't tell if it's a "Oh, you're so fucked, lucky you're pretty" type smile or a genuine one.

"You got them all right."

I blink at him. "I what?"

He turns the paper toward me. All that's there is red check marks next to each question.

"I did it?"

"You did it. You know the material, Asher. There's no reason you can't get at least a C if not higher."

Relief surges through me. Hey, it's only one subject, but it's one less I'll have to worry about.

"Fuck, thank you. Thank you so much." Without thinking, I lean forward and press my lips to his.

Then I remember that, one, when my mouth is on Kole's, I lose all sense of my surroundings, and two, I can never just give him a small, chaste peck.

I cup his face and tease his lips with my tongue. He opens for me but only for a couple of seconds before he pulls back. His gaze darts around the room, and I realize I've messed up. This thing between us isn't public, and even though there's only a couple of people in here, if someone saw who knew someone who could tell one of the team—or his *dad* ...

I pull back, and a feeling of never measuring up to him sits heavy in my chest. "Sorry. I got a bit carried away with finding out I'm a genius. Is this how you feel all the time?"

Kole laughs. "You should be invited to join Mensa."

"What's that?"

He snorts. "Never mind. Do you want me to give you another practice test? The more you use the formula, the easier it will be to remember it."

"What happens if I get them all right again?"

His hazel eyes turn my way. "What were you thinking?"

I lean in and whisper, "Really awkward anal in the back of my car."

"How enticing. However will I say no to that?"

My eyes narrow. "I can't tell if you're being sarcastic or not."

"Definitely sarcastic. But we can totally do other things in your car."

"Aren't I getting that anyway for being such a good boy and studying hard?"

Kole licks his lips, and I'm two seconds away from offering to do that for him. "You're right. Maybe I should start making the reward level higher. You have to get so many questions right without help before you get any *reward*."

I pull back. "What? No, that's not what I said. *At all*."

"Don't worry. I have faith you can do it."

"Because I'm Mensa smart?" Still don't know what Mensa is, but whatever.

"Nope." Kole leans in this time. "Because my mouth is worth it."

"So true," I murmur.

He slaps my shoulder. "Good. Then that's settled. You need at least eighty percent on this quiz before you get sex." He starts scribbling down some questions.

I'm starting to forget what I see in him, but there's no doubt Kole Hogan has some weird hold over me because I'll do anything to have his mouth on me again. Even use my brain to think all the things with the smart stuff. So much brainage. Braining?

I don't distract him as he writes out the questions. I'm just content to sit and watch the side of his face as he concentrates.

Kole passes me the new quiz, and I get to work. The sooner I can get these questions answered, the sooner I can touch him. Ah, I mean, the sooner his mouth will be wrapped around my dick. Obviously. That's what I want.

While I focus on the questions, making sure I don't rush it too much and miss important information that will change the whole outcome, someone approaches the table.

At first I don't pay them attention because I assume it's someone to talk to Kole—Katey probably—but then the sound that comes out of them makes me tense. It's deep and masculine, and the words?

"Hey, Kole, I texted you. Did you get it?"

My pen freezes on the page, but I refuse to look up. I'm not interested at *all* in the guy asking Kole to text him back.

For all I know, it's someone from his classes and is looking for notes. No need to jump to—

"Oh, yeah. I did. Sorry, I've been pretty busy."

—conclusions.

Okay. Not class related.

Still not going to look up. It's not my business. None at all. Nope.

My gaze flickers upward. Damn it.

A tall, good-looking, hipster type wearing an unbuttoned flannel shirt stands there smiling down at Kole.

I growl. Wait ... I growl? I clear my throat, and Kole's eyes meet mine. "I, uh, made a mistake." I scribble out the correct answer on my sheet and then wave my hand. "Carry on."

"Are you free this weekend?" Hipster Boy asks.

I automatically answer for him but don't take my eye off my paper. "We have a game at UConn."

I can feel their stares burning into me, and I lift my head.

"Sorry. I'll stop interrupting."

"He's right though," Kole says. "Sorry, Tray."

Of course his name is Tray. That's a douche name. Like Chet. Or Brad.

"Since when are you on the hockey team?"

"Since I lost a bet with my dad, and he forced me to be equipment manager this year."

Chet, Tray, what-the-fuck-ever his name is chuckles. "Damn. When do you get back? Sunday night?"

Out of the corner of my eye, I see Kole nod.

Hipster Boy taps the table. "Awesome. I'll text you, and we can hang out." He doesn't even give Kole a chance to answer him before he leaves with a smarmy grin.

Apparently, it's happening. Kole's got a date.

And I'm totally cool with it. One hundred percent. Even if we had plans to fuck or whatever. It's sex. Only sex. It never means anything.

Never.

Then why do I want to tell Kole he can't go out with anyone else?

And where the hell is that thought coming from?

"Sorry about that," Kole says to me.

"You can go out with whoever you want." As long as their name starts with *A* and ends in *sher*.

Ugh, shut up, brain.

"I'm so not going out with him."

Good.

I can't help the smile. "Oh?"

"Yeah. He's not my type."

"Apparently I'm not your type either, but clearly I do it for you."

"Eh. He's not boyfriend material. I'm sure he'd be fun for a few hours, but I already have a fuck buddy." He nudges me with his elbow. "I've never had one of those before, but I figure unless someone comes along with actual potential, I can just use you for sex."

Right. Sex. "Let's get started, then." I slide my paper over to him. "The last one is probably wrong because I was distracted, but I only need eighty percent, right?"

He checks my work. "Looks like you've earned yourself a reward."

Taking my hand, Kole pulls me out of my seat. I try to pack up my stuff, but he says, "Leave it," and drags me toward the back of the library.

"Where are we going?"

"Somewhere I can follow through."

"In the library?"

He turns. "Scared of getting caught?"

"No skin off my nose if we did." I definitely wouldn't mind that Tray guy finding us, but I keep that to myself.

Kole grips my shirt and pulls me down one of the aisles in between dusty books. "It's so much hotter when risk is involved."

"Oh no. I've become a bad influence on you."

"Are you sure about that? You have no idea what I got up to before we met." He pushes me up against the wall while my mind drifts to all the possible dirty things Kole could be into.

"Nah, I don't buy it. You're all … innocent."

Kole steps closer. "Need I remind you that I jerked you off in the locker room where anyone, including my dad, could catch us?"

"Mm, how could I forget? Maybe *you're* the bad influence here."

"I call bullshit on that too. It's obvious you've slept around. Of course, I thought it was with only women at first, but you exude sex."

I'm already hard behind my jeans, and I grip Kole's hips and bring him against me so I have something to grind against.

"My freshman and sophomore years basically consisted of me making up for lost time," Kole says.

"Lost time?"

"I was … not good-looking in high school. Think braces, acne, and then of course, my giant reading glasses I had to wear during class. No one wanted to date me."

"Your glasses are sexy as fuck."

"The face underneath them wasn't."

I gently push him off me so I can look him in the eye when I say, "I don't believe it. You're all …" I screw up my face. "I was going to say beautiful, but—"

"Eww, gag."

I laugh. "Right? But I mean, you're drop-dead gorgeous."

"I am now."

"Wow. And you're so modest about it too."

"Once the acne cleared up and the braces came off, it was easier to blend into society as one of the more fortunate-looking people. I think sleeping around made me feel validated in a way. It's why I did a lot of it."

"How much is a lot?"

"Oh, are we doing numbers here? Are we sure we want to go there?"

Hmm, if he tells me his, I'd have to tell him mine, and nope. "No fucking way."

Kole lets out a relieved breath. "Good. Phew. Bullet dodged."

"Although, maybe …" The fact he's so adamant on keeping quiet has me curious.

"Nope. We're not doing that. Not here. Not now." He reaches between us and rubs over my cock.

I throw my head back and close my eyes, loving the sensation of his hand moving up and down over my jeans.

"How do you feel about getting your dick out in public?" he whispers.

This is different than in the locker room. It's less risky in some ways because the chance of any of my teammates or Coach finding us is next to nothing, but at the same time, *anyone* could see us here.

"Depends on what you're planning to do with it," I say cautiously.

Kole leans in and nips my earlobe. "Anything you're comfortable with. I could get down on my knees for you. Jerk you off. Rut against you until we both leave a big mess."

I shudder. I want *all* of that.

But there's a part of me that wants to protect Kole's dignity if we were to get caught, even if he doesn't have the same reservations about it.

I want to protect it. Protect *him*.

"I want it just like this," I whisper and pull him against me.

He rotates his hips. "Are you going to be able to get there fast enough? The longer we're here, the more chance of someone coming by."

"Mm, true. Maybe this will help get us there faster." I reach between us and undo my jeans, but I don't lower them. "Use your hand."

Kole wraps his long fingers around my cock while I go for his belt buckle, but he shakes his head. "I don't need it. You're so fucking hot." He ruts against my hip.

His voice goes straight to my balls, and I want him to keep talking.

"Tell me what's going to happen this weekend," I whisper.

He pauses and stares up at me, Kole's hazel eyes clouded with lust and confusion. "What?"

I lower my head to his ear while I thrust into his hand. "Tell me how you want me to take you. How you want me to get you ready. With my fingers? My mouth?"

"Both?" he squeaks, and I love it.

"Then what?"

Kole breathes heavily as he rasps out, "I want you to suck my dick while you finger fuck me. I want you to find that spot inside me and press against it over and over again until I almost fall apart. I want to get so close to the edge that I think it's past the point of no return, but at the last second, right before I think I'm going to come, you'll pull your fingers out of me and fill me up with your huge—" He grips my cock tighter, adjusting his rhythm.

The sensation of his hand on my dick, mixed with his words that are filled with such heat and anticipation—

"I'm close," I grunt.

Kole doesn't slow down. If anything, he starts grinding on me harder.

His ashy hair falls across my eyes as he nips at my earlobe. "After we're done and maybe napped, when we wake up …"

I can't wait for what he's going to say. We'll do it all again? We'll make each other come so many times, I'll need extra tutoring because my brain cells will be mush?

"I'll flip you over and do the same to you," he finishes.

And fuck!

I have to bite my lip to stop the long moan of release as my dick erupts between us.

"Oh, shit. I didn't think you'd like that idea that much." Kole moves against me once more.

His muscles are coiled tight as he stiffens in my arms. He's better at staying quiet while he comes than I am.

You'd think with how much chaos I live with and how many people I have to schedule alone time around that I would've learned to be stealthier.

Kole's head drops to my shoulder. "This weekend can't come fast enough."

"Unlike me, right? That was pretty fast."

"That's not something you should be bragging about, but sure, buddy. Good job."

"You told me—" I don't realize my voice is loud until Kole uses his non-cum-covered hand to silence me.

"We should get out of here and clean up." He steps back and pulls his shirt down over the wet patch on his jeans.

"At least we have our books and stuff to cover up?"

Kole shakes his head with a laugh. "See, this is why public hookups are a bad idea. Too much mess to make disappear afterward." Then, he makes eye contact and licks my release from his fingers.

I pull him back to me and touch my lips to his. "This weekend. You, me, hotel bed."

I can't fucking wait.

KOLE

The snow crunches underfoot, and Hades pulls desperately at his lead, trying to get to the dog park. He's always been a pain to walk, but seeing his happiness the moment he's let off the lead is my favorite part of the day.

Unfortunately it's now getting way too cold to run around with him.

I hunch down into my coat and pause at the top of Asher's street. In all the afternoons I've walked past, I haven't seen Asher around … until now. He's out front with who I'm assuming are two of his siblings.

Even from here, heat pools in my gut. Tomorrow. Tomorrow is Friday and we'll be on the bus to Connecticut for the next away game. And while I love what we've been doing, it's like we've been edging each other this whole time.

I give Hades a massive tug to redirect down the street and get a whine of protest for my efforts. That is until we're two houses away and Asher spots us.

"Hellhound!"

The sharp tug of the leash is so unexpected it pulls from my hand, and my dumb dog takes off. He launches himself into Asher's arms and knocks him straight over. Hades is barking like a madman at all the attention, and Asher's having a hard time keeping the dog's tongue off his face.

"He's a terrible judge of character," I say when I finally walk up the path.

"Like his owner?"

I reach a hand down and help Asher back to his feet. "At least I know when I'm—what did you call it? Slumming it?"

A whine comes from Hades, and I glance down as he starts to hump Asher's leg.

"Aw, another thing he gets from his daddy," Asher says, pulling away.

"I told you that you exude sex appeal. We're the innocents in all this."

One of the kids comes running over before Asher can respond, which is probably a good thing. "Whose dog?"

"Did I say you could stop?" Asher throws back.

The kid huffs and turns to run back over to the other ... well, his twin, actually. I blink for a moment, watching them run back and forth, thrown by how identical they look.

"Wait, are they doing suicides?"

Asher shrugs. "They've been fighting since I got home. Figured they needed to expel some energy."

Unconventional, maybe, but it's effective. "They look like they're about to pass out."

"You think?" He cocks his head. "Em, Ben, back in the house. If you two cause shit again, we'll be out here all night."

"You can't give your kid brothers frostbite."

"Yeah, but they don't know that."

The twins go running past, and Hades takes off after them into the house. "Oops, let me just—"

A shrill scream comes from inside, and Asher reacts like he's on autopilot. He bounds onto the porch and through the front door, and I trail after him, completely unprepared for what I'm about to find.

There's a girl standing on the dining room table as Hades struggles to get to her. One of the twins is restraining him, while the other is keeled over laughing. I sniff and tilt my head toward the kitchen.

"Asher, is something burn—"

"Fuck!" He darts past me into the kitchen, and I go retrieve Hades, managing to wrangle him outside into their backyard.

"Sorry, boy." I slide the door closed on him and turn to look around.

The house is … well, to put it nicely—umm … okay, there's no way to say a complete shithole and make it sound nice. Okay, so not a total shithole because it's not like we're in an episode of *Hoarders* here, but it looks as though no one has been bothered to look after the place.

Given how busy West and Asher are, and that their siblings are all young, I really shouldn't be surprised.

I walk over to the girl now sitting on the table. "You okay?"

"I am *now*." She looks around me to the back door. "What was that thing?"

"My dog. He's really friendly, just … loud and excitable. Sorry."

She presses a hand to her chest. "My heart is beating so fast. I was *not* prepared for a dog to come running at me like that." Her eyes sharpen. "Who *are* you?"

"I'm Kole. Friend of Asher's."

"I'm Hazel."

"Nice to meet you."

She drops back into her chair and pulls her laptop toward

herself. Right before she puts her headphones back on, she looks back up at me and says softly, "I like that he has a friend."

She can't be much older than the twins, but she's a whole lot quieter than them. Which they prove a moment later when a loud crash comes from the front room.

"Asher! Emmett broke the controller!"

"Bennett did! He's lying."

They start to argue until a piercing voice comes from upstairs. "*Ash-er!*" A second later, two pairs of footsteps thunder downstairs, the arguing from the twins recommences, Hazel starts humming behind me, and when I walk through to the kitchen, I find Asher with his head in his hands, large pot of burned pasta in the sink.

"Asher!" A blonde teen girl storms into the kitchen. "Rhys has been in my room, *again*. He went on my laptop. You told me he'd stop. You *told* me he'd be grounded if he did it again." She's practically shaking with anger, and a moment later, a boy around the same age walks in and leans casually against the doorframe.

"Zoe has a boyfriend."

"Fuck off, Rhys."

"He messaged her—"

"I said *fuck off!*"

I didn't realize a voice could go so loud.

Asher finally raises his head from his hands. "Zoe, go back upstairs."

"Asher—"

"I'll talk to him."

She huffs and storms off. Asher turns to Rhys.

"Could you save annoying her for when West is here? Please."

Rhys scowls. "I was bored."

"You can't go into your sister's computer. It's not right."

The kid scowls, and *holy shit* he looks like a blond Asher when he does that.

"Rhys—"

"Whatever. When is West home?"

Asher's expression grows tight. "I have no idea."

Rhys walks to the fridge, grabs a Coke, and pretends to sniff the air. "Dinner smells delicious, by the way."

Asher's hands fist at his sides before he takes a long breath. "Can you please go away? Is Charlotte home? Can you annoy her parents?"

"Why? I'm having fun."

There's another crash from the front room that makes Asher cringe. "Just go upstairs and stay out of Zoe's room."

When Rhys leaves, Asher slumps.

"When *will* West be home?" I ask.

"Who knows? He says he's doing something for the team, but I'm pretty sure he's getting his dick wet. Not like he's much help when he's here anyway. He can't even tell the twins apart."

In his defense, it's hard. "Kind of goes with the whole being identical thing, right?"

"I can tell them apart. Emmett is the quiet one."

There's a quiet one?

"Okay, so what do we have to do before West gets home?" I point to the pasta. "I take it spaghetti is off the menu tonight, so what are we going to cook?"

"*We?*"

"Sure. Though, I *can't* actually cook, so you're going to have to direct me, but an extra pair of hands is never a bad thing, right?"

He looks conflicted for a moment, like he's going to tell me to get out of his house.

"You know I'm good with my hands …" I taunt, wiggling my fingers at him.

"Fine." He walks to the fridge and starts grabbing vegetables and throwing them my way. "We'll do the Asher special. Everything in the pan with a jar of sauce on top. Start chopping."

We both jump as a door slams upstairs. "Stay out of my room," Zoe screeches.

"Want to go deal with them?" I ask.

"You'll be okay here?"

"I'm sure I'll manage."

He leaves, and I duck into the front room to find the twins throwing batteries at each other. *Wonderful.*

"Hey, do you two have a tennis ball?"

"Yes, why?"

"Hades loves to play fetch."

One of the twins jumps up, looking excited, while the other stares at me blankly.

"Can I go play with him?" the excited one asks.

"Of course."

"Coming, Ben?"

"Nope."

At first I think Emmett is going to stay inside too, so I give him a little nudge. If the suicides didn't wear them out, maybe separating them is best. "Hades is all yours, then."

He disappears into the backyard, *Ben* switches their Xbox back on, and I get my ass in the kitchen again. I set to work finding a chopping board, a clean knife, and a pot. Then I peel and cut up everything he's given me, dump it into the pot with the jar of sauce, and set it all on the stove.

Asher's still gone, but the constant noise that was filling the house has calmed.

Now, it's time to calm Asher.

I find a bottle of vodka in the cupboard above the fridge and pour out two small drinks with juice. Neither of us has time to be getting drunk, but hopefully this will help him loosen up a little.

When Asher is still gone, and I have nothing else to do, I stand at the window watching Emmett and Hades.

By the time Asher appears behind me, the sauce is in the pot bubbling away, and I've stacked all the dirty dishes in the dishwasher.

Not going to lie, I'm totally a domestic fucking goddess right now.

"Thank you," he says as he leans against the sink.

I hand over his drink. "Don't thank me. I was worried if I left and you went full meltdown mode, you'd never come back from that. Then who would suck my dick? Totally selfish move on my part."

He manages a smile and takes a long mouthful. "I'm so not cut out for this."

"No offense, but I can't imagine many people would be. You and West have been dumped with *five* kids. That's rough."

"It is."

"He, umm, mentioned hiring someone to help out. Has he done that yet? I figured with him not being at away games—"

"Oh, he has never gone to away games. Zoe was only fourteen last year, so there was no way we could leave them alone all weekend. That's a stipulation in his contract because of the kids. We have a babysitter for after school until West and I get home from practice, but there's no point having a babysitter when we're home, you know?"

"Well, I guess I could—"

"Nope." Asher puts down his drink and moves to stir the food on the burner, thank fuck, because not knowing when it was ready was starting to give me anxiety. "I know you want to help, because that's you, but this is my crazy. You're already doing way more than enough."

I don't *feel* like I am though. Making sure Asher stays on the team is a big one, of course, but after seeing all this …

I'm really starting to see how lucky I have it in life.

And why Asher is so closed off.

The itch to help is still there, but I don't doubt he wants me to keep hands off here. He seems protective of his family, and it's another one of those things that has me convinced Asher is a good person.

"In that case, feel free to continue using me as stress relief."

"That's an offer I'll hold you to."

Asher and I have another drink together before dinner is done, and then I help him spoon it all out into bowls, tidy up, and grab Hades.

He walks me to the front door, looking more awkward than I've ever seen him. "It was really cool of you to hang out. Just having someone here made it not seem so bad."

"Asher … is that … *sincerity* I hear?"

He shoves me. "Don't get used to it."

"Today will forever be marked as the day that Asher Dalton showed gratitude."

He laughs and steps forward, then before I know what's happening, he leans in and kisses me. And if this is his way of thanking me, I accept.

Because *damn* he can kiss.

I bite his lip before pulling back and speaking softly so his siblings can't hear. "We need to stop before *I'm* the one humping your leg."

He kisses me again. "Tomorrow. Away game. Condoms."

"Still have the box packed."

He hesitates. "The *whole* box?"

His tone reminds me of that growly little voice he had when Tray was talking to me at the library. I think I like it. "Completely unopened," I assure him. "You just have to promise not to get a concussion this time."

"I didn't have a concussion *last* time."

"That's your story."

He didn't, but I won't be sorry for playing it safe.

"It's times like this that make me regret not getting my own place," I say.

"Yeah, after last time at your house, even the thought of hooking up there is an instant boner killer."

"Good thing we have tomorrow, then."

When he finally steps away, he has to reach down and adjust himself. "Be prepared to study *all* night."

I don't need the warning. With how long I've been waiting, he's going to struggle to get me off him.

ASHER

I MIGHT HAVE THE SAME MENTALITY AS A DOG BECAUSE POSITIVE reinforcement makes me try harder. Not only when it comes to academics but hockey too. The sooner I can beat UConn on the ice, the sooner I get to have all the sex. All of it.

Even if my theory is flawed because a hockey game is three periods no matter what. There's no way I'm letting this get to overtime.

The team has been on a winning streak, and tonight is no different. Finally, since Coach threw the lines together at the start of the season, we're acting like a team, and it's showing where it counts—the scoreboard.

Plays are crisper, our passes smoother, and tonight alone, I've already scored a goal in each of the first two periods. It's getting down to the buzzer, and we're up by four, so we're basically in it for the fun at this point. All we have to do is run out the clock.

The opposition is getting desperate and frustrated.

I fly down the ice, but UConn's two defensemen are waiting. I try to split them up, but they only converge closer. I need to break either left or right or pass the puck. A quick look shows neither

Simms or Kaplan are open, and now defense is on me, and I have no way out.

All I need to do is keep possession of the puck. That's the only aim.

Well, that and to not get hit in the head.

Right before one of the mountainous bruisers is about to slam into me, I spin. That guy runs into my back and tries to knock me down, but I don't let him. The other tries to trip me.

I can't get out of this, so I need to get rid of the puck any way I can, even if that means having to shove my stick through my legs, shoot in what I hope is the right direction, and pray for a miracle one of my guys picks it up.

It's the most ungraceful play, and as the puck goes flying, I firmly fall on the ice. Luckily my pads save me from another hit to the head.

No concussion protocol this time, thank you very much.

The play is so fast, I'm still trying to work out where the puck went. I don't realize I found the actual goal until my line mates are pulling me up into a hug.

I glance around. *Wait, what?*

Then I smile as if to say, *Oh, yeah, I totally did that on purpose.*

I'm probably going to regret it when that becomes the play of the night. Fluke shots are amazing, but I'd prefer to look at least a little bit cool while pulling them off.

As we skate back to the team box for a shift change, my gaze finds Kole's where he sits in the corner of the box. He shakes his head, and I bow.

Coach gives more ice time to the lower string lines until the clock runs down. I already know I'm not going back out there tonight, which is probably why my gaze keeps darting behind me instead of focusing on the action.

UConn ends up scoring one more time, bringing their entire total to two. Our offense has kept the puck in our attack zone for most of the game. You can't score from the wrong end of the ice.

Everyone's on a high when we reach the locker room, but Coach Hogan, as usual, feels the need to remind us that we have another game tomorrow night, and any partying will result in missing out on playing that game.

Simms sidles up to me as we strip down for the showers. "We have to celebrate that fluke shot though."

I agree. I just think we have two very different ideas on how that celebration should go. Mine involves Kole naked and a lot of lube.

"Tomorrow night. After we kick their asses again."

Though I assume I'll want to celebrate the exact same way I plan to tonight.

Simms punches me in the shoulder. "You're on. We killed them."

"Don't get too confident or it can all fall to shit tomorrow. We don't want a repeat of regionals."

At least if we do lose tomorrow, we'll still be high on the leaders' list for this season.

We're sitting comfortably. A lot more comfortable than we were this time last year. We barely scraped into the playoffs and then fought our way through to regionals. We were only two wins away from winning the whole damn thing when it all fell apart.

I don't want that disappointment this year.

Kole's cleaning up after us, putting all our shit in its place, and as I walk by him to go to the showers, I can't help myself and send him a wink.

His cheeks pinken the tiniest bit. I can't wait until his whole body is flushed that same color.

The sucky thing about away games is it doesn't matter how quick you shower and get out to the bus, you have to wait for everyone else, and apparently, everyone else is too busy goofing off and delaying hotel curfew because they're still coming down from the win.

Kole's the last on the bus, and he takes his usual seat next to his dad. Not that he had many other options. Simms is next to me, blabbering on and on about my fluke shot.

I don't take my eyes off the back of Kole's head as I say, "It wasn't a fluke. It's all talent."

Simms scoffs. "If you say so. I think it could win play of the year and best blooper. The way you tripped on your own stick and landed on the ice …"

"It takes a lot of talent to look that stupid," Kaplan adds from the seat in front of us.

I lean forward and give him a noogie. Because apparently, I'm one of them now.

And this is normal behavior for us.

I don't know when that happened, but there it is.

When we pull up to the hotel, it takes all my strength not to run to the room. That wouldn't be obvious or anything.

Totally casual.

Completely.

"Where's the fire?" Simms calls out behind me.

I guess I'm not pulling off this casual thing, after all. And I've also lost Kole somewhere along the way. I get in the elevator and hit Kole's and my floor, but then Schofield holds the door open for everyone to join us.

My dick complains. No, wait, that groan is coming from my mouth. Kole's on the other side of the elevator, and he smiles in my direction. Apparently my groan is *loud* too.

We stop at a million different floors, and I begin to think

everyone is conspiring against us. Maybe the universe is trying to protect Kole from someone like me.

But as I meet his gaze, and those hazel eyes fill with heat, there's no doubt in my mind that Kole's only in this for the sex. He's too smart to fall for someone so ... damaged.

It's a shame, really, because our chemistry is on fire, and I actually *like* him. I don't like many people. Sure as shit don't get along with a lot.

Which is why if I had any sense, I never would have started this thing. Too late now. He's already got me hooked.

We finally reach our floor, and I itch to grab Kole's hand and hold it while we walk down the corridor to our room, but we're not the only ones staying on this level.

Kole can barely keep up with me as I march ahead. I'm buzzing, and I haven't even touched him yet.

I'm going to rectify that as soon as we're through the door. My hands shake as I try to push the key card into the slot, and I miss three times.

Kole steps up beside me and takes over. "If this is how you are at fitting things into holes designed for that purpose, we're gonna have some problems."

I burst out laughing, but then I realize I'm nervous. Why the fuck am I nervous? It's just sex, and Kole and I have gotten each other off countless times. Granted, we've seen each other naked a lot less because public hookups and blowjobs in cars are not ideal places to strip. He's seen me naked plenty around the locker room, but that's different.

Kole opens the door and spins, walking backward into the room while gripping my suit jacket and pulling me with him.

I thought I was going to be the one to pounce as soon as we made it across the threshold, but no, apparently, this is all Kole.

We drop our bags by the door, and he immediately shoves me

against the wall. Then his mouth is on mine, his perfect lithe frame blocking me in. His tongue is strong and commanding, and he tastes like breath mints. I guess he came even more prepared than I thought.

He eagerly grinds against me, and the familiarity of his body moving with mine comforts me some. The nerves slowly dissipate the more he touches me, and as much as I have loved what we've been doing, how hot it is, and I'll gladly take more of it, I can't miss this chance to get inside him.

I want to strip him bare and kiss every inch of him.

The words he whispered in my ear while jerking me off in the library spring to mind. He wants me to drive him crazy, bring him close to the edge, and then back off.

"I can promise to take my time later," I rumble. "But I need inside you now."

"You won't hear me complaining."

I reach for his pants and undo his belt. We're unceremoniously clumsy as we try to undress each other.

We pull apart to shed our shoes and socks, my jacket, and his shirt, but then I need more of him and go back to nipping, licking, and sucking on his lips and neck.

"Mm." His skin tastes salty, and it only makes me want to suck on something else delicious.

I rush to get the rest of his clothes off and push him down on my bed.

His long, lean body with his cock sticking straight up is a mouthwatering sight.

Fuck, I have to prep him, and my dick so doesn't have time for that. I grip the base hard to bring me back down from the edge.

"Lube," I grunt.

"Bag. Front."

"Speak in sentences?" Not that I'm much different.

"Your dick turns me into a caveman. Can't help it."

I quickly grab the supplies while Kole squirms impatiently. We're both too keyed up for this to last, and as much as I'd like to take a breath and slow this down, I've been waiting way too long to get inside him.

I drop what I need next to me on the floor while I sink to my knees.

Kole's quick to lift his legs and inch his way to the edge, exposing his tight hole.

"Fuuuck," I pant.

"Asher, I need … Need …"

I know exactly what he needs. I don't hesitate to bury my head between his legs and lick my way from his balls to his hole. My hand flies to his cock, stroking him, while I use my mouth to soften his entrance.

Kole whimpers because I'm not gentle. I'm not slow.

I could eat him out all night, but maybe another time. I'm on a mission, and I need to prep him quickly. With my free hand, I feel around for the bottle of lube I dropped and uncap it.

I move my hand from his cock so I can grab the condom and coat myself and my fingers in lube because once he's ready, I'm not pausing for a second for my dick to catch up.

Kole complains when I stop giving his cock attention, but then I push my tongue inside him, and he shuts up again. Unless you count the muttered curses under his breath.

It's no secret I've had plenty of experience, but trying to put a condom on by feel because my mouth is too busy is a new one for me. It takes a while for it to work, though I'm sure Kole isn't complaining.

He writhes like he's trying to push my face farther between his legs and makes a guttural sound I can't decipher. He's either frustrated and wants more or is doing his best to restrain himself.

Perhaps it's both.

And as much as I'd love to keep at it so I could work it out, I need inside him.

With my fingers well and truly slippery, I move my lips up to his balls and suck one in my mouth while I press my index finger against his hole.

He relaxes, and it's easy to push in to the first knuckle before his ass clamps down around my finger.

He needs more distraction, then.

I lean over him and grip his cock, guiding it to my mouth. I feel him watching, can sense that heated stare on me, but I'm too busy concentrating to pay him attention. He can lie back and enjoy the show.

There's no faster way to get a guy ready than to bring my A-game blowjob skills while pegging their prostate with my fingers. He just has to open up enough for me to get there.

I suck him down and hum around his hard dick, and my finger moves inside him a little more.

"I can take it," he breathes. "Give me more." His hips move, taking me deeper, and when I hit his prostate, his body takes over.

He becomes this oversexed fiend. He thrusts up into my mouth and down on my finger. I add another finger, and he adjusts quickly. When I get to three, his large hand grips my hair to keep me in place. I've blown him before, but not like this.

Not where he's fucking my mouth while fucking himself on my fingers.

Kole quickly becomes frantic, and even though I want to glance up and watch him, I can barely keep pace with him.

Until his long, low moan breaks my concentration, and I slip. My gaze flicks up, and the sight of him with his lips parted, his ashy hair falling across his forehead, and his eyes an intense hazel that are locked on mine ... it has my cock leaking.

I can taste precum from him too. Salty and heady.

It's tempting to swallow him all and keep going until he comes down my throat because I know from experience he tastes so good, but I want all of him tonight, and I want him now.

I pull off his cock with a wet pop but don't stop fingering him.

His eyes are glazed. "I'm ready. Shit." He throws his head back, and the tendons in his neck stick out as he grits his teeth. "Fuck me before this is all over."

Yes.

I stand, my cock already sheathed and lubed up, ready to go.

The hotel beds are lower than ideal, so I tap Kole's leg to get him to shuffle up a bit. I climb on top of him and then kneel between his widened thighs.

I run my hand down his chest and lower, toward where his cock points upward to his belly button. His surprisingly thick thighs rest over mine, and I drink in the amazing sight.

Then, I reach for my cock, guiding it toward his slick hole, and slowly push inside.

Kole lets out a loud, concentrated breath but accepts me easily.

The pressure surrounding my cock is insane, and I'm two seconds away from embarrassing myself.

Kole's skin flushes. His chest rises and falls in rapid bursts, and as I push in further, I try to look for signs that it's too much or he needs to adjust, but all that happens is he breaks out into a lazy smile.

"You don't have to be scared you'll hurt me. I've taken a dick or two in my day."

That instinctual growl that came out when Hipster Boy asked

to see Kole this weekend reappears. "We're not talking about that while I'm inside you."

"What, that I've been with other guys? Worried you won't compare? Getting a little stage fright?" The fucker smirks, and I thrust harder, hitting his prostate.

It's hard to be smug when you're shuddering in pleasure.

"I know you're taunting me to get me to move faster, but if I do that right now, I really will worry about how I compare when I'll be a two-pump chump."

Kole reaches for me, cupping my face. "Aww, if that happens, you can blow me instead. I'm generous like that."

I snort. "So generous. But give me a sec, and then I'm going to show you what you've been missing out on with your no-jocks rule."

"Promises, promises," he whispers and then leans up to kiss me. His hand moves behind my head and grips my hair tight, holding me to him.

His mouth is demanding—it's distracting—and before I know it, I'm moving in and out of him, breathing him in, and savoring the sensation of being inside him.

Kole breaks his mouth away and tilts his head back, exposing his neck. I lick a path from his collarbone to his jaw. "I need more," he pants.

"Yeah?" I straighten up and pull him with me so his ass is off the bed and practically in my lap.

I grip his hips hard and slam inside him, and then pull out and do it again. And again, and again, and again, until we're two trembling bodies chasing release.

Kole reaches for a pillow next to his head and white-knuckles it while he muffles the sexy sounds gasping from him.

I want to tear it off him and hear it all, but the walls in the hotel rooms we stay in are pretty thin, and the sounds falling from him are positively sinful. And *loud*.

I'm tempted—so fucking tempted—to slow down and frustrate the hell out of him before doing it all again and building him back up where he's on the brink of losing control, but I'm too far gone, too keyed up, and I know I'm at my point of no return.

I'm already skirting the edge, and it feels so good. His ass squeezes me tight, and every thrust sends tingles to my aching balls.

I need to come, but shit, I need him to come first.

I reach between us and wrap my hand around his cock, stroking hard and fast.

"Asher, I'm gonna ..." He doesn't finish his sentence as he erupts and shoots all over his stomach. I keep jerking him as ropes of cum hit his skin and slowly run down to his chest.

The sight alone triggers my own release, and as I push inside him two more times and fill the condom, a full-body orgasm hits me. It's not only in my cock and in my balls. My skin warms, my gut fills with butterflies, and when I come down from the high and pull out of him, another rush of pleasure shoots through me.

I collapse on my back next to him and breathe heavily. I need to get up and get rid of the condom, but that can wait because that was ...

"Eh. I guess you're all right," Kole says.

My head turns so fast I see stars. "What did you just say? I don't think I heard you correctly."

Kole laughs. "I'm kidding. Fuck, I needed that." He slowly sits up and looks around the room. "I guess I should get cleaned up and get into my bed."

"Nuh-uh. Well, yeah, go get cleaned up, but come back here." I pat the bed beside me.

"What, you want to cuddle?"

I move closer to him while taking off the condom. "Who said anything about cuddling? Once I can get it up, we're doing that again."

Kole's eyes fill with heat, and his cock twitches. Oh yeah, he's so okay with that plan.

20

KOLE

I blink groggily awake, my body sore in the best possible way after two nights of really. Hot. Sex.

I'd never underestimated how good it would feel with Asher inside me, but I didn't realize how quickly I'd become addicted to it. We fucked twice on Friday night, and once after his game last night, and even though the plan *had* been to switch it up, when we'd got back here—*oops!*—I'd accidentally ended up back on his cock.

No regrets here.

Especially because this morning is my turn.

I roll over toward him and press a kiss to his shoulder while my hand follows the smooth skin of his back to his ass. He lets out a low hum as he wakes, and my dick stirs at the thought of holding him facedown and slipping inside him. Just as I'm about to plaster my body to his, someone bashes on the door.

"Get your asses up, you're late!"

Dad.

Asher obviously recognizes the voice too, because he jolts upright, and his head smacks straight into my nose.

"Shit!" Pain shoots across my face, and my vision swims as water floods my eyes. "What the hell?"

"Are you okay?" He pulls my hands back and lightly touches my nose. The pain is ebbing slightly, but *fucking ouch.*

The pounding on the door comes again. My head is all scrambled, and I can't concentrate.

Asher gives me a little shove as he passes me for the door. "Get off my bed."

Bed. Right. I press my hand to my nose a few more times. No blood. Pain is dimming. Then I drop onto the side of my mattress, and *nope!* Pain is back but in a whole new area.

Maybe letting Asher fuck me until the lube was wearing thin after months of my ass being closed for business wasn't the best game plan?

But when I shift and get hit with the low burn again, it has me reminiscing over the last two nights. Being fucked by Asher is something I'm not going to forget in a hurry, and the dull pain is going to help bring those memories back fresh and clear.

"You boys ready?" asks Dad's voice.

"Almost. Just finishing packing," Asher replies.

"We're meeting downstairs in five."

"Got it."

"You need help getting there on time?" Dad's tone is wary, almost suspicious.

I catch a glimpse of the used condom lying on the floor, and I don't know who I need to swear my soul to, but I'm *praying* he doesn't step foot in this room and see it.

"Nah, everything's under control here, Coach."

And Asher has every right to sound that cocky when he scored the winning goal last night.

Dad leaves, and Asher hurries back over to me. He takes one look at my face and starts to laugh.

"Well, I don't think anything's broken, doc."

"Your concern is smothering."

"Ah, come on. It's just a bit red." His smile is wide and *so* pretty. I forgive him instantly.

"I can't believe that actually happened."

"Need me to kiss it better?"

"Like there's time." I try hard not to pout. "We were supposed to wake up early."

"You're the one who begged for my dick last night."

"You were sore after your game. *Of course* I was going to ride you."

He pulls me to my feet. "Only three weeks until our next away game."

"Three *weeks*?" I drop my head back on a groan that abruptly cuts off as he pulls me into a kiss.

"Unless we can find somewhere else to do it, you're going to have to admire this ass from afar."

Can't say that's a tragedy.

We pack and make it downstairs five minutes late, and since we skipped showering, I'm paranoid I smell like sex. So when we climb onto the bus, instead of letting Asher go sit with the team, I push him into the front row and take the seat beside him.

He shoots me a confused look.

"We both stink. I'm saving the others from enduring it. Or worse, speculating why we smell the same."

Asher leans over and pitches his voice low. "Think my breath still smells like your cum?"

He's teasing because even though we didn't shower, we *did* brush our teeth. Even still, it's a definite turn-on to think about us smelling like each other. For people to know what we got up to last night, even though I don't want anyone to *actually* know. The thought of it is hot, but having to face Dad and the team and defend what we're doing ... that's a no from me.

Dad's obviously thrown when he climbs on board, but he moves to the row behind us with Beck and thankfully doesn't call out the weirdness of us sitting together.

"What the hell happened to your nose?" he asks instead.

"Allergies?" Not that I actually have any of those, and December definitely lacks pollen in the air. I'm pretty sure Dad knows I'm lying. Still, him guessing the real reason my nose is discolored is a long shot.

I connect my earbuds to my phone and hand one to Asher. It's a long drive from UConn back to CU, so we might as well settle in. It's sort of ... nice. We're sitting close enough that our shoulders are touching while we whisper stupid shit back and forth.

Seeing Asher like this, open and relaxed, really highlights how far we've come as friends. And sure, the sex has something to do with it, but beyond that, it feels like we've actually connected.

He's not a pet project, and I'm not a means to pass his tests and stay on the team.

We actually enjoy each other's company.

Not that Asher makes it easy sometimes.

I crack a smile and let my eyes drift closed. The rock of the bus is settling, and I zone out to a happy, content place for most of the drive while Asher flicks between songs.

The sound of screeching wheels breaks my contentment, and we're flung forward violently in our seats. The bus swerves into the gravel on the shoulder, flinging me into Asher, before veering back onto the road.

"What the hell?" I gasp. My heart rate has kicked up to nauseating levels, and I have to work on my breathing to try and bring it back down again.

"Fucking deer, I think," someone a row or two back says.

"Moose." The driver grunts. "Just missed the damn thing."

I exhale slowly. Even in a bus, that wouldn't have been a great sight.

It takes a minute for the shock to wear off.

The noise from the team has kicked up so loud, it takes me a moment to notice the short, sharp pants coming from Asher.

He's pale and looks freaked-out. Okay, the shock has clearly not worn off him.

The need to *do* something grips me.

"Hey, it's okay. It was only a moose." I go to take his arm, but Asher jerks it from my hold.

"I know, I'm fine." Except his voice is anything but fine.

"Asher—"

"*Leave it.*"

I flinch at the tone, because even when Asher's pissed off, he's controlled. He holds back. This …

His chest is working overtime as he tries to hold it all in, but he can't hide how his fists are shaking in his lap.

I want—no, *need*—to comfort him. To tell him everything's fine and being a bit panicked over a near miss like that is totally normal, and that it's the adrenaline hitting his system. But his eyes have taken on this savage look I've never seen on him before, and I'm feeling a little out of my depth.

It physically hurts to hold back from offering my support.

It takes a good ten minutes before his breathing sounds normal again.

"Are … are you okay?"

He nods and turns to look pointedly out the window.

Message received.

Since he's okay, I give him what he needs and back off until we reach the CU campus. I plan to just move on and pretend like it didn't happen. Except when we climb off the bus, Asher still doesn't look at me.

He grabs his bag from under the bus and beelines it straight for his car.

I'm supposed to make sure everyone gets their shit, but instead, I dart after him. "Hey, what's going on?"

He doesn't stop, so I grab his arm and force him around to look at me.

"What the hell?" I hiss.

"It's nothing."

"Sure as shit doesn't seem that way."

"I freaked out. It's no big deal. Why can't you let it go?"

"Because you're acting weird."

"And since when does that have anything to do with *you*?"

I reel back for a moment. "Since we're *friends*, asshole."

"Friends?" he snarls, and the ruthlessly haughty look I'm used to seeing him direct toward other people crosses his face. "Yeah, because what we did last night was so fucking *friendly*, wasn't it?"

I don't catch on with what he's saying at first. "So what, you freaked out today, who cares? It could happen to anyone."

"Leave me alone, Kole."

"Not until you tell me what's wrong."

"I don't have to tell you shit. Don't come at me like a stage five clinger because we had sex. Don't make this into something it's not."

Something it's not? I cross my arms. "So what *is* this, then?"

"You're there and convenient. And hooking up with you is obviously helping me win games."

The nonchalant way he throws it out there should be raising red flags, but even though this wasn't anything beyond sex and platonic friendship, I'm hurt. "I was an easy lay." This whole friendship, was it just a way for him to bang the coach's son and win some hockey games?

Asher shrugs, and his complete lack of emotion makes me angry.

I turn my head to make sure the team can't actually hear us. "You know what, fuck you. Just because you got what you wanted, that's no reason to be a stereotypical dick over it."

He looks like he wants to say something but must change his mind because he heaves his bag over his shoulder, spins on his heel, and heads for his car before I can swallow down the lump in my throat. He climbs in and starts the engine, and the wheels kick up dust for a second as he takes off out of the parking lot.

What *was* that?

It was like a flipped switch with how quickly he did a one-eighty, and I'm still struggling to even figure it out. All my brain seems stuck on is that we made it back here, and he ditched me as fast as he could.

It's not supposed to *hurt*.

"Hey, Kole?"

I quickly relax my features before I turn to Dad, but he doesn't look much better. He's staring off at the place where Asher disappeared, eyebrows drawn in worry.

"I wanted to catch Asher before he left. Is he okay?"

I try to play it off. "Just Asher being a dick like usual."

Dad shakes his head, and something strikes me as odd. Normally seeing a player act like a testosterone-filled meathead would have Dad turning red and ready to bench them, but instead, his face pales.

"I'm gonna call West."

"Why?"

"Give him the heads-up."

"I'm pretty sure he knows what Asher is like."

Dad steps closer. "Has he told you how his folks died?"

I'm not expecting that question. "N-no ..." But I'm starting to get a gross sinking feeling that maybe ... that really *was* Asher being Asher. Not him being a *dick*, but him trying to protect himself. I almost don't want to ask. "How?"

"A car crash. They hit a moose and drove off the road."

Fuck.

Dad leaves, and now *I'm* the one struck dumb.

My heart gives this painful little throb, and I jog up to where Dad's walking back toward the arena.

"Can I take your car?" I'm seriously regretting getting a lift with him. "Mom can come and pick you up."

Dad looks confused. "I'll only be half an—"

"*Please*, Dad."

"Where are you going?"

Hmm ... truth or lie? "I need to find Asher."

I'm expecting him to tell me that West will handle it, but instead, he reaches into his pocket and pulls out his keys.

"Let me know he's okay. And *drive safe*."

I promise I will before I cross back over the parking lot and jump in Dad's car. My hands are tight on the steering wheel as I drive, and I remind myself to calm the hell down because that's what Asher needs right now.

I'm a dumbass. But I'm going to make it right.

Asher said himself no one *wants* to look out for him, but I do, and screw him if he thinks I'm not going to be there for him after something like that.

Friends ... Study partners ... Fuck buddies ... None of that matters. All that matters is that Asher knows he doesn't have to be alone all the time.

When I get to his place and see his car in the driveway, relief hits me. He made it here okay, at least.

And maybe he won't want to see me while he's upset, but he's going to know I *tried*.

I knock on the door, and his brother Rhys answers. "Hey, I need to see Asher."

"Sorry, man. Away game."

"We just got back." I point at Asher's car, and Rhys glances at it, confused.

"He's not home. Check his room if you want." Rhys wanders off, leaving the door wide open.

But if Asher's not here, the last thing I want is to be found in the house by Coach Dalton and then have to tell him what happened.

I stare at Asher's car for a moment. If he's not here …

Then I'm pretty sure I can guess where he's gone.

ASHER

I couldn't walk in that house. All that bad energy—the permanently simmering anger—is too close to the surface.

I actually don't remember the drive home. All I remember is wanting to get away from that bus. Away from everyone. Even Kole.

Damn it, I said some fucked-up shit to him, something I'll need to apologize for later.

As soon as I pulled into my driveway, I got out and started walking with no real direction in mind, but that's how I ended up here, in the same park where I found my brother with his girlfriend.

I don't care where I am, as long as it's nowhere near my younger siblings. They can't see me like this.

My hands are still shaky, my breath not coming out right. The buzzing energy inside me ebbs and flows at a dangerous pace. I want to punch things, pace … scream. Instead of doing any of that, my eyes well up.

What in the fuck is this shit?

I wipe the few drops away, but that only makes more flow.

I ... I don't know what is happening. I haven't cried since their deaths. I thought there was no need for tears. Death happens. That's life. The end.

Then why the hell does one stupid moose unleash all this grossness. Oh great, now my nose is running.

Someone calls my name, but I can't make out who it is, and I don't want to turn around like this.

Dry, you stupid tears. Dry.

I take a deep breath and shove everything down, but when I spin on my heel and see Kole approaching, I almost break again.

Shaking my head, I try to hold on to the tiny bit of strength I have left.

"You shouldn't have come after me," I rasp. Shit. I clear my throat.

"You can tell me to go away if you want. Tell me to leave you alone. But I wanted you to know that I'm here. If you need me."

"I don't need anyone," I snap.

Kole purses his lips.

"I'm sorry I was an asshole to you, okay? I didn't mean any of it. I wanted to escape, and I did it the only way I know how."

"By making others mad at you so they won't care what you do or what happens to you."

Exactly. "Get out of my head," I grumble. "Maybe you should become a shrink instead of an MD."

"Nah, why listen to people whining all day when I have you for that?"

I try for a laugh. I really do. In fact, I think it starts as a laugh, but then all at once, it collapses into uncontrollable sobs.

Kole doesn't hesitate. He steps into my arms, which only breaks the dam, and buckets of tears fall from my eyes. "I'm here," he whispers. "We can talk, I can just hold you ... whatever. Just let it all out."

Apparently, my body thinks that's a brilliant idea.

I soak Kole's shirt with snot and tears—so sexy—but I can't stop it. I'm not even trying anymore.

For the first time since my father and stepmother died, I let go of everything I've thought I needed to hold on to.

I've been trying to keep the lid on tight for so long. The ironic thing is I've been waiting for West to break down. I've been anticipating it.

Nope, turns out it's me who doesn't have their shit handled.

Kole tries to pull back, but I hold tighter, gripping onto him so hard I fear I might be crushing him. He doesn't fight it. He runs his hand down my back and whispers soothing words like "I'm not going anywhere" and "I got you."

I know we can't stay like this forever, but fuck, I want to.

Right here and now, there's only Kole, me, and a whole mountain of baggage I can't let anyone else see. If Kole wasn't so … *Kole*, he wouldn't see it either.

Minutes pass, but I can't tell how many. Ten, twenty, forty-five. Every time I think I'm getting the gut-wrenching crying under control, it starts again.

"Come here," Kole says. I let him pull back and lead me toward a park bench. He sits with his arm running along the back and gestures for me to sit next to him..

When he pulls me in close, I can finally let some of the fight I'm holding on to go. He makes me feel warm even though I'm near frozen.

Being in his arms is the safest place I've felt in a really long time. As long as he keeps touching me, I think I'll be okay.

Here with him, I don't have to worry about what my siblings will think. I won't have to worry about their future or mine. I don't have to be strong for them.

I don't have to pretend I'm not struggling.

Because I am struggling.

"I wished it was me," I mumble.

"What?"

"When Dad and June died, I wished it was me."

Kole's arms tighten around me. "Oh, Asher."

I realize how it sounded now. "No, no, don't think I'm suicidal or anything like that. When they died, I couldn't help feeling guilty that they were gone. They were really good people and put up with a lot of shit from West and me. Nothing too serious—typical angsty teenager crap—but they dealt with it, you know? And raised their own five kids. Why did they have to die? It seemed like such a waste when we all know it's me who's a waste. I don't take anything seriously, I hate everyone—"

Kole nudges me. "Hey."

I roll my eyes. "I hate *almost* everyone. I'm not … I'm not a good person. They were. I just … don't understand."

"It sounds like you're suffering from a very complicated and rare disorder."

I turn my head. "What?"

His lips turn up at the edges. "Grief."

"For a moment there, I thought you might actually have an answer for me."

"I hate to say it, but the only treatment for grief is time. Eventually it will get easier and easier to get through the day without being an asshole."

"I hate that my brothers and sisters have to grow up without them. I hate that they're stuck with me and West."

Kole shifts, and I get the feeling he wants to say something but is holding back. He could ask me anything right now. I don't have the strength to fight it anymore. I'll also give anything to stop my train of thought and rambling musings about how life is so unfair and why I can't seem to be a half-decent person when I know how privileged I am.

"Ask it," I say.

"Ask what?"

"What you want to ask but are worried it'll piss me off."

Kole's fingers link through mine on my thigh. "What's the deal with you and West? Your relationship is confusing. Sometimes it feels like you hate him, sometimes it sounds like you think he hates you when I know for a fact he loves you and wants to protect you, and then other times …"

"Other times, what?"

"It seems like you're two sides of the same coin."

"Where to start with that mess?" I sigh. "When Mom passed away, Dad depended on West to look after me a lot. They had him when they were eighteen. Me when they were twenty-four, and then Mom died when she was twenty-six. I don't even remember her, but West was eight."

"How did she die?"

"Pulmonary embolism. They didn't know something had happened until she didn't pick West up from school. I was with her, but I don't remember."

"You were two. That's understandable."

"Dad looked to West a lot to help with me. At least until June came along."

"He was a kid."

"I know, and it's why sometimes I feel like he resents me." I flip Kole's hand over and draw circles against his palm to avoid thinking too much about what I'm saying. "Even though I was little back then, I felt it. I thought it was 'Oh, my annoying little brother wants to be like me, and I'm the best' which is why I fought playing hockey for so long. Then when I found out hey, I'm actually really good at hockey, possibly even better than—" I mock gasp "—Westly fucking Dalton, it suddenly became a competition I don't think either of us wanted to play. Constant comparisons, all the questions about if I'd hoped Boston would draft me so I could play with my big brother. And when I was drafted to Buffalo, then there was speculation of which brother would come out on top. It's like the world of hockey has been trying to pit us against each other from the beginning, and we played into it."

"And now?"

I shrug. "Now I just hate that he acts like he has it all figured out when he doesn't."

Kole chuckles.

"That's funny?"

"Like I said, two sides, one coin. You do know why he's like that, right?"

"Because he thinks he's better than me?"

Kole full-on laughs now. "Why do you act the way that you do? Why do you act like a dick to your own teammates?"

I don't want to admit it aloud. *Because I don't want them to see I'm broken and fragile.*

"They see you the exact way you see West. He acts strong because he feels he *needs* to so your family can grieve and move on without falling apart. He's trying to hold it together for all of you even if he's broken up inside."

His words hit me square in the chest, and each time I run his words over in my head, it's like *punch, punch, punch.*

I rub my sternum. Kole's right. I know he is. I've probably known it all along, but it's taken someone else to point it out for me to really see it.

"Shit," I mutter and stand.

"What?"

"I need to go do something."

"O ... kay?"

I glance at him over my shoulder. "You coming?"

Kole catches up with me, and I loop my arm around his shoulder and hold him close as we head for my house in silence. I can tell he wants to ask me what I'm doing, but I'm scared if I say it out loud, I'll chicken out.

He pauses where he parked his car on the street. "You need me to go home, or do you want me with you?"

"I want you with me. I'll be super quick, and then we can hang out in my room with a big sign that says 'No kids allowed.'"

"Will that work?"

"Nope. Clothes will have to stay on at all times."

"I think I'll be able to manage."

I step forward and kiss the tip of his cold nose. "Thank you."

"For what?"

"For coming after me when I probably don't deserve it. The things I said ..."

"I know you didn't mean them. Well, I thought you did at first, but then Dad told me how your parents died, and I put it together."

"I'm sorry." I've never been more sorry in all my life. And that's saying something because I've fucked up countless times.

"I know that too," Kole says softly.

"How?"

"Because you're not this big tough *no emotions* guy. I've known that from the first night I met you and you were freaking out over your missing little brother. You're not an asshole no matter how much you want people to believe you are."

I didn't know I needed to hear that until this moment. Kole sees me. Really sees me.

"I'm here if you need anything," Kole murmurs.

"I need the courage to do this. Can you give me that?"

"Do *what* exactly?"

I pull him inside the house, and we make our way to the kitchen where I can hear West rummaging around.

His green eyes meet mine. "Hey, you're back. I streamed the games. You—wait, why is your face all splotchy?"

I pause and hesitate for a millisecond, but like earlier when I decided it was time to let it all go and bawled like a baby, I do it again. It's not intentional, and I'd fully intended to get through telling West what needs to be said without them, but one look at him and *nope*. Only this time, I don't try to hold the tears back.

I cross the room and throw my arms around my stupid big brother. "I love you. You're a great brother, and you're doing a great job."

West doesn't react at first, but then he hugs me back, and when I try to pull away, he won't let me. "What happened? What's wrong? Are you hurt?"

I shake my head. "Not hurt. Just an idiot."

"I've been trying to tell you that for—"

I slap the back of his head and step away. "Not cool."

"I don't understand where this is coming from. I appreciate it, but ... yeah, surprised, I guess."

"There ... there was a ..." Nope, I can't say it.

Kole says it for me. "There was a near miss on the way back. The bus had to swerve to avoid a moose."

"I've been an emotional wreck ever since. You're welcome." More tears come. "Jesus H. Christ, how much water can your eyes have?"

"You're okay?" West asks and then turns to Kole. "Is everyone okay?"

"Yeah. No one was hurt," Kole says.

"It gave me some perspective. Well, the near accident made me freak out, and then *Kole* gave me perspective. That, maybe, possibly, bottling everything up is not healthy? Because when you do that, you end up like this." I wave my hand over my face. "And he pointed out how much you and I are alike, and well, I thought you might need to hear that you're not alone and you aren't screwing it all up."

I see the moment all the tension and stress leaves West's stance.

"Even if I still can't tell the difference between the twins?"

"Even then. Though if you want, I can shave an E and a B in the back of their heads."

"We'll save that as a last resort." West comes closer and hugs me this time. "And I love you too."

22

KOLE

What is it about two brothers showing emotion to each other that warms me inside?

I'm so soft after seeing Asher and West hug that, yes, I'm in danger of tearing up too. They finally part, and Asher sniffs before swiping at his eyes.

"Okay, I'm done with this shit."

"It suits you, little brother."

"Fuck off, West." Aww, even the insult is missing his usual aggression.

I'm so preoccupied by all the happy feels that it takes me a moment to notice when Asher takes my hand and tugs me toward the kitchen door.

My gaze immediately darts to Coach Dal—*West* as he crosses his arms and leans back against the counter.

"Why *is* Kole here?" he asks, voice heavy with suspicion.

Asher's hand tightens around mine for a moment. "Studying." Then he pulls me away down the hall.

"Your brother totally knows," I whisper.

Asher opens a door and motions for me to go first down the

stairs. "He doesn't know shit."

"You sure about that?"

He doesn't answer immediately as he follows me down to his room.

It's … well, a basement. There's a washer and dryer with a basket of dirty laundry along one wall, then a bed, couch, and TV tucked into the opposite side of the room.

Asher walks over and drops onto the couch, then pats the spot beside him. "Would it be so bad if he did know?"

"If he told my dad, yes."

"It's just sex, right? It's not like there's much to tell. We're adults, we can do that."

"Yeah, as far as Dad is concerned, I'm still a kid who makes dumb choices. Do you really think him finding out I'm sleeping with you is going to help that perception?" I shift around so I'm facing him. After what happened, I want to be as close to him as possible, but I can't tell him that.

Apparently I don't need to, because Asher reaches for my legs and pulls them over his lap. "I *am* a dumb choice."

His joke falls dead when he doesn't even try to inject any humor into his tone. It makes me want to argue back that's not true at all, but …

"Come on." I cup his jaw and tilt his face toward me. "*We* know that's not true, but we also know Dad won't see it that way. You don't make it easy for people to like you." I stroke my thumb along his jaw, before meeting his eyes. They're still a little red, which makes the green even more vibrant.

"And yet, you're here anyway."

Even though he phrases it like a statement, I can feel the question between us.

Why?

Why didn't he scare me away like he does with everyone else?

"I've always seen through your bullshit."

"And called me on it."

"Which you liked."

He leans into my hand. "I think I did. Even while I hated it."

"You're welcome, then."

He snickers. "So sure of yourself, aren't you?"

"I have no reason not to be."

Asher's stare drops to my lips. "You really don't."

His mouth presses softly to mine as he steers me onto his lap. The kiss itself isn't a surprise, but when he wraps his arms around me, holding me close, and makes no move to deepen it or speed things up, it is.

One hand moves to my hair, running softly through it before trailing his fingertips over my neck. A shiver racks through me, and I pull back.

"Should we, ah, study first?"

He meets my eyes. "No."

No. That's the only answer he gives me before he's kissing me again. He's more confident this time, but he still doesn't make a move to heat things up. His touches to my back, my face, my arms are light and filled with purpose and some meaning I can't catch. It sits heavy between us. Makes me shake with need.

And after sex last night, and our closeness this morning, and Asher's vulnerability this afternoon ... the more turned on I get, the more I want to crush Asher to me and never let go. Like my heart is connected to my dick, and both feel equally as needy for his attention.

Is a heart-on a thing?

I'm making it a thing.

"You sure about your clothes-on rule?" I pant against his wet lips.

"Mhmm. You never know when one of them might come thundering down here."

"No fair." I grind my hips down into him. "Why get me all worked up, then?"

He brushes my hair back. "How are you such a brainiac when you're always thinking with your dick?"

"You make me dumb." He does. Dumb in the best possible way. He makes me turn off from everything. He reminds me to feel and experience and live. I've always known this thing with Asher was a terrible decision, but I made it anyway.

And now I'm struggling to remember what was so terrible about it.

Because I'm starting to think this isn't just sex. There's friendship between us. Trust. Asher's vulnerability and the swelling feeling that hits deep in my chest whenever he passes some stupid quiz.

Uh-oh.

No ...

Nope.

That ... that sounds suspiciously like *feelings*. Something I promised Asher he'd never have to worry about.

I break the kiss and look down to find him staring up at me, no barriers in place, almost like ...

I jerk back off his lap and drop into the couch beside him, giving an awkward laugh. "Guess there's no point kissing if it's not going to lead anywhere." Even if that felt really, really good.

Especially because that felt really good.

Kisses and no sex equals a relationship, and Asher's made it clear that's not what he wants. He's been through a lot today, and he doesn't need this from me when he's already feeling vulnerable.

I was doing so well to keep the lines clear. Friendship only. Then studying and sex. That's it. That's what we are.

Two very clear, separate parts of our lives.

So why won't this swirly feeling in my gut get the memo?

Asher blinks at me a few times, and I can't blame him for being confused when I'm acting weird and jittery. "Right."

"If West says anything, deny it," I say. "You're right. He can't prove we're hooking up."

"Of course."

I finally look at him properly. "There's no point worrying Dad when it's nothing. I've already disappointed him more than enough that …"

I don't know how to finish that thought. The truth is, Dad's disappointment isn't something I can control. When it comes to important things, things that are worth standing up for—like being attracted to men, and quitting hockey—I'll risk disappointing him all day long. I'm not going to be miserable to please him.

And if this thing between me and Asher was bigger than it is, if we were dating, or—*fuck*—in *love*, I wouldn't hesitate to tell him.

There's just no point in causing us *all* headaches when it's only a bit of fun.

"Kole …" His voice cracks.

"I should probably go." I jump up and hesitate. I can't help it. All my feet have to do is keep walking, and even though I need my distance, I also need Asher to know I'm not running away from *him*. These emotions are my problem to deal with. Asher's had enough for one day.

We were both clear about what this was. I overstepped.

And no matter what, I'm here for him. I want him to know that.

I reach back down and take his hand so he knows I'm sincere, and I can safely say that even with all these confusing emotions, this part comes from pure friendship. "I know today was hard, but I'm glad it happened. That you trusted me and then West. That you finally let go of some of that pain." And this part might be pushing it a little, but it needs to be said. "And if nothing else, I want you to remember this, not because I said it, but because it's true. You are *never* a waste."

Especially not to me.

Then I flee his room so fast, I wouldn't be surprised if I left dust clouds behind me.

Because if I stayed for one more second, I'm worried he would have figured out exactly what was going on in my head.

I drive straight to Katey's share house and walk in without bothering to knock. Her car's in the driveway, and after quickly checking the kitchen, that only leaves her room. She hates socializing with her roommates, so tends to avoid common areas.

Except when I walk into her room—

"*The* fuck?"

I slap my hands over my eyes to avoid the naked bodies greeting me.

"Most people knock, sweetie."

"How many people do you have in your bed right now?"

She laughs, and *damn* what it would be like to have no shame like her. "Let's make a deal. You keep your eyes closed while they get out, and you never have to know."

"Sounds good to me." And even though my hands are sealed

over my eyes, I turn my back on them to be sure. There's hushed conversation, but eventually I sense people pass me, and the door closes.

"Your eyes are safe."

I turn back slowly and thankfully find her sitting on the bed in a robe. "I guess I should apologize?"

"We were pretty much done. I'm sure Jessa will finish Liam off."

"Jessa and Liam? Wait. Your roommates?"

She cocks her head. "Since when are you such a prude?"

"Cut me a break. It's been a day."

"What kind of day?"

"Well, I just saw my best friend's tits—something I never had on my bucket list—and I was already spinning out over these *horrible, unwelcome, completely not wanted* feelings that I might be having over Asher Dalton."

Her mouth forms an O. "Yeah, okay."

"That's it? 'Okay'?"

She pats the bed beside her, and I shake my head.

"No way in hell am I sitting on those sheets after what I saw."

"Fine. But I wouldn't sit on the couch downstairs either. Or that bookshelf."

"Bookshelf? How in the—you know what, I don't want to know. Desk chair?"

"Questionable, but not recently."

"Floor it is."

She waits until I'm settled, then turns an uncharacteristically serious look on me. "I know I joked about not falling for him, but can I ask why it's a bad thing?"

"It's *Asher*." I give her a pointed look like *duh*, but the second the words are past my lips, I don't even know what they mean. Asher is ... well, before I really knew him, he was a flippant jerk who didn't seem to have much time for anyone. Now ... now I know how desperately he wants someone to see him. To connect with him.

"He's a player." Katey nods. "Got it."

I want to dispute that because as far as I know since we've been sleeping together, he hasn't once hooked up with anyone else. At least, not that he's told me.

Would he tell me?

"It seems pretty simple to me," she announces. "You guys are becoming too reliant on each other. You, what? Sleep, go to classes, do your hockey thing where Asher is, study *with Asher*, hook up *with Asher* ... That's bound to start feeling a bit relationshippy."

"You think?"

"There's a reason friends with benefits can start getting messy. One person confuses what's happening with something else. You like the guy, and you're friends, but that doesn't mean you're falling for him just because you've had his dick in your mouth."

She's right. It's a proximity thing. It would happen with anyone. And if I'm honest, I really, *really* don't want to feel this way. I'm scared if I do, it'll complicate things and I'll lose him.

For some reason, that thought is unbearable.

"So what do I do?"

"I don't know. I haven't really had to deal with all that." She chews on her thumbnail. "If it's because you guys hang out a lot, stop seeing him so much. Get a bit of distance. Or ... when was the last time you hooked up with someone who wasn't him?"

I try to think. "Over the summer sometime."

"Maybe you need to fuck someone else for perspective?"

There isn't a single cell in my body interested in that idea. In fact, the thought of some other guy sucking my dick makes it want to retract into my body. "No."

"Did you ever message Tray back?"

"Double no. No Tray. No other guys."

She looks at me like I have two heads. "Why?"

"Asher wouldn't like that." I wouldn't either.

"Kole … are you two exclusive?"

I open my mouth to say no, but if he's not sleeping with anyone else, and I'm not sleeping with anyone else … "Not officially."

"Which means …?"

"We've never talked about it, but I'm pretty sure he hasn't been with anyone else either."

For some reason, that makes her laugh. "Oh, honey …"

I frown at the endearment because it always precedes something condescending. "What?"

"You want my brutally honest advice?"

"Always."

"You're *both* fucked."

23

ASHER

I get the distinct feeling that Kole is avoiding me. There's a chance I'm reading into it, but I swear when I walk into the locker room every day, he's rushing the other way. He doesn't have time to study, which is fair because I have been taking up a lot of his energy just trying to understand the basics. He's premed which would be intense, and he needs time to focus on his own studies.

But when a week goes by and I realize I haven't even kissed him in that time, let alone had a chance to talk to him other than passing greetings, I begin to think it's more than that.

I probably scared him off with all the sobbing. Tears are a sex repellent. This is why you should never show emotion.

I decide I'll confront him about it and promise to never snot all over him again. We have an away game this weekend, and I was really looking forward to flipping our dynamic around. My ass is worried that's not going to happen now.

After practice, I make sure to go slow in the shower and with getting dressed. Kole's always the last one out because he has to make sure everything is in its place after the herd of unkempt cavemen have destroyed the locker room with jockstraps and towels left everywhere.

He has the worst job.

When it's only him and me left, I stand and stalk toward him. He either pretends he doesn't know I'm coming, or he's really focused on throwing those towels in the laundry bins.

Damn his ass looks good in those jeans he's wearing.

I wrap my arm around his middle and pull him against me. He stiffens for a brief second before melting into me.

"I've missed you," I hedge. I lower my head and kiss his neck. "Missed touching you."

A small shiver runs through him.

"Are we still good for this weekend?" I ask.

"Weekend?"

"The away game. This time I won't let you jump on my dick first. My ass is lonely."

Kole snorts. "You know, there are other things that could help with that?"

"Like what?"

"Toys—"

"In a house where teenagers could snoop and find them?"

"Someone else …"

My hands drop faster than if he'd pushed me. "Oh."

Kole refuses to look at me.

I step back. "Is that what's happening here?"

He wants to put an end to this arrangement. I ignore the disappointment, but it already sits heavy in my chest.

Finally, he turns to face me. "I mean, we're casual, right? You could go out and fuck anybody. You don't have to wait for me to be available."

Yep, this is definitely the blow-off speech.

It shouldn't get to me, but it does.

Kole's obviously realized he can do a lot better than someone like me. Someone who he can't have a future with. Who isn't worth disappointing his father over.

And whoa, apparently I'm thinking of further ahead than the next away game.

"Got it." This is where I'm supposed to walk away or something, but I can't bring myself to do it.

What we have ... it started as a way to get me to study, but I've found myself wanting more and more of Kole.

He's someone I can actually let my guard down with. Or, I thought he was. Now, suddenly, he wants to pull back. It can't be a coincidence that it happened right after I had a breakdown in front of him.

"Is this because of all the emotional shit? Because I can totally go back to being an asshole. You're a ... twatwaffle." I wince. Okay, maybe I can't be an asshole *to him*.

Kole laughs. "No, this isn't because you cried over your parents' death. I mean, you're a monster for it, *of course*, but it ... it's not why I ..." He swallows, and his Adam's apple bounces.

"Why you're ending this?"

His hazel eyes widen. "Wait, what? Is that what I said? All I said was you're welcome to go get sex from someone else if you're missing it because I've been too busy."

I step forward. "Is *that* what *I* said? I believe my words were I miss *you*."

"You can't," he blurts.

"I can't miss you?" I move even closer, and he stumbles, his back hitting the side of the cubbies.

"It's ... against the rules." His words hold no conviction, which I find interesting. "Total casual hookup violation."

"You going to give me a penalty? Five minutes in the sin bin?"

Kole narrows his eyes. "I'm serious, Asher. This whole kissing when we're not studying and sharing a bed after sex ... it ... it blurs lines."

Holy shit.

Holy. Shit.

"Is Mr. It's Impossible to Fall For You Because You're A Stupid Jock catching *feelings*?" I can't stop the smile from taking over because the idea of that? My heart wants to damn explode.

"No," he whines. It's way too emphatic and high-pitched to be the truth though. He clears his throat, looks me in the eye, and tries again. "*No.*"

I sing. "I think you like me." I add a little dance in there too. "You really like me."

"I don't like you so much right now," he mutters.

"It was the crying, wasn't it? You have, like, a tear fetish, and the tears of your partners really gets you off."

"Nailed it," he says dryly.

"Dude, I thought you were smart. You're stupid if you have feelings for me."

Kole sighs and folds his arms. "Are you done yet?"

"No. I'm not going to stop until you admit it."

"I don't like you." He pushes off the side of the cubbies and tries to leave, but I quickly jump in his way. "You're infuriating."

"You like me anyway."

"Asher—"

"Go out with me," I say.

He steps back again. "What?"

"Date me."

"You're not the dating type."

"Hey, I've dated a lot of people before. I've even had a girlfriend." I mockingly gasp.

"Dating you would be detrimental for my health."

"Went to the doctor a few weeks back, actually. All negative. So ..."

Kole grunts. "That's not what I meant, *at all*."

Wow, he's really adamant about not dating me, huh. I should be offended and disappointed, but I'm not. Because I know why he's doing this. At least, I'm pretty sure. He's starting to feel something for me, but it scares him because one, I am not his usual type—fair enough. Two, when it comes to being someone you bring home to the parents, I definitely do not fit that description. Three, he's premed, I'm NHL bound—hopefully—and our schedules are nuts. Could there really be a future when we don't know where either of us will be in two or three years?

There are so many reasons for him to want to push me away and ignore that there's something really good between us, but I'm hoping the one reason I have to give us a shot will win out.

I like him too.

There has never been anyone in my life I've let in like I have Kole. Last year, I made friends with Cohen, but we never talked about real shit. I would purposefully make him uncomfortable by being blasé about everything wrong with my life because I could make offhanded comments and not think about it too deeply.

With Kole ... I'm not sure when it happened or how, but I feel like I could tell him anything and he wouldn't judge me.

He accepts me, bad behavior, baggage, and everything else that comes with it.

I lean in and whisper, "You're allowed to be hesitant. I know I would be if I was dating ... uh, me. Although, I've done plenty of that too." I wink.

"It's nothing against you. You're great. I just don't have time for anything serious."

"You don't have time for anything serious with a fuckboy. You do realize we've been spending most of our free time with each other already? Well, until you caught the feels and decided you needed to avoid me. Not cool, yo."

He almost smiles. "What will it take for you to drop this?"

Easy. "A date."

"Oh, sure, when should we schedule that in? After practice, during midterms, at an away game, or when you're looking after five minors?"

"Hmm …" I tap my chin. "How about now?"

Kole's sexy mouth opens and then closes just as fast.

"Ha, you can't come up with an excuse. Buckle up, big guy. A date with Asher Dalton is like a date with—"

"A pushy, insistent jerk whose head is so big it's surprising he doesn't fall over when he walks?"

"I was going to go with something cliché like destiny, but yours might be closer to the truth."

"If I do this date thing and then tell you I don't want another one, will you let it go?"

I want to say no, but I also don't want to be one of those pushy guys. "Yes," I say instead, and I mean it. If I can't make him admit to me with this one date that he really does have feelings for me, then we should step back.

I didn't think Kole could ever look at me as more than a jock who can't pass a basic health course—and who can give him amazing orgasms. If there's a chance? Even if I don't deserve it? I'm going to give it everything I have.

I wait for his reply anxiously but try not to let it show.

He relents. "Fine. Take me to your date place."

Yesss. Okay, date mode.

"Hmm, which McDonald's do you think is more romantic? The one in Colchester or South Burlington?"

Kole pauses and glares at me.

"That was a joke. Geez. Calm down. Five Guys is much

better. And you can say things like 'Five Guys filled me up, and now I can't even walk.'"

Kole pats my shoulder. "You're really selling me on this date thing. It's going to be so hard for me to say I don't want another one by the end of it."

Little does he know I'm messing with him.

Prepare to be wooed, Kole Hogan. I'm bringing out the big guns.

24

KOLE

I'M NERVOUS. I CAN'T REMEMBER EVER BEING NERVOUS AROUND Asher before, but now that he knows how I feel about him, things have shifted. I'm in a vulnerable position I don't like. One my playful and charming attitude won't get me out of.

I almost kick myself. If Asher—poster child for flippant emotion—can break down and show me himself at his lowest, I can suck this shit up.

A week wasn't enough to turn these feelings off.

A week was *painful*.

The whole time, I tried to focus on coursework and spending time with Hades, and flirting with guys in my classes was a total fail because the more I worked to actively *not* think about Asher, the more he occupied my mind.

I have committed the ultimate friends-with-benefits crime. I'm not just falling for the guy.

I've fallen.

And now I have to hope it doesn't freak him out completely.

I try to study his face again, but it's neutral as he concentrates on driving. His black hair is curled over into his eyes a little, and his biceps flex as he flicks the turn signal.

"Wendy's?" I ask through a grin.

"Only the best for you."

"Well, it's not McDonald's."

"No, this is way classier." He turns into the drive-thru. "And since it's a first date, I'll even let you order from the regular menu. I should warn you though, second dates and onward are deal items only."

"I thought you were supposed to be convincing me to *want* a second date?"

"What's not convincing about that?"

We place our orders, and after they're handed to us, Asher pulls up in the parking lot.

"This isn't our date, by the way," he says around a mouthful of burger.

Joke's on him though, because I really don't care what we do together. I could easily make an excuse of telling him this is all I have time for, but the last week has caught me up completely on schoolwork, and now I'm with him, I'm too weak to walk away.

"Where are we going, then?"

"You'll see."

I pretend to be unamused, but teasing has always looked good on him. He grins as he takes a long slurp of his thick shake and then swirls his tongue around the straw.

"Oh, no, stop, I'm so turned on," I say in the flattest voice I can manage.

He leans over and licks his cold tongue along my bottom lip. "You had sauce."

"Sure I did."

My phone lights up on the console between us, and we both glance down.

Dad: *Where are you?*

"Umm ... I might have forgotten to tell him I was leaving."

Something pinches in Asher's face, but it disappears quickly. He balls up his garbage and puts the car back in drive as I text back.

Me: *Sorry, out with a friend.*

Then I check that Asher isn't watching and add, *Might stay at Katey's tonight, I'll let you know.*

Because even though there's no way I'd be getting sex at Asher's, and we'd have to stay fully clothed, the idea of stretching out beside him is an addictive one, and if this date goes well, that's where I want to end up.

We're on the road for fifteen minutes, and Asher has chosen a radio station with Christmas carols playing. It's painful torture, and when "Jingle Bells" starts for the second damn time, I lean my head back and try not to groan.

I swear the car is full of Asher. His scent, his warmth, his presence. I really need to touch him. Not his dick, but that would be nice too. Just ... him. His hand or his face or to feel his arm tight around my waist again. From a week of nothing to something so ... *claimy*, I'd loved it.

We turn into a residential street lined with cars, and Asher slows as he looks for a parking space. There doesn't seem to be much of anything around.

"If our date consists of your dropping me off at some rando's house and expecting me to find my way back, I've gotta say, I don't think I love it."

He laughs softly and pulls into a free spot. "Definitely not what we're doing, but it's great to know you have such a high opinion of me."

"Ooh, does that mean I can drop *you* here and have you find your way back?"

"Wouldn't work. I've been here too many times."

Way to make a guy feel special, Asher. "With that girlfriend you mentioned?"

"With my parents." He turns off the car and climbs out, and I rush to undo my seat belt and follow him. He waits for me on the footpath, and as soon as I reach him, he takes my hand.

I squeeze it. I can't stop smiling. "Have you been here since?"

"Not before I left for the juniors. Christmas last year was pretty shit, if I'm honest."

I can only imagine. "You're not going to start crying on me again, are you?"

"Well, now I know how much it turns you on ..." He pretends to sniff, and his lip quivers.

I punch him in the arm. "You're an idiot."

"Well, you bring out the best in me."

I really hope that's true.

Asher lets go of my hand and wraps an arm around my shoulders instead. I lean into his touch as he starts to walk, and it only takes a block to realize where we're heading.

"Christmas lights?"

We've reached a cul-de-sac, and every house is decked out with festive displays. The road has been blocked off, and there are people caroling and others selling homemade, well, whatever, and the smell of cinnamon and something fruity is heavy on the air.

"How have I lived in Colchester for six years and never knew this was here?"

"Your dad doesn't exactly seem like the festive type."

That's true. It's always hilarious seeing his face when he unwraps the ugly matching Christmas sweaters Mom buys us. By this point, I think she does it to screw with him.

Asher leads me to a stand selling hot cocoa, which sounds amazing given how damn cold it is.

We wander for a while, taking it all in and pointing out badly placed decorations. In particular, one that at a certain angle looks like—

"Do you think Santa's fucking that reindeer by choice?" Asher asks.

"That's what I was wondering. Either way, Mrs. Claus doesn't look impressed."

"Maybe that's her turned-on face."

"You know, I always wanted to visit the North Pole as a kid. Now, I'm having reservations."

Asher pulls me a bit closer. "Total sexfest up there, I swear."

We move on to the next house, and when the carolers start on "Jingle Bells," I find the song a whole lot more enjoyable this time.

It's cold, and the wind is biting at my cheeks, but everyone around us has massive smiles on their faces. Kids are goddamn everywhere, building snowmen and shrieking at their parents, and we have to dodge a few rogue snowballs, but it all adds to the atmosphere.

It might be an unconventional first date, but Asher's showing me a side of himself he never lets out. Trusting me to get him through revisiting a place that he finds special enough to share with me. It's that, more than anything, that helps me to stop worrying about how I feel.

Sure, I might have fallen for him.

But Asher doesn't open himself up like this to just anyone.

Even though he's the one constantly saying he doesn't feel worthy, I have the strongest need to prove that *I* deserve *him*. So I pay attention and try to read how being back here is making him feel. He shifts between joking and introspective, and whenever I notice his eyes start to darken as some memory takes hold, I yank him back to this moment with me. Even with those little slips, he's more relaxed than I've ever seen him outside the bedroom.

Once we've walked past all the houses and made it back to the top of the street, I turn to him. "Thank you for bringing me here."

He shrugs, playing it off like usual. "Well, I figured if I wanted a second date, I had to emotionally manipulate you into it, so—"

"Nope." I pinch his cold nose. "No joking it off. This meant a lot."

"Shut up."

"You're doing that *vulnerable* thing with me again."

"You're gross."

"Admit it. You sort of like it."

"I like *you*." He looks me straight in the eyes as he says it, and my heart gives this weird jitter. "And I'll never say you make this shit easier because *eww, emotion*, but sometimes it's maybe sort of cool the way I don't have to think about who I should be when I'm around you."

I lean in and brush a quick kiss over his lips.

"So, did I earn a second date?" he asks.

"Who says this one is over?"

I drag Asher back to the car, check that no one is around, and then shove him into the back seat. If he agrees with my suggestion of staying at his place tonight, I'm going to need to get off before sleeping next to ... well, all *that*.

Fuck me, he's sexy.

And maybe he's onto something about an emotional kink, because I swear every time he shows that extra layer of himself, it makes me want him even more.

I pull the door closed and straddle his lap, then kiss him the way I've wanted to for weeks. There's no hesitation on his side, and as our tongues press against each other, I hurry to undo his pants and pull out his cock. It's already starting to harden, and by the time I free myself as well, he's full and needy.

I break the kiss to spit into my hand and wrap it around us both. "We better hurry."

His answer is to grip my ass and pull me tight against him. The feel of his cock against mine as I thrust, his sloppy kisses, the sound of me jerking us off all work to push me close to the edge.

His mouth breaks from mine, and he works down my neck, making me tremble.

"You're so fucking gorgeous," he murmurs against my skin. "And you're mine. All mine."

My balls tighten, and my orgasm shudders through me. I barely have enough time to yank Asher's shirt up out of the way as I start to come on his delicious abs.

"Mm, that's hot," he grits out, bucking his hips up into mine. "Kole … *Fuck, Kole* …" His eyes squeeze closed as his cock throbs in my hand and his cum joins mine.

I've taken the edge off, but my heart feels so full it's not enough. I want more. Always more.

Before he's even recovered, I sink to the floor between his knees and start to clean off the mess with my tongue.

"Kole …" He cards his fingers through my hair and tugs me up to look at him. A weighted silence passes between us before he whispers one word. "Mine …"

I nod. "I'm yours."

ASHER

"You're coming back to my house," I say on the way home.

"Kidnapping is a crime."

I cock my eyebrow at Kole.

"But I totally had the same idea," he finishes. "Why else do you think I mauled you in your back seat? I needed to take the edge off if we're going to sleep next to each other without being able to actually do anything."

"Oh, I didn't tell you the loophole rule? My siblings sleep like the dead. Once they're asleep, we have a six-to-eight-hour window where clothing is optional. So long as we either set an alarm to get dressed the next morning or clean up and dress before we pass out."

Kole sucks in a sharp breath. "When's bedtime?"

Yesss. "The twins and Hazel should be in bed already. It's the older two we'll have to wait for."

"Maybe we can work in some study time for you while we wait."

I slump. "I was kind of hoping now we're boyfriends, the studying in exchange for sex would stop."

"I was never helping you for the sex. You *want* to stay on the team, don't you?"

"Of course I do."

"How have things been progressing?"

"Slowly, but I'm managing. Even got Eckstein to offer me an extra-credit assignment to bring my average grade up."

"How'd you do that? He never offers extra credit."

I honestly don't know. "I think West talking to him might have helped. He probably pulled the sob story of our parents."

"That's usually your job."

"I tried, but Eckstein wouldn't even let me get it out. I figure maybe with West being faculty, he actually listened."

I turn the car onto my street and pull into the driveway to park, but before I can open my door, Kole grabs my arm.

"What will your brother say?"

"Do you want to tell him or still keep it quiet? We can always say we're studying. Which apparently you're going to make me do anyway, so it's not a lie."

Kole looks hesitant, but then his eyes soften. "You really meant it, then? What you said in the back seat? I'm yours? That wasn't some post-sex rambling?"

"Not at all. I called you my boyfriend, didn't I?"

His smile is blinding. "Then maybe we could tell West. But … after my dad?"

"Hmm, I dunno. I might need West there to protect me when your dad finds out. Actually, I might need all of my siblings."

"You think the nine-year-old twins can take my dad?"

I scoff. "Ben and Em could take him by themselves. You should see the shit they do to each other. I'm surprised neither has landed in the hospital yet with the way they fight."

"Is that … normal?" Kole asks, and I have to laugh.

"Aww, my precious little only child." I pat his head. "You'll learn."

I open the car and round the hood to meet Kole. He moves toward the door, but I take his hand and pull him against me to smack a quick kiss to his lips seeing as I won't be able to do it inside.

Ten pm. We only have to make it one hour, and then we can safely go downstairs without interruption.

Only, when we do step inside, the usual chaos that happens is there to greet us.

"Bennett, Emmett, why aren't you in bed yet?" I bark.

They're in their pajamas at least, so that's something.

"West didn't tell us," Ben complains.

"West isn't here," Zoe calls out from the kitchen. "I told them to go to bed, but they don't listen to me."

"Where's the babysitter?" I ask.

"West came home and told her to leave. Then he burned dinner, ordered pizza, told me to watch the kids and ... disappeared." Zoe looks panicked.

I take out my phone, but there are no messages or calls or anything for me to come home. I glare at the screen and then slip it back into my jeans and get into big-brother mode. "Okay, twins, bed. Now."

They go running toward the stairs.

"Wait. Brush your teeth. Then bed."

They're not so fast now.

I turn to Zoe. "Where's Hazel and Rhys?" If she tells me Rhys went to see his girlfriend, I'm going to lose my shit.

"Hazel's in bed, and Rhys is in his room. I think he's sexting with Charlotte."

I do not want to deal with that. Zoe first.

"And are you okay?" I ask. Our family dynamic is a mess.

West is the kids' legal guardian, so technically all the pressure is on his shoulders, but when he asked me to help out, he put some of that burden on me, and then I know we both put some of it on Zoe. It's not fair, and I hate when we do it.

The babysitter situation has helped a lot, but I have no idea what happened tonight.

"I'm tired," Zoe says, "but the kitchen is still a mess—"

"We've got it. You go on up to bed."

"Thank you," she mumbles on her way past me.

I sigh and turn to Kole. "I guess we're on cleanup duty instead of all the fun things I had planned."

"That's all right with me, but … I just want to do something first."

"What?"

He steps closer to me and wraps his arms around me. "I thought you might need a hug."

"Mm, not gonna lie, that feels good, but what's it for?"

"You're twenty-one—"

"Almost twenty-two."

"Still, you're way too young for this kind of responsibility. Even teen parents aren't thrust into raising five kids at once."

"Unless somehow they get pregnant with quintuplets."

"Not my point."

Being told how unfair my whole situation is makes me want to defend it because it's instinct to say I'll do anything for my brothers and sisters, but at the same time, getting the acknowledgment that I'm doing something other twenty-one-year-olds would run screaming from … it gives me a sense of accomplishment that trumps my shitty behavior.

Hey, I may act like a dick, but I'm a decent human being deep down. They cancel each other out, right?

"I hate to ask," I start, but Kole cuts me off.

"I'll clean the kitchen while you go do whatever you need to do."

"Thank you." I don't care if one of the kids comes in or West miraculously reappears and tears into me for kissing Coach's son. I lean in and do it anyway. "I have to go try to pry a thirteen-year-old's phone off him so I can make sure he's not sexting with his girlfriend."

"Good luck."

I'm going to need it.

I run upstairs to Rhys's door first on the right. My hand reaches for the handle, and I'm about to barge in when I think better of it. Thirteen-year-old. His own room. If he is sexting, I don't want to see something I'm pretending he doesn't do yet. Even though I think that's *all* I did at his age.

I knock instead.

"Come in."

Immediate response. That's a good sign.

I open the door, and Rhys blinks up at me from where he sits on his bed. I hold out my palm. "Phone."

"What did I do?" he complains.

"Nothing. I just want to check something."

"What do you need to check?"

"The Wi-Fi."

My little brother narrows his eyes but hands it over.

I open his messenger app and click on Charlotte's name.

It doesn't take long for him to catch on to what I'm doing. He stands and tries to take the phone off me, but I turn my back to him while I scroll through the messages. There's only sweet "I miss yous" and "school sucks" and Rhys complaining about living with so many goddamn people.

Amen, brother.

"What are you doing?" he screeches.

I hand him his phone back. "Zoe said you were sexting with Charlotte. I wanted to make sure before sitting you down for a really embarrassing talk that would be awkward for both of us."

"And you believed her?" The hurt in his tone is evident.

"After our talk a few weeks back about my virginity? Yeah. I wanted to be sure you're not doing anything you shouldn't be. You're *thirteen*."

Rhys looks like he wants to argue, but he doesn't. "That's fair. But you could have asked me."

"Again, you're thirteen, and I know how much I used to lie to Dad and your mom when I was your age. It's not a trust thing, it's a teenager thing."

"First you believe Hazel when she said I was meeting someone online, and now you believe Zoe that I'm sexting? It *sounds* like a trust thing to me."

"You're forgetting one very big important element here."

"What?"

I smile. "I was a thirteen-year-old boy once, and I know what I got up to. If I find you doing half the shit I did, I'll kick your ass. Got it?"

"What kind of stuff?"

"Please, I'm not going to give you ideas." I turn to walk out, when his softer, smaller voice stops me.

"Thank you."

I pause and look over my shoulder. "Thank you?"

"You're the only one who's honest with me."

I spin to face him completely. "You do realize I just lied to you to get into your messages, right?"

"You're honest when it counts. I get the feeling West keeps trying to do what Dad would have done, and it doesn't work. And by the way, West has already tried to give me the awkward sex talk, but I held up my hand and informed him Dad beat him to it. By about three years."

"Yeah, but Dad also gave me his version of that talk, and it missed all the important things that he didn't have to deal with as a kid. Like, don't send nudes. Don't ask for nudes. Social media changes things."

"I'm smarter than that, and I actually like Charlotte. I'm not going to ask her to do anything like that. Not until we're sixteen."

"Eighteen," I argue.

"*You* were sixteen." The fucker's got me there.

I relent, I guess. Fair is fair. Though it's cute he thinks he and Charlotte will still even be together in three years.

"Do you know where West went tonight?" I ask.

Rhys shakes his head.

"Okay. Maybe we should all ... go to bed. It's been a day."

"Goodnight."

I make my way back downstairs, where I find Kole still in the kitchen, barely making a dent in the mess all around. "Damn. I was hoping I was up there long enough that I missed out on all the fun cleaning."

"No such luck." He holds up a saucepan. "I tried to salvage this, but I think it's toast." He shows me the charred black marks at the bottom.

"I'd say so." I take it out of his hands and put it in the sink. "I'll do the dishes in the morning. Come to bed."

Kole presses against me. "I like that idea, but I can go if you've got family drama to deal with."

"My plans to get you naked probably won't happen because I don't want to be about to come when West walks through the door and I need to yell at him. Screaming about irresponsibility while wearing only a towel compromises my argument. But I want to wrap myself around you while we wait for him."

Kole buries his face in my shoulder. "That sounds even better."

"My dick is offended."

"No, it's not."

"Is this what having a boyfriend is like? No sex and dealing with whiny kids?" I lead Kole to the stairs that go down to the basement.

Kole chuckles. "Sounds like marriage, actually."

We get to my room, and I throw back the covers. "Been together for a few hours and we're already talking marriage? Might want to slow down there."

Kole shoves me. "Definitely no marriage. Ever."

That surprises me. "Ever?" I ask as we climb into bed and he snuggles into my side.

"It's not my thing."

"Huh."

"What was that huh for?"

I shrug. "Granted I don't remember my mom, but from what I've heard, she and Dad had this fairy-tale romance. And then he found another great partner in June. Dad made two marriages work—literally until death did they part both times. I kinda …" I slam my mouth shut.

"You kinda what?"

"Nothing. It's stupid."

"What?"

Seeing as he loves it so much when I share shit … "I thought I'd have that one day. While growing up, I always thought I was going to have a wife, maybe some kids, and then when I was with the juniors, I started discovering that a person doesn't have to be a certain gender for me to be attracted to them, and that opened me up to a whole lot of other partnering possibilities, but … I guess I always figured I'd settle down. At *some point*."

Kole's hand runs down my chest over my shirt. "If you were NHL-bound, that would make sense. All that attention, you were likely to find someone who'd tolerate you. At least enough for the paycheck."

I poke his ribs. "Hey."

"It's kind of sweet, actually. You like to show off this 'I don't give a shit about anyone' attitude, but you only have to spend a short time with you for you to come out of your shell. Anyone who really knows you can see you care a lot. Especially about your siblings. It's cute. I can see *that* guy getting married in the future."

A life with a partner and a white picket fence sounds absurd to me, but the imagery of it is still super appealing.

My eyes drift close.

"Asher?" Kole whispers.

"Mm?"

"You can't fall asleep. West isn't home yet."

"Keep talking to me."

"Okay." He does, but I couldn't repeat anything he says.

His voice lulls me into sleep.

Damn it.

When I wake up, the room is bright, and the noise of our old washing machine's dials being cranked echoes in my ears.

Apparently West came home at some point.

He stands at the machine punching whatever buttons he needs to press, and then he turns to face me and folds his arms.

The scowl on his face makes me think I'm in trouble when he's the one who abandoned the kids last night with no word about when he'd return. No phone call to tell me to come take over.

"That better not be who I think it is." He nods toward Kole, who's still asleep.

I slip out of bed. "We—"

He puts his hands over his ears. "Nope. No. *No*. The only way I can play ignorance is if I don't actually know anything."

"Where were you last night?" I ask.

West averts his gaze. "Is that why you're in bed with my boss's son? Because I needed a break from …" His mouth closes, and I get the impression he was about to say he needed a break from the kids but doesn't want to actually voice it aloud because the thought of any of them hearing and making them feel guilty would devastate him.

And I get it. I so get that he needs a break. I think all seven of us could do with a fucking break. But he can't just run off on them without telling any of us where he is.

I wave in Kole's direction. "That, and what we're doing, has nothing to do with you."

"You really expect me to believe that? You thrive on making the people around you as miserable as you are. If someone does something you don't like, you lash out and hurt them in ways that actually scare me. First Ezra and now Kole? You'd put my job on the line just to get at me? What is wrong with you?"

"I knew you were more pissed off about Ezra than you let on. That was a mistake."

"Sure it was. It wasn't at all to piss me off because he and I …"

I frown. "He and you … what?" I don't think I want to know the answer.

West gives me his *are you fucking kidding me* look.

"Nooooo. You and Ezra? He's your best friend. And since when? No. No, no, no, no, no, and *eww*. I need to wash my dick."

"I'm really worried about your hygiene if you haven't bathed since you and Ezra hooked up."

"I meant I'm going to scrub my dick until there's no skin left."

"Charming."

"You and *Ezra*? Why didn't you say anything?" I shudder and try to shake off the icky feeling of Ezra's hands all over me, but I end up doing some weird interpretive dance of what happens when hookups go wrong.

West's eyes narrow. "Are you seriously telling me you didn't know? You can't tell me you hadn't heard all the shit going around about me. It's not exactly a huge secret."

"About you not being as straight as you appear, yes. About you and Ezra? No. Hell no. Fucking fuck no. If I knew, I never would've touched him."

Shit, thinking about it now though, I guess it makes sense. Ezra is out and proud, and West is vague publicly. They're "best friends."

"I'm sorry. Wait, were you guys together when he and I—"

"No. We weren't technically together at all. Sort of. We were, but we weren't. It's complicated. And you know Ez. He'll never settle down. After Dad and June passed, I ended it because it was easier to sever that part of my life completely. All the partying and casual sex ... yeah, I couldn't bring any of that with me here."

"Where were you last night?" I ask.

He scowls. "Where did you disappear to after practice?"

Nice try at deflecting, Westly. Really.

"Out. With my boyfriend." I wave in Kole's direction again. "I didn't realize I was needed here or I would've come home."

West's face slowly falls from deflective anger to something worse—utter confusion. "B-boyfriend?" He groans. "Coach Hogan is going to kill me."

"And me, but that's not the point. Where. Were. You?"

West crumples and hangs his head in his hands. "It's ... I was with ..." He blows out a loud breath. "It was too much. I stepped out on the back deck for some air and some quiet. And then ... Fuck, I should not be allowed to be in charge of this family. I've been holding it together, but Christmas last year sucked, and I don't want to deal with it this year. It's hard, and they're so loud, and—"

"West, breathe," I say. "You're allowed to be overwhelmed. I know it's hard. But you can't run out on them without telling at least me so I can come home."

"I have to stop putting shit on you. And Zoe."

"We all need to pull our own weight around here. I can stay home this weekend—"

"No, the team needs you."

"I'll tell them I'm sick."

West is adamant. "No. After my breather last night, I'm better. I can get back in there."

"I'll try to be home more, then. Kole can come here to study. We could make it a reality show. Extreme studying. The challenge is memorizing shit while things fly at your head and the sound of an imploding house surrounds you. If Kole's going to run away, he should do it now."

"I'm not going anywhere." Kole's croaky voice startles both of us. He slowly climbs out of bed, and I wonder how much he heard.

West's eyes dart between us. "We're going to have to talk about this."

"West!" one of the twins calls from upstairs.

West sighs. "Which one was that?"

I snort. "I can tell the difference between their faces, not their voices."

"You still need to teach me that trick. Go back to bed. Your away game is tonight, and you need to be rested. We can deal with you and Kole later."

"If by deal you mean give us your blessing and not tell his dad until we're ready, there's nothing to discuss."

West's gaze hardens. "There are things to discuss."

That sounds ominous.

West heads upstairs, and I turn to Kole.

"Did you hear that? He said we should go back to *bed*." I emphasize it with as much sex in my voice as I can manage.

"He also said you have an away game, and you need to rest. I should get home anyway. I'll see you tonight."

"I'll drop you home."

"Nah, I'll walk. You should get some more sleep. You have a *big* night ahead of you."

I pull him against me. "I think I remember a deal we had for this away game."

He kisses me, just enough to get me hard, and then he pulls away. "Don't get a concussion tonight."

"No way. I've been waiting for this for so long."

With one more kiss, Kole shoves his feet into his shoes, throws on his sweater and coat, and takes the exit directly outside instead of trudging through the house past my siblings.

26

KOLE

When the hotel door clicks closed behind me, it's barely a full twenty-four hours since we decided to make this official, and I swear I've been turned on since he called me his boyfriend this morning.

I've never actually had a boyfriend. I've dated, but never like this. Never with someone I find so consuming that my limits are breaking down fast. Never with someone I've even considered asking *this* question.

Asher's fingers link through mine as I lead him toward the bed. It was torture to sit through that game and then clearing out the locker room, when all I could picture was fucking my boyfriend.

Bare.

Lips find the back of my neck as Asher reaches around for the button on my pants, but I stop him.

"Before you get too turned on, there's something I wanted to ask you."

"You're an idiot if you think I'm not hard already."

I laugh and separate from him before pushing him down on the bed. "That'll help get some blood to your brain for a minute."

He pouts, and it's so damn sexy.

"Did you mean what you said yesterday? About getting tested."

Asher's lust-filled stare shoots to mine, and it's clear he knows where I'm going with this. "Three weeks ago. After the whole condom issue …"

"I got the all clear at the end of summer. You're the only one I've been with since."

"You going to fuck me bare, Kole?"

I'll take his taunting tone as a yes. I pull him up against me and slip his jacket from his shoulders as my lips find his ear. "I want you to feel every inch of me."

"Yes …" He almost pops his buttons in his hurry to undo his shirt, and between the two of us, we have him stripped naked in under a minute. I step back and yank my shirt over my head, then push down my pants and briefs in one go. My dick is already standing at attention, but I take a moment to let myself drink him in. All that warm skin, stretched over lean muscle. Broad shoulders. A small amount of dark hair leading down into his trimmed pubes.

And that thick, mouthwatering cock.

"Lie back."

Asher flops down into the middle of the bed, watching me the way I'm sure I'm watching him. The heated stare sends a thrill through me. The confidence his arousal gives me is addictive, and I don't think I'll ever get over the high of making someone feel this way.

But knowing it's *Asher*? That takes it to the next level.

I want to give him everything.

I want to make him come over and over, with zero care about getting off myself.

It's why I love sucking him off so much. Driving him crazy is *such* a massive turn-on for me.

I climb onto the bed and crawl over until I'm straddling his chest. When I look down at him, there's amusement mixed in with his lust, and it makes me smile.

"You're going to suck my cock and get it good and wet so I don't hurt you," I tell him.

His head darts forward immediately to do just that, but I grab his hair and yank him back out of reach.

"And once you're done … I'm going to do the same to your hole. Now open up."

Asher's mouth drops open, and I rub the head of my dick over his lips. It's so hot watching someone as strong and usually stand-offish as Asher, ready and waiting to take my cock.

I slowly slide into the wet heat of his mouth. He clamps down over me, tongue stroking the underside like he's on a mission, but I force myself to keep the steady pace. Each thrust takes me deeper until I bump the back of his throat. "Come on, Asher, I know you want to let me in."

He grunts and angles his head, and on the next thrust, I sink deep inside him. *Holy fuck* it feels so good. Asher locks eyes with me as my hips start to move faster, and if the grip I have on his hair is painful, he seems to be enjoying it. He hasn't bitten my dick off, at least.

But shit, I'm about to get off if I keep this up. I tell myself one more thrust, just one more, but I can't break his eye contact or make myself stop. It feels so good.

I close both hands over his head as I use his mouth.

Asher suddenly shoves my hips back so I pull out. "I swear if you come now instead of in my ass, I'm gonna be pissed."

The sudden loss of his warm mouth brings me back down, and I zero in on Asher's swollen lips. I crash my mouth against his and kiss him until I'm panting.

"Do you have any idea how hot you looked fucking my face?" he murmurs.

"It can't have been anywhere near as hot as it felt doing it." I break from his lips and press kisses to his nose, his forehead, his cheeks, his neck. Everything about him tastes so good. Tastes like my Asher. "Turn over."

"Yes ..." he hisses and rolls onto his stomach.

Hovering above him, I drag my hands down his body, trailing my thumbs along the deep groove of his spine until I reach his bubble butt. There are two depressions above it, either side of his spine, and as I grab his hips and press my thumbs to them, they remind me of instructions.

Hold here and fuck.

I hurry to grab the lube from my bag beside the bed and move to kneel between Asher's spread thighs. Then I grab his firm ass, spread his cheeks, and cover his hole with my mouth. His hips jerk at the contact, and I follow, wanting, *needing* more. I want to taste every inch of him, and as I work the spit up in my mouth, I start to push my tongue inside.

He's tight, and I have no idea how long it's been since he's bottomed, but the small grunts he's trying to hold back and the way his thighs keep clenching tell me he wants this as much as I do.

I get my tongue past that tight ring of muscle and start to pump it in and out. His hips shift with me, and it takes me a moment to realize he's rubbing his cock over the mattress. I pull back, and there's a loud *crack* as my hand connects with his thigh.

"You do not come until I'm inside you."

"Then hurry up back there," he whines.

That needy tone makes me desperate. I cover my fingers in lube and reach down to pull his cock back between his legs while I push a finger inside him. The resistance around my digit lasts just long enough for me to wrap my lips around the head of his cock, and then he starts to relax. I suck and stretch until I'm able to slip a second and then third finger in.

"*Kole* ... Fuck, come on."

We are so on the same wavelength. I give his dick a solid stroke before I pull away, grab the lube, and coat myself with it. I completely overdo it in my eagerness and don't even care, because I've been wanting this so long I can barely believe it's about to happen.

Knowing my luck, the fire alarms or some shit will go off before I can get inside him, and that thought has me scrambling to position myself between his legs.

Asher tilts his hips up toward me.

"Ready?"

"Yes, yes. Do it already." His begging almost has a high-pitched note to it.

I press my cock against his hole and start to push inside.

I could sob it feels so good. Nothing between us. Nothing to dim the pleasure.

One long, smooth stroke and I'm finally seated deep inside him. I have to stop for a moment. I press my forehead to his back as I try to stave off the building orgasm. "You feel so good."

His back muscles shift beneath me. "*Damn*, I didn't know how much I needed this."

"What?"

"You. Inside me. Owning me. Fuck, Kole, you're all I can feel. It's ..." Whatever it is, he doesn't have words for. He reaches down and grabs my hand, linking our fingers together. "Please ..."

I lean in and press a kiss behind his ear. Inhale the smell of locker room soap, which used to remind me of pressure and disappointment, but now reminds me of Asher. My thrusts start slow and deep as I hold him tight against me. What he's feeling, I'm feeling it too. It's overwhelming. Perfect. I want to feel every minute. His hard chest under my palm. The bead of sweat on his neck. His strong legs pinned under mine. The press of my balls against his with each thrust.

Skin and warmth on the outside. Words like *claimed* and *owned* and *mine* on the inside.

I press in deep against his ass. "Does that feel good?"

He responds by grinding up against me. And as incredible as this feels, I'm not going to be able to hold out for much longer.

"Time for you to come."

I steer his hand to his dick, then release him and kneel up to grip his hips. There's no more teasing, no more dragging it out. I pound into him over and over, and Asher meets every thrust with a backward one of his own.

The slap of flesh, the smell of sweat, my hard breaths, and Asher's moans, and … shit. It's too much, too much—

Asher clenches tight around my dick, and my legs jolt as my orgasm hits me. It's so intense I'm barely aware of Asher slumping forward until I land heavily on top of him, and my cock gives one final twitch inside his ass.

I can't do anything but breathe and hold him tight while I wonder if it's possible for an orgasm to send you blind because that was …

"Have you ever barebacked someone?" I finally ask, bonelessly rolling off him.

"No, never. Why?"

"Holy shit, are you in for a surprise."

Asher starts to laugh, and as he flops over and pulls me tight against his chest, I snuggle in, sure I could pass out at any moment. For once, I have no smartassed words for him; I just let my eyes drift closed as he kisses my temple.

"Hey," Asher says.

I look up and could almost melt at the tender look he's giving me. He has no barriers up, and he's never looked so damn beautiful. "Was that okay?"

"Oh yeah. Except now my ass feels gross and sticky. I'm going to have to shower."

"I don't think I can move."

"The joys of being the one doing the fucking." He trails a finger down my cheek. "God. You're perfect, Kole. What are you doing with me?"

It's not until he asks that question that I realize I already have the answer. Asher is sweet and kind and hurting. He has big dreams about family even though he could easily resent that whole thought with all the siblings he has to look after. Sure, there are days I could strangle him, but deep down, Asher only wants to be loved.

I kiss him, a bit overwhelmed at the thought.

Because I'm beginning to suspect that Asher could be way too easy to love.

I'VE DECIDED I hate the bus ride home from games. Asher and I agree to sit separately, because there's no way in hell we'd be able to keep our hands off each other, and I really don't want to deal with Dad while I'm trapped on a bus full of hockey players.

Then we get back to Colchester, and I can't even kiss him goodbye. I'm tempted to go with him to his place, but he's planning to take over from West so West can have a break, and I don't want to interrupt him spending time with his siblings.

Which means I head home with Dad and try not to act like one of my limbs has been forcibly removed.

Dad's talking through last night's game, and even though they won, he's focused on what they could have done *better*. Because superstition forbid he acknowledge that the team's really coming together. Positivity is like Frozen Four repellent.

I could tell him now. Four words.

I'm dating Asher Dalton.

But he's driving, and I don't feel like ending up in a ditch. Then when we're home, he's tired from the trip, so it doesn't feel right then either.

Besides, should Asher be here with me? Should I give him the heads-up? Check the house for potential weapons first?

The familiar nerves that have hit me a couple of times before are coming on strong. I love Dad, and disappointing him is never something I take lightly. The thing is, I don't *want* to disappoint him this time, because I don't want *Asher* to be seen as a disappointment.

He's not.

And I know if Dad knew him a little off the ice—outside those walls he puts up with everyone he's not close to—Dad would see that. If he could see him with his siblings the way I've seen him.

That first day we met, he was closed off in the locker room, but when he was searching for his brother in the park that night, all the bullshit was put aside for genuine worry for Rhys. Dad would only have to see that side of him to approve—I'm sure of it.

"Hey, honey." Mom's sitting at the kitchen counter when we

walk through the door, thumbing through her phone while she eats lunch.

"Hey, Mom." I walk over and kiss her on the cheek, then steal one of the tomatoes out of her salad. "Fun weekend without us?"

"Cried myself to sleep," she answers dryly. "What about you?"

I think of lying with Asher, touching, kissing, joking. "Yeah. Good."

"Don't tell me you're finally enjoying hockey."

Hell no. But watching Asher play hockey is something I'm here for. "I guess it's good for me to do something other than school and studying."

"And picking up used gym socks is worth it?"

I laugh. "Good thing I have two weeks off without school *or* gym socks."

"That reminds me, your grandparents are flying in for Christmas in two days since it's our year to host."

"Lucky you're such a good cook." My voice is heavy with sarcasm. The one year she tried to do Thanksgiving lunch, we ended up eating five hours after we'd planned.

She throws a slice of cucumber my way. "Grandpa and your dad will be in charge this year."

"None of the others are flying up?"

"They'd planned to, but they can't get away."

So it will be my two grandparents, Mom, Dad, and me. I'm going to be fussed over like nothing else. I sort of wish we were going to Miami this year with all the cousins and millions of aunts and uncles. But then I wouldn't get to see Asher. Not that I'll get to spend Christmas with him anyway. Unless …

West said the other morning that their Christmas last year was shit. *Would* Asher want to spend Christmas with me? I can't see him wanting to be apart from his siblings, but ... well, why couldn't they come too?

It'd give my grandparents *actual* children to fuss over, I'd have Asher with me for the day, Dad would see him with his siblings, and it would get them away from their house where all they'd be thinking of is the two people who should be there spoiling them.

"I have a question. And heads-up, it's kind of wild."

Mom puts her phone down. "Consider me warned."

"How would you feel if I invited some people to Christmas this year?"

"Like a boyfriend?"

I don't answer.

"Maybe we need to redefine your definition of wild," she says. "Or did you forget that you already came out to us years ago?"

"First, cool it on the boyfriend thing. He's a friend, and he lost his parents, and I thought it might be nice to get him away from his house for the day."

"That's horrible. Of course he can come. We have plenty of room."

"Enough room for a few more?"

"How many more?"

"He has some brothers and sisters ... who are obviously just as lonely with no parents."

"How many brothers and sisters?" she asks cautiously.

"Uhh, there's seven of them altogether."

"*Seven?*"

"It's *Christmas*." I'm trying not to laugh at her shock. "The more, the merrier."

"You *had* to lead with the orphan thing, didn't you? There is no possible way for me to say no to that."

"Good thing too, because I need you to say yes."

She shakes her head at me. "Fine. Yes. Of course they can. Shit, now I need to buy more presents ... I want names and ages, Kole."

"You don't have to buy—"

"Of course I do. I'm not having someone leave here empty-handed on Christmas. What is wrong with you?"

Ah, my mom. Yes, she's being dramatic, but yes, she's actually serious.

Still, that opens up a whole new question. Am I supposed to get *Asher* something?

Maybe this wasn't such a good idea after all. What if I get him something and he has nothing for me? Or I don't and he does.

Argh. No. Too much stress.

I whip out my phone and send off a text.

Have we been together long enough to buy each other Christmas presents or can we just bypass it this year? Also, you and your siblings are having Christmas dinner with me and my parents. You're welcome.

Now, I hold my breath.

ASHER

"Em, put your shoes on," West yells. "We're already late! Rhys, you can't wear a shirt that says, 'Fuck Christmas.' Where did you even get that? Go change. This is my boss's house. Everyone on their best behavior."

I'm starting to regret taking Kole up on his offer to spend Christmas at his place. Not that it was an offer so much as an order.

Emmett sighs from beside me while I put the finishing touches on a salad I'm taking to Kole's parents' place. Salad: the one thing I can't burn. "One day he'll get it right, won't he?"

I glance down at where Emmett is fully dressed and ready to go, so that means West is yelling at the wrong twin again. "Maybe soon he'll learn to not use either of your names when he yells."

Emmett laughs. "At least when we're teenagers he won't know which one of us is in trouble, so he won't know who to yell at, and then he won't punish either of us."

I turn and pat his head. "You keep thinking that, buddy."

It's smart in theory, but knowing West, he'll probably punish both of them for the one crime. Is it bad I'm happy I won't be here for that?

By the time the boys hit thirteen, I'll have graduated CU, both Zoe and Rhys will be out of the house, and West should be able to handle the other three on his own.

By that point, I'll be playing in the NHL. Hopefully Buffalo will still want me, but if not, my exclusivity contract with them will have lifted, so I can try as a free agent to any team who wants me.

I just have to pray a team will want me.

Then I think of Kole. He'll be in med school then, and I could be anywhere. I quickly shake that thought free. What are the chances Kole will put up with my shit long enough we have to talk about what will happen when he's in med school?

Pretty fucking small.

I need to milk this relationship for every second I can get with him.

The immediate future is the only thing I should be worried about. Which includes spending Christmas Day with my boyfriend's parents.

What was Kole thinking? And why was the idea of spending Christmas with Kole more alluring than risking it all by actually doing it? We want Coach to like me, not to see how much of a screwup I am off the ice.

I turn to Emmett. "You know how I'm your favorite big brother?"

"Are you?"

I glare at him, and he giggles. "Please behave today. Maybe stay away from Bennett while we're there."

"Why?"

"Because …" I hesitate. "It's important."

"I don't understand why we're not having Christmas here."

"Because last year we got takeout, and we were all depressed because West and I can't cook as well as your mom could, which only reminded us that she's not here, and it was depressing."

Emmett slumps a little, and I regret bringing up his mom at all.

"Sorry," I mumble and cover the salad with saran wrap. "My point was we're trying to do something to distract us from being sad this year."

"I think it will always be sad."

I wince. I turn to him and kneel to his level. He's nine, but the twins are a small nine. "It will be, but maybe having dinner with another family will make it less lonely."

The thought of each of these kids feeling lonely in a house with six other people isn't lost on me.

"Can I take my iPad?"

I sigh. "Sure."

If the twins are distracted with screens, they'll be less destructive of Coach's things.

West pops his head in the kitchen. "Are we ready?"

"Guess so." Because sure? Let's get this shitshow on the road.

Merry Christmas.

I'm thankful we agreed on not getting each other presents—that would have been another stress I didn't need.

It would help if Kole hadn't been so vague about what he actually told his parents about us. He said he just asked if a friend could come over for Christmas and then played the orphan card. Shit, I'm a bad influence on him, for sure. But still, it's not clear how Coach feels about this.

And as we pile into the seven-seater minivan to drive the few blocks to their house and arrive on the Hogans' doorstep, I think I get my answer.

Coach opens the door with a scowl on his face. I'm not sure if it's completely because of me or the ugly-ass sweater he's wearing.

"Merry Christmas?" I croak and then clear my throat. I hold up the salad as if to say, "*Look, I'm not completely helpless.*"

He eyes me and then the salad.

"Merry Christmas, Paul." West shakes Coach's hand.

Coach steps aside. "Come in."

Okay, I know he's usually a stoic man, only showing emotion when we lose and that's always negative, but I dunno, it's Christmas. Where's that softer side of him I keep hearing about?

He was kind in hiring West, and he let me onto his team when he didn't have to—although, I'm sure that has more to do with replacing an NHL-bound player with another one.

But he has a nice side. I know he does. Am I reading into it that he's this uptight?

Is someone paranoid? a voice sings in the back of my head.

It's not just me though. As we enter the house, and the kids barrel past us to go say hi to Kole and Hades, West leans in and whispers in my ear, "Kole didn't tell his dad about you two, did he?"

"I don't think so? But Coach is acting weird, right?"

"Yeah, that was intense."

"Hello." Kole's mom appears in front of us. "You must be Westly and Asher. Paul talks about you two all the time." She hugs us both, and I get an overwhelming mother vibe. I hate it and love it and maybe want to hold on to her hug a little bit longer than normal. She pulls back and looks me in the eye. "I'm so happy to have you here."

"Umm, thank you for having us."

She smiles and leads us farther into the house to Kole's grandparents. "Mom, Dad, this is Westly, one of Paul's assistant coaches, and Asher, one of his players."

Whether or not Kole's told them we're together isn't clear, but it is obvious he played up the orphan angle because Kole's grandparents' eyes soften in sympathy. It looks like they're two seconds away from getting out of their seats and fussing over us.

The dining table is perfectly set in gold, red, and green decorations with a huge centerpiece and individual napkins on plates with Christmas patterns. It's definitely fancier than anything we would've had back at home.

Hopefully the kids will feel like they're getting a regular Christmas experience. We did Christmas presents this morning where West spoiled everyone with extravagant presents. The younger kids appreciated it, but Rhys and Zoe shared a suspicious look. When we were getting ready, I overheard them talking about how West has all this money but has kept Mom and Dad's crappy house and the minivan.

I don't think they understand that while West was playing for the NHL, it's not like he put aside a shit ton of his earnings. They're not privy to West's old party lifestyle. He told me he has some saved up, but he's now going to be responsible for five college degrees. So while he bought them all new iPads and game consoles and whatever, there's a big difference between that and buying a bigger house or newer car. I made a note to talk to them about it later, but today is not the time for that.

All of us got an insurance payout when our parents died, but the kids' shares are in trusts for when they're eighteen, and it's nowhere near enough for everything. I've worked out mine will support me during college, but after that, it will nearly be all gone.

Kole's family stares at us expectantly, and I squeeze West's shoulder. "I'm going to go check on the kids."

Quick! Escape!

I find them all in Kole's living room. Rhys and Hazel are

tapping away on their new phones, and Zoe and the twins are on the floor playing with the ugly-ass dog, who's so ugly he's cute to me now.

Kole's watching them from the entryway, and I join him. I want to reach for him and wrap him in my arms or kiss his cheek in greeting, but I hold back. Christmas is not a day for dying.

I open my mouth to say hi, but then Hades sees me, and my siblings are no longer entertaining. I open my arms. "Hey, Hellhound."

He runs into my arms and tries to lick my face, but I hold him back a bit.

"No peeing on me, please. Not in the house."

Kole laughs. "Anyone would think you're the only one who gives him attention."

A throat clears behind us, deep and husky. Coach is there watching me. I stand again and pat the dog's head.

"Uh, good boy."

Hades won't leave my side.

"Go play," I encourage.

He still doesn't leave.

I turn to Kole. "Your dog is clingy."

"He has horrible taste in people," Kole deadpans.

Coach's footsteps disappear down the hall, and I let out a breath.

"Does he know?" I whisper.

"I haven't told him."

That doesn't answer my question. I'm going to try to avoid him for this whole dinner.

"But … I was thinking about it," Kole says. "That maybe today …" He reaches for my hand, but I reflexively look around and flinch away. "Or not."

I slump. "Shit. Sorry. No, we should. Maybe. How about at

the very end. Like, after I leave, you can tell him. Give me a head start. I don't really want my younger siblings to witness my murder. They've already been through enough. Think of the kids!"

Rhys, who's clearly eavesdropping, pipes up. "Please. It's obvious you two are doing it."

I frantically slash at my throat. "Zip it."

Rhys rolls his eyes. "I'm just saying, Kole comes over and helps clean up the house. His dog knows you. I know hockey players are dumb, but are hockey coaches too? I'm guessing Kole had something to do with you showing up home half-naked that day."

"What day?" Kole asks.

"The day he was fleeing a hookup."

"Rhys," I groan. "Please for the love of everything, shus—"

"So you're the one who broke the porch gutters." The deep, authoritative voice almost makes me shit myself.

Coach Hogan is back.

Oh goodie.

28

KOLE

Something in Dad's jaw twitches, and I hear Rhys snicker from behind us. Hades is still panting at Asher's feet, and I swear even the twins have gone quiet.

Tension stretches between us all.

Even though I'd been planning to tell Dad pretty soon, this probably isn't ideal. *Merry Christmas, Dad, I'm dating the team brat.*

I'd wanted him to see how Asher is with his siblings first. To get to know him properly.

Maybe I can still salvage this. Maybe I can—

Emmett's little voice comes from behind us. "Rhys, we're supposed to be on best behavior for Asher's boyfriend."

My stare immediately darts to Asher, who goes so pale he looks like he wants to be anywhere but here.

Hades growls at the lack of attention, and Zoe squeaks and slaps her hand over Emmett's mouth.

I swear Dad's head is about to shoot off.

Everyone in the room is so. Damn. Tense.

I can't help it.

I burst out laughing.

Asher's looking at me like he's asking what the fuck I'm doing, and Dad seems concerned for my sanity. But honestly, screw this. Me having a boyfriend shouldn't stop time.

I loop my arm around Asher's waist and tug him to me before smacking a kiss against his cheek. "Dad, you've met my boyfriend, right?"

"This is how my life ends," Asher mutters, which only makes me laugh more.

"Kole, a word?" Dad turns and heads back down the hall for his study.

Well, shit.

Normally I'd grab Asher's hand and drag him in there to face my dad with me, but I'm low-key worried about exactly what Dad will say. The last thing Asher needs to hear is the same negative shit repeated back at him that he's constantly telling himself.

If they're all going to be dramatic idiots about it, I'm going to act like this is all no big deal.

Let's not focus on Asher being the *only* boyfriend I've ever brought home and skip right to the part where it's Christmas and we're all celebrating.

"Sup, Dad?"

"Cut the shit, Kole. You're dating Asher Dalton?"

"That is usually what the word 'boyfriend' means."

"What part of 'leave the kid alone' didn't you get?"

I shrug and take a seat, pretending to be bored while a flicker of irritation sparks inside me. "The part where I'm old enough to make my own choices."

"Kole."

"*Dad.*"

He shoves a hand through his hair. "I thought you hated hockey. What's going on here?"

"I *do* hate hockey. Playing it, anyway. Watching isn't so bad."

"I just don't get it. You're a smart kid. What the hell could a hothead—a *talented* hothead—like Asher Dalton have to interest you?"

I'm thinking *his dick* isn't the correct answer here. I drop the flippant attitude. "He's not always like that. The guy he shows you and the team is a front. It's because he *wants* to keep his distance. With me, with his family, he's a completely different person."

Dad changes track. "You're premed. You need to be focused on that. Asher's a distraction."

"We've been seeing each other for a few months now, and I was helping him study before that. I'm still top of my class. I'm keeping up. If you want to talk distractions and time wasters, I'd argue that picking up sweaty jocks and weekend trips away are a bigger distraction than a boyfriend."

That makes him hesitate. "I ... I thought it might be a way for us to spend some time together."

"I know you did." Like Asher, people only see the surface level with Dad. He's gruff and focused, but underneath he's a giant teddy bear. "And we have. It's been good. But you can't use the excuse of me needing to focus on school instead of Asher when you have me doing that. Especially because we both know we wouldn't be having this conversation if it wasn't Asher."

He darts a quick look at me and away again. "You can quit the equipment manager thing."

"No. A bet's a bet. And I've liked spending time with you too. But Asher and I aren't breaking up."

"I'd say he doesn't seem like your type, but when it comes to people who are helpless or lost, they're the ones you can never resist."

I'd thought that about Asher at first too. "The fact you think he's either of those things proves you don't know him at all."

"And you do?"

"Maybe better than anyone."

Dad scoffs.

"I know you think I'm being naïve, but you can just go ahead and think that, old man. Because when we go back out there, you're going to treat Asher like you would any other boyfriend I brought home. You're going to be embarrassing and intimidating, but you're going to make him feel welcome. For me."

"You're too much like your mother."

I jump from my seat and round the desk. Dad looks surprised at first as I grab him in a rough hug and rock him back and forth in the most patronizing way I can manage. He pats my elbow, and when I think I've made him uncomfortable enough, I pull away.

"Oh, and I have a favor."

"Uh-oh."

I leave the office and dart upstairs, before returning with a wrapped package.

"What's this?" he asks.

"A sweater that matches ours. Mom got it for him."

"No."

"Yep. You're going to give it to him."

"There is no way in hell."

I pretend to pout. "If Mom finds out we didn't give it to him, she'll be pissed. And *I* can't since Asher and I agreed to no presents. You don't want me to make him feel bad on Christmas, do you?"

He gives me a flat look.

"It's *Christmas*. Besides, it'll mean so much more coming from you."

"Give me strength," Dad says, running a hand down his face. "I'm still not sure I even like the idea of you two together."

"Do you like the idea of me being happy?"

He sighs, knowing I've got him. "Pulling out the big guns, huh?"

"Whatever it takes."

He tosses the present on his desk, and I go to leave, but I'm still not sure he gets it. Not fully. The last impression I want him to have is that this is some kind of fling, or me acting out, or—I shudder—that Asher is a *pet project*.

I catch my breath, then slowly let it all out again. "This is, umm ..." Serious? I hope so. "I *really* like him. A lot. I don't know if we'll make it long term or whatever, because there's still a lot to figure out there, but when we're together, it's sort of hard to remember what it was like before him. I don't *want* to remember. Please don't screw this up for me."

He glances toward the hall where the unmistakable sounds of Em and Ben fighting echo toward us. "You better get back out there before he works himself into a fit, worrying about what we're talking over in here."

I let out a small laugh. "Don't act like that's not exactly what you wanted."

"You said I can still be intimidating." He stands, and I don't miss that he picks up the present. "Can't have him thinking that dating my son will cut him a break on the ice. We have a season to win."

There's the dad I know and love.

Asher's in the kitchen helping Grandpa, and when we get out there, Dad walks straight up to him and hands over the sweater with a grunted "Here."

He leaves, and Asher walks over to me. "What the hell is this?"

"Hmm ..." I tap my chin. "If only there was something we could do to figure it out."

Asher rolls his eyes and tears open the paper. "Oh no ..."

"Oh yes. Reindeer knit is my kink."

He groans as I take the sweater and force it over his head. "Why do you hate me?" Despite his words, he shoves his arms into the sleeves.

"Nonsense. Red, navy, and white is a good look on you." I actually don't think it's a good look on anyone, but Asher almost pulls it off.

Then I take out my phone.

"Oh, hell no." He lunges for it, but even with his hockey reflexes, he's too slow, and we end up play fighting in the kitchen while he tries to wrestle it off me.

"Just *one* picture," I say.

"No."

"But you're my boyfriend. It's basically a requirement."

"There is no damn way I want anyone on the team seeing me in this."

"For me?"

"Not even for that."

I pout. "I'll tell my dad you're being mean to me."

"And people think *I'm* the shithead." He pretends to be outraged but leans in and kisses me. It's soft and sweet and does nothing other than make me want more.

Then my phone is tugged from my hand.

"Hey!"

I don't get a chance to protest any more because Asher pulls me against his side and holds out the phone. "You owe me."

"Yeah, yeah." I lower my voice so no one else can hear. "I'll lick your jingle *balls* later."

He takes the shot, and when he hands my phone back, I'm sort of blown away by how good we look together. It might be the lighting, or the angle, but I'm pretty sure the main reason the photo is so good is because we both look *happy*.

"What's that face?" Asher asks.

I glance up from my phone to find him watching me closely. "I'm glad you're here."

"Figured." His gorgeous lips pull into a smirk as he plucks the front of his sweater. "There's no way this was from your dad."

"My mom, actually."

He steps forward and wraps his arms around me. "Was he okay with us?"

"Not really. Maybe still isn't that sold on the idea, truthfully, but I made it clear he doesn't have a choice."

For some reason, that seems to surprise Asher. "That simple?"

"At the end of the day, he wants the same thing as I do. Someone who will treat me right. And that's you, so he needs to deal with it."

"I don't think I've ever seen someone tell Coach to *deal with it* before."

"Lucky you have me, then."

The back door slams loudly, followed by, "Bennett, give it back!"

Asher drops his head onto my shoulder. "It's going to be a long day."

I tilt his face back up. "Totally worth it."

29

ASHER

I'm sitting at Coach's dining table. Next to my boyfriend. And I'm breathing. I was not expecting that. Though I can feel Coach's stare from the head of the table.

On my other side, Bennett tugs on my ugly-ass sweater and points to his plate. Out of all of us, Ben is the fussy eater. He'd rather starve than eat a vegetable. West is adamant he has to eat everything on his plate or go to bed hungry, but Ben would rather be hungry. There have been many nights where he has skipped dinner.

According to Google, kids won't starve themselves and will eat their vegetables if they truly are hungry, but Ben has my stubbornness, so yeah, I wouldn't put it past him.

I take his plate and separate his food so it's not touching each other the way he likes it and then scrape a good chunk of the stuff I know he won't eat onto my plate.

And now West is glaring at me too.

At this rate, Kole will be next. Maybe by the end of the meal, everyone will be glaring at me.

I figure I had the choice of fighting with Ben in front of everyone or giving him a smaller goal. He still has some vegetables on his plate, just not an overwhelming amount. If he eats any, it's a win.

"Asher," Kole's mom starts, "Paul says you're going to take the team all the way this season."

"It's a team effort," Coach grumbles, as if he doesn't want to acknowledge he's been talking about how good I am.

"I hope so," I say diplomatically. "The team's really coming together."

"And the good news is, we'll have Asher, Kaplan, and Simms for at least another season," West says. "They're really working together and are tight line mates."

Ugh. I hate that my chest swells with pride at my big brother's approval, but I focus on the praise because I know the resentment is superficial. It's been years of comparisons that we don't need to do anymore.

That's going to take some getting used to.

"Have you got big NHL dreams?" Kole's mom asks.

"I do. Until then, I just hope to do the school proud." All this acting like a respectful human being is making me gag. I reach for my water.

Kole leans in and mutters, "Kiss ass," and I practically choke on my drink.

I cough and splutter. "Thanks for that."

"The NHL is grueling," Kole's mom says. "Paul only played two seasons before becoming a coach. You have to be built for it and be committed. It doesn't leave much time for … the important people in your life. Oh, and don't even get me started on the trades. That only happened once with Paul, but the other WAGs would complain a lot."

"It's a big commitment, I know that." But that doesn't answer her implied question.

Do you think you could handle it and still make my son feel loved?

That's a question we're so not ready for.

"I don't want you to leave," Ben says beside me.

I ruffle his hair. "I'm not going anywhere anytime soon."

Kole catches my eye, and he's staring at me with such … I don't know what it is, actually. Awe? Like I've said something melt-worthy when all I did was tell my brother I won't leave him.

He smiles at me, so I return it and reach for his hand on top of the dining table.

"What do you think about these two being boyfriends?" Coach asks West while waving his fork between us.

My gaze darts to West's, and I silently plead for him to not be a dick.

West rubs the back of his neck. "Kole's been a good influence. It's the first time I haven't had professors tracking me down and telling me how poorly Asher's doing in school. Well, apart from one …"

"That's because Eckstein's a …" *Do not swear, Asher.* "Hard professor to impress," I finish and give myself a mental pat on the back.

West snickers because I assume he knows I wanted to call Fuckstain a dick.

"Is that why he was at your house the other week?" Kole asks.

"What? Why the hell would Eckstein be at my house?"

"I swear I saw him pull up there when I was leaving the morning after our date …" Kole trails off and throws a guilty look at Coach.

Coach snorts. "Staying with Katey, my ass."

Oops? But he knows we're dating now; surely Kole spending the night will be a given.

West quickly changes the subject, and it takes a few moments for his words to sink in. "Asher and Kole ending up together was definitely not what I thought would happen when I asked Kole to keep Asher in line at the beginning of the year. I thought Kole quitting his spot as equipment manager after a week was more likely than them actually liking each other."

I blink.

Under my hand, Kole's tenses.

"You asked Kole to keep me in line?"

"Well, to keep an eye on you mostly. It was the away games I was most worried about."

Is that why Kole wanted to room together?

"I told Kole to stay away," Coach says. "I guess we both set up the perfect storm."

He. And West.

I pull my hand out from Kole's and sit here stunned. I shouldn't be, but I am. The Coach thing makes sense, and I remember Kole mentioning Coach was worried about his grades slipping because of me, but West …

Kole grips my bicep. "That's not really how it all went down—"

Out of nowhere, Emmett screams, and when I look over, blood is gushing out of his hand.

I stand so fast my chair topples over. West is closer, and he's quick to put a napkin on Emmett's palm, but he's already looking green.

West and blood don't mix, and don't even get me started on the fact he's a hockey player who faints at the sight of blood. There's a reason West never got into fights on the ice, and it had nothing to do with having been a passive player because he wasn't. He was aggressive, right up to the point of fighting. Then he'd back off.

I get to their side and take over while West reaches for some water.

Emmett is still screaming his head off, and there's commotion around me—Kole's mom's saying something about Coach getting the first aid kit.

Kole appears at my side. "Can I take a look?"

I let Kole lift the fancy cloth napkin that's now covered in blood while I get Emmett's attention.

"Hey," I say softly. "It's going to be okay. It's just a little cut."

His screaming lessens but doesn't stop.

"It's going to need stitches," Kole says. "It's really deep."

And now Emmett's screaming at the top of his lungs again.

"We need to go to the hospital," I say and then look around the table at our millions of damn siblings. "Crap, we only brought one car."

"I'll drive you," Kole says.

I nod. "West, you stay with the others. I'll take him—"

"I'm his legal guardian," West says.

"Are you going to be able to take him without vomiting everywhere? No, so you should stay with the other kids."

"We can watch them if you need to go," Kole's mom says.

"I want to go with Emmett," Bennett cries.

Oh of course, now that Emmett is injured, suddenly they're best friends.

I take control of the situation and stand. "West, you stay with the kids and try to calm down Ben. Kole, you drive me and Emmett to the emergency room, and West, if you need to be there to sign him in or whatever, we'll call you, but I think it should be all right. He just needs some stitches. It's not like he's going to be admitted."

Even though Emmett's nine, he's still small enough for me to carry out to the car. It's hard, but when he refuses to get off his damn seat, I don't have much of a choice.

Kole keeps the napkin pressed on Emmett's hand out to his car, and then I take over once we're in the back seat and buckled in.

Kole jumps in the driver's seat, and we head for the UVM Medical Center.

Emmett is still sobbing next to me, but he's starting to calm down. "Will ... will it ... hurt?"

"Nah. They'll make it all numb first. You won't even be able to feel it." I look at Kole in the rearview mirror. "Shame you weren't already a doctor. You could fix him right up."

"You're a few years too early."

There's something weird in his tone I can't exactly pinpoint. "You okay? You're not feeling faint at the sight of blood too, are you? I don't know how successful a doctor you're going to be if that's the case."

He shakes his head. "It's nothing."

I frown. "O ... kay."

"Just, what West said ... I—"

Ah. I wave him off. "It's fine."

Is it though?

"But—"

Emmett cries out as I press tighter on the wound.

"We can talk about it later."

Not that I want to.

The thought of Kole only hanging out with me because my brother asked him to makes me feel ick, but can I really blame Kole? If I were him, I wouldn't want to hang out with me either.

Then there's the whole Coach mess, but again ... if I were Coach, I wouldn't want my kid dating a Dalton.

I sigh. It sucks, and I hate it, but it is what it is.

Having a shitty attitude doesn't get you far in this world, but that's all I know. It's all that I am.

So maybe I don't have a right to be mad that we started under false pretenses, but that doesn't stop it from stinging.

30

KOLE

Asher's right. Now's not the time.

In the scheme of things, Asher being pissed with me should be registering pretty low on the scale given the complete one-eighty today has done. All I'd wanted was for Asher and his siblings to have a better Christmas, yet here they are separated, one of them broken, another sick with worry, and Asher pissed with his boyfriend and probably his brother.

So yeah, his reaction to West asking me to keep an eye on him *should* be low priority.

But it's all I can think about.

The waiting room is packed with people who all thought Christmas would be the best day possible to injure themselves. I'd make a mental note to bitch Mom out about giving that knife to a nine-year-old, but I wouldn't have thought of that either.

What age do they get to use sharp cutlery?

Yikes. See? This is why marriage and kids are in the nope column.

Professionally, I'll be trained to keep people alive, but personally? How the hell do parents do it?

But ... I think of how passionately Asher wants all that. It sort of sounded nonnegotiable.

And I really, really like him.

So much that my gut is in metaphorical knots while I wait for Emmett to get stitched up so we can go home and talk out this tension between us.

Would the marriage and kids thing be something I'd be willing to compromise on? When it comes to something like kids, you either have one or you don't.

Do I want one?

No.

But also, I've always pictured my life working in a busy hospital and not having the time to dedicate to someone else. It never even occurred to me to think of the other person in the picture.

Even before considering kids, though, is the whole NHL thing. How do we make that work? Sure, it's forever away, but if I'm in med school and he's going pro, what then? Mom brought up a good point at dinner about the trades and moving and—

I stop and blink at the opposite wall for a moment.

Am I *really* thinking about marriage and kids and being a fucking WAG? And in this case, the *G* doesn't stand for *girlfriend*.

Holy shit.

I *am* thinking about it.

Not even in an abstract way either, as much as I want to trick myself into thinking that.

No, already my brain is trying to come up with logical and *feasible* options for us.

I want to stay with him. Long term.

That's more important to me than worrying about details.

It should scare me that there are zero doubts circulating in my head. The voice that usually tries to argue reason is suspiciously silent.

Like with Hades, I just *know*.

Me and Asher, we were meant to end up here. We were meant to be together. Even when I first saw him and assumed "trouble," there was always something there. Something that made me look a little longer, a little more carefully.

And now that I see him ... I want to keep him.

Possibly forever.

Definitely forever.

This terrible, achy feeling hits me in the chest when I remember the look on Asher's face at lunch. How his hand tensed over mine. He asked me. Early on, he asked me if I was there to *spy* on the team, and even though I hadn't lied, it's not like I put the truth out there. I barely knew him then.

And now I do know him ... I know that Asher is sensitive when it's anything to do with West interfering.

They've only just started to get their relationship to a good level—is this going to send it backward again?

And what about us?

My skin prickles like it's too tight for my body, and I shift in the uncomfortable waiting room chair to lessen the feeling. It's not like he'd break up with me over it ... right? I mean, it's not like I've been reporting back on him. West's request literally brought Asher to my attention, and the rest was inevitable. And to be fair, I'm pretty sure I would have been attracted to Asher anyway.

None of the other guys on the hockey team got a second glance from me, and it took me ages even to learn some of their names. Asher is ... special.

And if I've hurt the feelings he very rarely shows, that's going to devastate me.

I push up from the chair and pace to the other side of the room, needing to stretch out my tense muscles. I hate uncertainty, which is why I'm always an up-front person, and not being able to talk this out *now* is making me restless.

My chair is immediately occupied, and there's still no sign of Asher or Emmett, so I pull out my phone and call Katey. She's back in Atlanta with her family, but we always check in on Christmas night, so I might as well get it over with now.

Hopefully take my mind off Asher.

"Hello, my beautiful best friend," she answers, sounding deep into a vat of eggnog.

I chuckle. "You're enjoying the festive season."

"I *am*. Everyone's here, and I'm stuffed from dinner, and the Christmas lights are so pretty ..."

"And you're drunk off your ass?"

"Yes, but ..." Her loving tone turns sharp. "Why aren't you?"

"Because *I* had to drive my boyfriend and his little brother to the hospital after an accident at Christmas lunch."

"What the shit?" Her squeal is loud down the line. "Okay, whoa. Explain. *Boyfriend*?"

I've held off saying anything to her because I wasn't sure how Katey would respond to me being in an actual couple, rather than just fooling around. "I'm dating Asher. Officially. And I'm actually really happy about it, so this is one of those times where you don't need to be honest if you disapprove."

"Aww, baby ... listen to you being all gross and loved up. Now you're making *me* feel all gross and squishy inside, and you're lucky I've been drinking because I want to crawl down this phone and smoosh you in a hug."

"Okay, you're *really* drunk."

"I *really* am. Is the little brother okay?"

"Yeah, pretty sure he's getting some stitches."

"What's with the tone?"

"Tone?"

"The sudden *life has me so defeated* tone."

I shake my head. "There was no tone. But yeah, I'm kind of stressing over something, and I want you to talk me down."

"Shoot."

I fill her in on what happened over lunch.

She groans. "You didn't even do anything. If he's mad at you, I'm going to jump on the next flight back to Vermont and kick his ass."

"Easy, tiger."

"I will go for the gonads, Kole. *The gonads!*"

"I love that you're trying to make me feel better, but Asher is pretty sensitive about this stuff. The last thing I want is to hurt him."

"Oh my god. Is my little Kole in *love*? Oh, this is too precious!"

"Shut your face."

"Urg, I have to go. The war is about to start."

"Monopoly?"

"You know it. I've got a reputation to uphold."

A reputation. Sure. I know for a fact she cheats—and she isn't subtle about it. "You do realize you threatening to kick my boyfriend in the balls in no way solved any of my problems, right?"

"Oops, I guess? Looks like you'll have to sort this thing out like a big boy. *Bye!*"

She ends the call. I cringe because that conversation got me literally nowhere. Sure, I don't see Asher and me breaking up over this, but is there going to be an argument? A *fight*? Even the possibility is making me feel sick to the gut. And the thing with

Asher is he's so good at creating walls and doing whatever it takes to avoid getting hurt that he's a total wild card here.

Will a fight make him step back? We've never had one before, so I really don't know.

Urg.

"Kole!"

I jerk around to find Emmett running up to me, a huge smile on his face.

He holds up his bandaged hand. "I got three stitches. It was so cool. They sewed me together. Ben is going to be so jealous if I end up with a scar."

Nine-year-olds, I swear.

I high-five his good hand. "That was so brave of you."

"I didn't even cry!"

Even *I* know enough to not remind him of how uncontrollable he was before he got here. "Pretty sure that deserves dessert."

His eyes light up, and he yells across the waiting area to Asher, who's finishing up with the nurse at the desk. "Kole's getting me dessert! Let's go!"

When Asher's finally done a few minutes later, he looks tired, and he doesn't meet my eyes as he manages a quick "Thanks." He's still wearing that ugly sweater, but now it just feels like a naïve joke.

Asher loops an arm around his brother's shoulders and presses a kiss to the top of his head. Even when he tries to joke about Emmett's injury being a ploy to get out of eating dinner and going straight to dessert, the joke doesn't ring true.

I lead them to the car, not wanting to bring my worries up again, especially while Asher is sticking close to Emmett's side. That barrier is back up, and I can feel it like a solid presence between us, and since it's so rarely directed at me, I can't help feeling like I'm in trouble.

I want to make some flippant comment or a joke, but my brain has firmly switched to *battle stations, man the defenses!*

Asher's too in his head, and he's acting ... distant. "West texted to say they're all back at home now, so you can drop us off there."

"But dessert," Emmett whines.

"We'll swing by my house first and bring dessert to everyone," I say. "Mom always makes too much, and when she found out she had seven more people coming, she made enough for twenty more. You know, just in case."

Asher manages a small smile in the rearview mirror.

What I'd wanted to be a perfect day for Asher and his family is probably going to go down as the worst.

Total boyfriend goals, right here.

At the very least, Emmett's face when I run inside my place and bring out two full pies for him to take home perks my mood up a bit.

It's dark by the time we get to their house, and the only light in the whole place is a dim one in the front living room. Emmett jumps out of the car and races ahead, but Asher lingers a little. Before he gets a chance to suggest I head home, I grab the pies, jump out of the car, and start across his snow-covered lawn without him.

"Someone's in a hurry."

"Dessert is an emergency. Duh."

We climb the first few front stairs, and I brace myself for the usual chaos, but when Asher pushes open the door ...

We're met with silence.

I exchange a look with him. "You sure West said they were home?"

"Positive." He heads down the hall, and I hurry to follow him into the living room.

What we find ... I have to check we're in the right place.

West and Bennett—and now Emmett—are on the couch under a blanket. Rhys is sitting on the floor beside them, and Hazel and Zoe are squashed into an armchair. They have a few candles lit, but nothing is on fire, no one is yelling, and even though Zoe's eyes are all red, they look ... happy.

"W-what's all this?" Asher asks. His voice is so guarded I can't help but step closer and wrap my arm around him.

"Are those for us?" Rhys asks, spotting the pies.

"Yep. Who wants apple pie?"

West stands. "I'll go dish them out."

"I'll help." Asher follows his brother into the kitchen, leaving me with the kids.

They're all silent and ... calm. It's freaking me out.

I take out my phone and send Asher a text: *I think your family has been taken over by pod people.*

A short laugh comes from the kitchen. At least he still finds me funny.

Asher and Westly appear a few moments later with pie for everyone. They hand them out, and then Asher's fingers linger on mine when he hands me a bowl. He nudges me to follow and sit next to him on the floor.

I'm torn between feeling like I'm intruding and relieved that Asher seems to want me here.

"We were just talking about Dad and June before you got here," West says.

Asher shifts. "You were?"

"Yeah. We were sort of done, but if there's anything you—"

"No." He shoves a spoonful of pie in his mouth. "But, Em, what about you?"

"I used to love when Mom made chocolate milk with ice cream and sprinkles. And helped with the hard levels on the

Xbox. And how Dad used to take us to ride our bikes after school and sometimes let us watch movies with swearing in them."

West smiles. "That last one was one of Bennett's favorites too."

"I think it's funny that Dad couldn't tell us apart," Ben adds. "Just like West."

West shifts. "Dad couldn't tell you apart either?"

"Nope. And then when he could, we'd pretend we were the other one to confuse him."

Asher's lips purse like he's trying not to laugh.

"You don't do that to me, do you?" West asks.

The twins just grin at each other, and even with all the worry about Asher still hanging over my head, it settles something that's been coiled tight inside me for a while.

Maybe chaos is this family's default.

"That's not the only thing West got from Dad," Zoe says. "What about his horrible cooking skills. His specialty dish is anything burned."

Asher cracks up.

"You're not much better," Zoe mutters to him, and his face falls.

The rest of the kids think it's hilarious.

As we sit here, and they talk about their parents, and school, and the parts of today they actually *enjoyed*, West truly laughs, and both he and Asher relax for maybe the first time since I've known them.

"I'm tired," Asher finally says, and he sounds it.

I have a moment to panic that we didn't get to talk, and maybe now *still* isn't the time to bring it up. When Asher turns to me with tension lining his expression, I expect him to tell me to go home. Instead, he pulls me up and tugs me toward his room.

I swallow thickly and somehow still manage to say goodnight and sound remotely normal.

My feet drag as I follow him downstairs.

Even though I've been waiting for this moment all afternoon, I'm still not sure I'm prepared.

Fighting with Asher feels unnatural.

But I'm worried it's about to happen anyway.

31

ASHER

ALL I WANTED THIS CHRISTMAS WAS AN IMPROVEMENT ON LAST year. I'm not sure an awkward dinner with my boyfriend's family and a hospital visit is an improvement or more of the same shit.

At least the kids seemed happy when we got home, but it doesn't stop the feeling of utter failure washing over me.

It's important moments like this that make me question whether West and I are the right people for the job. It's a constant tide of thinking I'm acing this shit and thinking they'd be better off with real parents.

"Asher—" Kole starts as soon as we're in my bedroom, but I don't let him get any further.

I turn and bury my head in his neck. "All I wanted was for their Christmas not to be as crappy as last year."

Kole strokes my hair. "Hey, hospital visit aside, it was a pretty good day. And it ended with apple pie. Any day that ends with apple pie can't be terrible. It's, like, the law. Apple pie makes it all better. It's scientific fact."

I huff a laugh. "I thought it was the law?"

"Can't the law and science be the same?"

I step back and pull him down with me onto my bed.

We lie on our sides, and I run my thumb down his cheek. His dirty-blond hair falls across his forehead, but his hazel eyes stare at me intently—expectantly—like he's waiting for something.

"About West," he says.

Oh. Right. I shake my head. "Forget about it."

"No, I want to explain."

"You don't really have to. I mean, my brother asked you to keep me in line, but you and I both know that's not possible. Not if I didn't let it happen. Not only that, but logically I know you wouldn't be sleeping with me because my brother asked you to keep me out of trouble."

Kole places his hand on my chest and pushes back. "Wait. You just said *logically* and then made the very insightful argument I was going to make. Who are you, and what did you do with my hothead boyfriend who should be jumping to all kinds of conclusions right now?"

I pull him back closer to me. "What kind of conclusions did you think I was going to jump to?"

"That the only reason I'm with you is for the team?"

"You hate hockey. I don't see you pimping yourself out for the sake of it."

"Oh good, you don't think I'm a whore."

I lean forward and kiss him. "You can be a whore for me if you like."

"Hmm, how much will you pay me?"

I kiss him again. "Can't you give me a freebie? Is hooking like drugs? Give the first one for free and they'll keep coming back?"

"Umm, I think hooking is nothing like that, but I wouldn't know. Seriously though, you're not mad? I expected you to at least be pissed at West for even asking."

"Eh. I expect it from him. Last year, he literally forced me and Cohen to get to know each other better—"

"Did he lock you in my dad's office too?"

"No. He did the adult thing and set us up on a playdate like we were two-year-olds."

"In his defense—"

"Ha ha, I *am* a two-year-old. You're funny."

"Also, in your brother's defense, he never asked me to tutor you. I did that myself. Of my own free will."

That does make me feel a little better about it all. "Good to know."

"Also, also—"

I slam my mouth on his and lick my way past his lips. He lets me. Until he doesn't anymore.

He pushes against my chest. "I want to tell you everything. You might not be mad, but I don't want you to wonder. That first day I approached you in the locker room, I'll admit, I did it because your brother asked. But that same night, when Rhys went to the park and you were freaking? That was a total coincidence, and I saw something in you then that I knew you would never show the team. I saw a glimpse of the real you that night, and that's what drew me in. I ... I've been yours ever since."

Kole's eyes flutter shut, like he doesn't want to look at me while he confesses that, but I want to see those hazel orbs looking at me the way they do. He sees me. The real me.

I've broken down walls for him and let him in. I don't know why it was so easy to do when it comes to Kole, but I do know I wouldn't have made it through these last few months if it weren't for him.

He brought me back when I was on the brink of self-destruction. That wouldn't have been good for me or the kids.

He gave me an outlet to finally grieve over the loss of my dad and stepmom.

He helped me pass my classes so I could stay on the team and keep the one thing I know I can do well in my life.

He didn't *fix* anything, he was just there, offering what I needed and wanted. A safe outlet to work through my shit and stop fighting the world.

Kole has given me so much already, and even though I feel like I don't deserve him, I want to try like hell to keep him.

"Say something," he whispers.

"I'm trying to think of the exact moment I knew I was yours, but I can't find it. Maybe I lied to myself when we were fuck buddies, so I didn't notice how much I was falling until now."

"You're falling for me?"

"Well and truly. Which is super inconvenient."

Kole snorts. "Why?"

"Because our future is—"

"Our future. We don't have to think about it now. We have time."

"But if I get a contract with Buffalo, and you—"

"You know what I heard? I heard Buffalo has hospitals. Crazy, right? Maybe med school will suck. Hell, maybe we won't even make it until then. But shit, we can't hold back on the off chance someday in the future it will be too hard. We have at least two and a half years until you graduate. I'll probably go to med school at UVM—"

I gasp. "You traitor."

"Oh no, I can't become a catamount," he cries dramatically.

"I don't even know why we're discussing our future when clearly we don't have one. I can't date someone at UVM."

Kole just smiles.

"What?" I ask.

"You and your school spirit. Considering how standoffish you were at the beginning of the year, and from what I understand all through last season too, it's good to see you find your passion again. And be a nice human being."

I poke him. "You take that back. I'm not nice."

"Oh no, never. And you're *definitely* not the most adorable part-time guardian to your younger brothers and sisters either."

"Shut up."

Kole pushes me onto my back and rolls on top of me. "You're not sweet. At all."

"Nope." I throw my head back while my mean boyfriend leaves kisses down my neck.

"You're not patient—"

"Definitely not."

"Hmm, actually, yeah, you're not patient on the ice. Or in bed. But with your brothers and sisters—"

"Can you please stop pointing out all my flaws?"

Kole works his way down my body but looks up at me through his lashes. "That's where we're different. You see them as flaws. I see them as the things that make you mine."

I run my hand through his hair. "Yeah?"

He nods. "Because I'm the only person you let see you like that. If you opened yourself up like that to the other guys on the team, there's no way you can lose the Frozen Four this year."

"Mm, keep talking about my teammates and the team which your dad coaches. That'll get me hard."

Kole chuckles. "And there you go, trying to make light of this situation because you don't want to be vulnerable and admit you want the team's approval. You want to be their friend, but you're scared they'll judge you for who you are deep down, which is a sweet, caring man who's devoted to his family even though they're overwhelming."

"I think we need a safeword when it comes to all this emoting. No more."

Kole laughs more. "It's a shame there's a clothing rule in this house. We could do something other than talk."

With all my power, I roll us over so I'm now on top and snugly resting between his legs. "Bedtime loophole, remember? After everything that happened today, no one will be coming down here."

"It really was a good day. Don't beat yourself up for one minor hiccup."

"I don't think three stitches is a minor hiccup."

"It is. Kids always get injured. It's not your fault. It was a good Christmas."

I want to believe him. So bad. "It's not over yet."

He reaches between us, rubbing over my hard cock. "Want to wish me a proper Merry Christmas?"

I shudder on top of him. "More than anything. I want you inside me."

Kole sighs. "Fine. But next chance we have, it's going the other way."

"Our first game after break is an away game."

"Deal."

Having sex in a crowded house is risky and somewhat terrifying, but we go slow and take our time, breathe each other in, and bask in this new promise we've made each other.

I lied just now though.

I don't think I'm falling for him.

I've already fallen.

32

KOLE

A sea of Mountain Lions jerseys walks through the door of Bean There, and my eyes immediately land on Asher.

Even after a few months together, he still pulls an automatic smile to my face.

Apparently, I do the same to him because when he spots me, he lights up and breaks away from the group.

He fishes something out of his bag on the walk over, and by the time he's in front of me, I have a piece of paper shoved in my face.

"What's this?"

He doesn't answer.

Then I note the giant grade at the top.

"B plus?" A burst of elation hits me at how happy Asher looks with himself.

"Best grade ever," he says.

"That's incredible."

"Borderline miracle."

"You're right. Must be a total fluke." But we both know that's not the case. For two guys early on in their relationship, there's a whole lot more study than sex at the moment. It sucks, but we don't have a lot of options. I'm at the Dalton house a lot because Asher's spending what little free time he does have at home. It means West can get a much-needed break so he doesn't burn out and run off again, and it leaves Asher and me plenty of time to study and *not* have sex.

We have to take full advantage of away games and the back seats of our cars. It's surprising Asher can still perform on the ice when the team is away because he gets little to no sleep, and we fuck until our bodies are completely wrung out. Yet, he gets out there and kicks ass every single game. The team is right on track to go all the way.

Not going to lie, it's hard to keep my hands to myself whenever I see him.

Especially moments like now, when all I want is to kiss him and show him how proud I am, but his team is right there. We haven't mentioned anything to them because we didn't want anyone to accuse Dad of favoritism.

"Fitting grade though. B *is* for blue balls."

"And blowjobs?" He lifts his eyebrows.

"Is that the reward you want?" My cock twitches. It's been *so long* since I had his dick in my mouth.

"Actually no."

Huh? That derails images of us both naked together and crashlands me back in the café. "Then …"

"I actually thought …" He shifts his eyes away from me. "That maybe it might be time we told people about us?"

His clear discomfort makes me unreasonably happy. "Aww, are you nervous?"

"No. I don't do nerves. Shut up."

I pat him on the head, and he gives me a blank *cut the crap* look. "Of course you don't, sweetie. You're a big bad hockey player."

And as much as he tries to look like he's not impressed, his eyes are soft.

"So what's the plan?" I ask. "I'm pretty sure none of your teammates know either of us is queer, so did you want to make it some big coming out thing, or …"

He takes my hand. "Nope. Come with me."

I grab my coffee and follow him to the table where Rossi, Simms, Kaplan, and Stalberg are already sitting. Asher steals a chair from another table, and before I can grab one of my own, he sits down and pulls me onto his lap.

I tense, and Asher's holding his breath.

But there's barely a break in the conversation.

Slowly, I relax in Asher's hold and chance a quick look at him. He's confused, and I can't blame him. Are they ignoring us on purpose?

Asher steals a quick sip of my coffee and loops his arm tighter around my waist. "Really not going to say anything, huh?" he finally asks.

Rossi looks over. "What, are we supposed to act surprised?"

"You *knew*?"

The four of them exchange looks, and Simms cocks his head. "Wait, did you guys think you were subtle?"

"Well, yeah." Don't they realize how painful it's been to keep our hands to ourselves?

"Let's review," Rossi says, clearly amused. "Asher waits for you after every practice, you arrive together, you study together, you share a room at away games—where you really could try to be more quiet, by the way—West treats Kole like another brother, Coach can't look at Asher without scowling, more so than usual, and if I have to hear the phrase *Kole said* one more time, my brain will start leaking out of my ears."

I'm ... kinda shocked. "And people say jocks are stupid."

"You forget I was friends with Foster, and Beck and Jacobs, and Cohen. I've given up assuming people are straight, and you two have been behaving just like those other idiots."

It's the first time I think I've actually been glad to be outsmarted by jocks.

"Who else knows?" Asher asks.

"Literally the whole team," Simms says. "We've known for ages."

"And no one said anything?"

Stalberg screws up his face. "No offense, man, but none of us want to know about your sex life. That's a strictly kiss and *don't* tell situation."

"Pity," Asher says, and his tone gives me a split-second warning. "Because Kole sucks the best dick. You guys have no idea what you're missing."

Rossi sighs, and Stalberg clears his throat, and Kaplan looks like he's trying not to laugh. Asher is lucky I don't get embarrassed easy, but he's *so* going to pay me back for that one later.

"Oh, I'm sorry," Asher says casually. "Did that make you uncomfortable?"

Simms gives him a deadpan look. "You really think we're not used to your shit by now?"

"Worth a shot."

"You're going to have to try way harder than that these days," Simms says.

"I'm sure I can come up with something."

"What, you can get even more unpleasant?"

"I can try," Asher taunts.

"And yet no one is surprised."

Even though they're goading each other, hearing them go back and forth makes me feel all warm. Because there's no longer an undercurrent of tension. In fact, Asher's smiling. Like, an actual one, not a shithead smirk meant to get under people's skin.

I shift around to face him properly. "Look at you making friends and everything."

"Safeword. *Safeword.*"

"Yeah, 'safeword' isn't a safeword, and nothing is going to stop me from pointing out how much I love seeing you crawl out of your cocoon to become a beautiful social butterfly." Knowing how much Asher likes to continue the act of keeping up his guard, there's nothing more fun than pointing out how amazing he is in front of other people.

I just, umm, *overdo* it sometimes.

He sighs. "This is for the sucking cock comment, isn't it?"

"It's cute you think I'll let you off that lightly, my snooky wooky ... ah, *booky*?"

"Fuck no."

"I'm going to buy pom-poms for your next game and wear a T-shirt with your face on it."

"I will end you."

"But I'm so *pretty*."

His eyes sweep over my face.

"Dear God, can you turn him off?" Kaplan asks.

"I prefer the opposite," Asher replies, getting a groan out of someone.

And oh yeah, this is going to be fun.

Asher pinches my chin and presses a quick kiss to my lips.

"We're going to have to get used to that, aren't we?" Simms asks.

"Sure are. I have no plans to keep my hands off my boyfriend just to make other people comfortable."

"Eh," Rossi says. "You guys can't be worse than Beck and Jacobs."

"Sounds like a challenge to me," I say.

Apparently that's the right answer because Asher presses another kiss to my cheek. Then he slaps my ass hard and orders me to stand up.

"We're out," Asher says. "See you guys at practice later."

When we get outside, he takes my hand as we walk back to campus.

"I'm surprised that went so well," I say.

"I'm not. You plus me equals perfection."

"I think I'm beginning to understand why you were failing math."

He tugs me to a stop, and where I'm expecting some smartass comeback, he just goes on smiling. "I mean it, you know."

Aww, he's being soft Asher. "I know."

"Even in the hard moments, being with you is easy."

"I *could* make a joke about how easy we both are when the other is hard, but instead … I have a theory."

"What's that?"

I step closer, meeting his green eyes as all that syrupy warmth flows through me just from being around him. "Either you've contracted some deadly disease that's messing with your thoughts, or … you're in love with me."

The smile slides from his face, and he cups my cheeks in the way that I love. "Definitely the second."

I suck in a breath, because with Asher, I really had no idea if he'd acknowledge it or not.

"And I have bad news for you," he continues. "I think it's contagious."

A shiver runs down my spine. "Uh-oh, I think you're right."

"Yikes. Have we caught the love?"

"Gross."

"So gross. And so you know," Asher says, "I blame you for this."

"I *am* pretty irresistible."

"I'll have to do something really dirty to you later to make up for it."

I laugh and then kiss Asher, long and hard, not giving a shit who sees us. I've always been a pretty happy person, but this, right here, is a whole new level of happy. "I really love you," I breathe.

"Yeah, Kole." He clears his throat. "I really love you too."

33

ASHER

We're all itching to get out of this locker room. It's spring break, and everyone's already gone on vacation, except for us.

Coach doesn't want a repeat of last year, so we've been working our butts off in the rink and in the gym for the upcoming regionals. We will not fail this year. And I'm sure as fuck staying away from any foods that could make me hurl for two days straight.

Never. Again.

But Coach is finally giving us a few days off, and we have plans. I have two whole nights where West has given me time away from the kids, Coach is letting us out into the wild, and Kole, well, he's going to be mine over and over and over again.

Somewhere in there, we're heading up to Montreal to catch Foster Grant play, to take Kaplan to a bar where he's legally able to drink, and we're going to blow off some steam for once.

Coach knows it too. "I don't want to know what you're all getting up to on your two days off, but here's what you're not going to be doing: no drinking, no drugs, no getting arrested, no—"

"Dad, you might be giving them ideas," Kole says from across the room but sends a pointed look my way.

Hey, I'm a good boy now.

The contrast in what "blowing off steam" used to be to now is unrecognizable. Before, I'd go out, get hammered, pick a fight, fuck someone I'm not supposed to, and do anything I could to alienate as many people as possible.

Blowing off steam now is literally going to a bar with friends, having a few drinks but not so many I'll be hungover the next morning, and taking my man back to our hotel room to make each other come as many times as possible while we have the chance to be alone.

That's what life with Kole will be like. If it's not the kids, after graduation it will be med school and the NHL getting in our way, but the thing is, now that we're both all in and I know Kole loves me, there are no doubts floating around my head.

When we're busy, we're busy. There's no rush to spend every free moment together, as long as we make the moments we have count.

Kole is my future.

Coach grumbles. "Just don't do anything to jeopardize our season. Go and have fun."

We all stand.

"But not too much fun," he adds. "There will be a random drug test when you get back."

I approach Kole while everyone low-key whines on their way out. "Is it still random if he tells us it's going to happen?"

"I'm willing to bet there is no test. He just doesn't want everyone going out and partying when regionals are next week."

"Maybe this is the one time your dad is happy you were stupid enough to fall for me because he knows you'll keep me in line."

"I'm not your keeper," he says.

I lean in and whisper in his ear, "I like it when you keep me though."

When I pull back, he grips my shirt, and those hazel eyes slay me. "I mean I don't want to hold you back from doing things you want to do. I want to be your partner, not your parole officer."

"I don't see you that way. Although, that could be a hot role-playing game. Do you have handcuffs by any chance?"

He shoves me. "I'm serious."

"So am I. But you want to know why you'll keep me in line?"

Kole's eyebrows rise in anticipation.

"Because with you, I don't have the need to hide who I am. I don't have to pretend to be strong. I don't need to do stupid shit to prove I can't be hurt. All of that excess anger I was keeping inside that would erupt in forms of self-destruction aren't there when I'm with you, and it's not because of anything you do or say. It's because I'm my true self around you. No pretenses."

Kole smiles and leans in to kiss me, but—

"Let's go," Rossi says, sticking his head back inside the locker room.

"On it, Captain." I drag Kole toward the door. "Two whole nights."

"No kids."

"No exams. Just my two favorite things. Hockey and you naked in my bed. Or in a bathroom. On a table. Against the wall. On a couch." Damn it, now I'm hard, and Montreal is two hours away.

We meet the guys out in the parking lot—Rossi, Simms, Kaplan, Beck, and Jacobs are coming, and when we get up there, we're meeting Cohen, who's a PR assistant for the Montreal team. He scored us tickets to the game.

"We have room in our car," Beck says, and Kaplan and Simms look our way.

Cohen might have warned me against getting into Beck's car. Apparently two hours in a confined space with him can drive anyone mad.

Rossi goes with them, while the four of us pile into Kole's car.

"Do you think Coach sent Beck to spy on us?" Kaplan asks on the way up north.

The three of us laugh at that absurdity.

"You have more chance of Kole ratting one of us out, and he loves me," I say.

"You weren't here the last two years when Beck was one of us," Simms says. "Trust me. He's the least of our worries. He'll always be a man child."

"Really?"

I don't know why Kaplan is surprised, but then I really think about it, and Beck has been more subdued this past year. "Maybe he's growing up."

"Thank fuck I still have another year before I need to do that," Simms says.

I turn to him from the passenger seat. "You and me, next year, we're getting every agent's attention. We're keeping you out of law school."

We fist bump.

"I'm, uh …" Kaplan starts. "I'm thinking of entering the draft next year." His voice pitches at the end as if he's asking our permission to do it.

"That settles it," I say. "We have to win the Frozen Four this year and get everyone to our games next season."

"Aww, look at you three being a team," Kole says. "I didn't think this would ever happen at the beginning of the season."

"I don't think any of us did," I murmur.

"Say, 'thank you, Kole.'"

Simms and I flip him off as though on cue.

When we finally make it to Montreal, I text Cohen to say we're here, and he replies he'll meet us in our hotel bar for pregame drinks.

And as we dump our stuff in our room and head downstairs, my old line mate stands to greet me with a hug while his boyfriend scowls at me. It's cute because Seth Grant is not an intimidating guy.

Cohen still has his kind face and goofy grin. "Rumor has it you've stopped being an asshole this year, but I told Beck he's full of shit because I didn't think that was possible."

"I'm a delightful human being, you complete cockwomble." I don't even need to look at Kole beside me to know he's rolling his eyes.

"Ah, there's the guy I know," Cohen says.

I pull Kole close. "This is my boyfriend. Kole, this is Cohen and Seth."

"Oh, so you're the reason he's not an asshole anymore?" Cohen asks and shakes Kole's hand.

"Nope. He loves me even when I'm an asshole." I pull Kole closer.

"Unfortunately, that's true." My boyfriend sighs.

Cohen laughs and grips my shoulder. "You do look happy, so that's something. I've also been keeping tabs on your games. You guys are killing it this year."

"Aww, are you checking up on me?" I ask in my flirty tone.

Beside him, Seth growls.

I throw my hands up. "I'm sorry, but it's so easy to get under your skin, and I love it."

Kole nudges me. "I can see why you had the reputation you did when I met you."

"Whatever. I'm totally innocent."

None of them believe me.

"Drinks!" Kaplan yells and puts a tray of shots down. "First ones I bought legally. I love Canada."

Cohen introduces himself to the freshman and greets Simms. Behind them, Jacobs, Beck, and Rossi enter the bar and beeline it toward us.

"Just in time." Kaplan hands out a shot to everyone. "What should we toast to?"

Cohen holds up his drink. "To line mates, old and new."

We all clink the small glasses and throw them back except for Cohen, who hands his to Seth, who downs both.

I cock my head at Cohen. "Pregnant?"

"I'm on PR duty tonight," he says. "Are you all ready to head to the arena?"

We walk the couple of minutes, my arm around Kole the whole time, and I can't think of a better way to spend the few days off I have than with him and a group of guys I'm quickly becoming close to.

I never realized how important true friendship was until I met Kole.

They're an escape from all the shit that drags me down.

Cohen scored us seats in the fourth row, really close to the ice, and Foster Grant's partner is already there waiting for us. Cohen kisses Seth on his cheek and leaves to get to work while we settle in.

I'm taken back to going with Dad to watch some of West's games whenever we could, and his voice rings in the back of my head, telling me that I'll be out there soon.

His dream of having both sons play for the same team at the same time in the NHL will never come true now, but I also think that was a pipedream. I was drafted to Buffalo, West played for Boston. If anything, all it would have done was cause a bigger rift between us, so it's probably good that's not happening.

Things with West are improving. Ever since he admitted he hasn't got his shit together, I've been sympathetic. I used to see his holier-than-thou attitude as a way for him to always put me in my place, but the truth is he's as clueless as me when it comes to expressing himself.

Hopefully one day he'll meet someone who'll be there for him the way Kole is for me.

"I can see me doing this in the future," Kole says next to me. His arm is looped through mine, and he glances around the arena like he knows one day it will become his second home.

"Going to hockey games with me?"

He shakes his head. "Going to see you play hockey in the NHL."

"That's the plan." I link my fingers with his. "I kind of can't wait, but at the same time I want to enjoy having the time we have together now before life gets even more chaotic."

"It's hard to believe our lives could get *more chaotic*."

"Hey, if we can handle spending nights in my household with that many kids, helping them with homework and putting them to bed, I'm certain you and I could handle anything. The NHL, a hospital residency ... pfft, it'll be a cakewalk."

"I hope so, because I kind of have plans for you."

"Oh, do you? What might they entail?"

"Hmm, doing my residency in whichever city you sign with. Getting a small house with a yard for Hades."

"Careful, that's starting to sound a hell of a lot like a white picket fence future you were so against."

Kole smiles at me and leans in to brush his lips against mine. "Maybe a white picket fence future with you wouldn't be so bad."

As the teams take to the ice, that calling I've always had since slipping on a pair of skates reaches for me. The ice is my future, but so is the guy right next to me.

There will be times when it's difficult because hockey schedules and a doctor's shift schedule don't exactly line up, but I know we can do it because no one has ever made me step back and look at myself the way Kole does. No one's ever been there for me the way he is.

Like I told him, I can't wait for the future to be here, but I also love where we're at now. Because when I'm with him, there's nowhere else I'd rather be. Except maybe alone with him.

I lean in and whisper in his ear. "How long do you think we should stay for the game?"

"You want to leave in the middle of it? You. *Mr. Hockey.*"

"You're more important to me than hockey. I'm desperate for you."

I'll always be desperate for him.

"After first period, we'll leave."

"I was kind of hoping for sooner than that, but deal. As soon as we get back to the hotel, I'm going to strip you bare and taste every inch of your skin until you're writhing and begging for my—"

Kole stands abruptly. "Changed my mind, let's go now."

Yes.

It seems he's just as desperate for me as I am for him.

When we get back to the hotel and I lay him out beneath me, I can see this.

Us.

For the rest of my life.

THANK YOU

Thank you for reading Line Mates & Study Dates.

While the plan was to feature all students in the CU hockey world, we couldn't help feeling a little sorry for a certain assistant coach who deserves his HEA. Someone older. Someone who might be a professor or something...

Puck Drills & Quick Thrills is in the works!

If you'd like to keep up to date with either author, here's where you can find them:

Saxon's Facebook Group:
www.facebook.com/groups/saxonssweethearts/
Eden's Facebook Group:
www.facebook.com/groups/absolutelyeden/

Alternatively, you can subscribe to our newsletters here:
Saxon: www.subscribepage.com/saxonjames
Eden:
https://landing.mailerlite.com/webforms/landing/d4e2a5

ABOUT EDEN FINLEY

You can follow Eden on any of the following platforms:

https://www.facebook.com/EdenFinleyAuthor/

https://www.facebook.com/groups/absolutelyeden/

https://amzn.to/2zUlM16

https://www.edenfinley.com

OTHER BOOKS BY EDEN FINLEY

FAMOUS SERIES

Pop Star

Spotlight

Fandom

Novellas:

Rockstar Hearts

FAKE BOYFRIEND SERIES

Fake Out

Trick Play

Deke

Blindsided

Hat Trick

Novellas:

Fake Boyfriend Breakaways: A short story collection

Final Play

VINO & VERITAS
Sarina Bowen's True North Series

Headstrong

STEELE BROTHERS

Unwritten Law

Unspoken Vow

ROYAL OBLIGATION

Unprincely (M/M/F)

ABOUT SAXON JAMES

Follow Saxon James on any of the platforms below.

www.facebook.com/thesaxonjames/

www.amazon.com/Saxon-James/e/B082TP7BR7

www.bookbub.com/profile/saxon-james

www.instagram.com/saxonjameswrites/

OTHER BOOKS BY SAXON JAMES

NEVER JUST FRIENDS SERIES

Just Friends

Fake Friends

Getting Friendly

LOVE'S A GAMBLE SERIES

Bet on Me

Calling Your Bluff

And if you're after something a little sweeter, don't forget my YA pen name

S. M. James.

These books are chock full of adorable, flawed characters with big hearts.

www.amazon.com/S-M-James/e/B07DVH3TZQ

Printed in Great Britain
by Amazon